Learning To Die

For A.

Learning to Die

Thomas Maloney

SCRIBE
Melbourne • London

Scribe Publications
18–20 Edward St, Brunswick, Victoria 3056, Australia
2 John St, Clerkenwell, London, WC1N 2ES, United Kingdom

Published by Scribe 2018

Typeset in the UK by Avon DataSet Ltd, Bidford on Avon,
Warwickshire B50 4JH

Printed and bound in the UK by CPI Group (UK) Ltd, Croydon CR0 4YY

Scribe Publications is committed to the sustainable use of natural resources
and the use of paper products made responsibly from those resources.

9781925322170 (Australian edition)
9781911344308 (UK edition)
9781925548266 (e-book)

CiP records for this title are available from the British Library
and the National Library of Australia.

scribepublications.com.au
scribepublications.co.uk

2011

1. Hard water

'I do not teach; I relate.'
Montaigne

Since he is carrying a sack of rubbish in each hand, and thinking guiltily of the glass of wine he has just poured himself rather than the interaction between breezes and buildings — guiltily because his wife is in hospital with multiple injuries — Daniel Mock leaves the back door open on his way through the mid-terrace house and out into the street. He encourages the sacks to settle against the low front wall. He glances automatically at those left out by his neighbours on each side to confirm the well-established fact, faintly satisfying even on a night like this, that he and Mrs Mock are less wasteful than some.

He turns back to the house, remembering the waiting warm-smacky glass of rosso with a feeling that his last duty is done, just as the front door slams in his face with theatrical violence. He stands staring at it for a few seconds, gives it a forlorn push, then looks down at himself. He is wearing a shabby towelling dressing gown and a pair of slippers. He sinks his hands speculatively into the gown's pockets but they encounter only a couple of well-used tissues of unknown vintage. He leans and peers through the living room window, where between the

3

casually closed curtains he can plainly see the rim-glistening chalice on the table.

He steps back and looks left and right at his profligate neighbours' windows, which are uncharacteristically and unequivocally dark; the spare key will not be forthcoming. His wife has a punctured lung and is not about to come to his rescue. He turns to the street and looks up at the drifting urban-orange Friday night sky. A pale smear, a nocturnal emission beyond the high-rise, might be the moon. He puts his hands back in his pockets.

Meanwhile, in his lop-sided bedroom in the north-eastern coastal village of Merryman's Bay, James F. Saunders is feeling anything but merry. The couple next door are at it again. They must like the way the headboard thumps against the wall, otherwise why not move the bed back an inch or two? He has to admire their stamina: they go at it hammer and tongs for a few minutes, then subside into faint moaning and shuffling, and then, just as James begins to drift off, they're at it again. Bang, bang, bang, moan, moan, moan, faster and faster, until he begins to worry about the plasterwork, then a few slow, emphatic crashes like someone trying to shoulder down a door, another hiatus of recuperating sighs, and then it begins yet again. He cannot suppress the thought that it was never quite so gung-ho with Becks.

Of course what depresses James most about his neighbours' weekend performances, as he lies in his winter pyjamas in his own bed, is that despite himself he gets aroused. When the woman — Trudy is her name, late thirties, wary eyes, new-age type — moans or yelps or calls out something stupid she heard on TV, James' jaded body responds. Like a decrepit retired soldier stubbornly heeding the call of duty, making a fool of himself.

He adjusts his pyjama trousers sulkily, rolls over and closes his eyes. There is a merciful pause in the fucking, and the last sound he hears is the restive sea pawing the ramp outside the Bay Hotel: it is a spring tide.

Tomorrow he will begin.

Natalie Mock is in the Royal Berkshire with a punctured lung, concussion and a smorgasbord of bumps and bruises.

When the Mocks were house-hunting in Reading in the spring, she was impressed by the water pressure in what is now their bathroom: she always tested the shower, and this one was a belter. Cleaning the bathroom is Dan's job, and he is pretty reliable (Nat is in charge of the kitchen). But Reading water is not like the sweet moorland run-off in Sheffield, where they went to university, or Manchester, where Dan grew up. Reading water is a groundwater soup of calcium ions, and these too are house-hunting.

This morning the showerhead, hopelessly clogged with scale, shot off the pipe like a champagne cork and struck Natalie on the right temple. A slight young woman still makes quite a crash. The riot-hose cascade soon roused her to a consciousness of sorts, but early attempts to sit up met with failure. Her back was apparently pressed not against the bottom of the bath but on a bed of nails, and it hurt to breathe. Blood, diluted by the deluge to something like raspberry juice, was trickling impressively between her breasts and pooling in her belly button, which it treated as a sort of roundabout, turning neatly to the right and overflowing around one throbbing hip. A faint but conspicuous stripe of raspberry juice was running down the side of the bath from one of the ornamented prongs of the shower's cradle. She'd never liked the fittings in here.

'Krovvy,' she murmured, the word blossoming from nowhere. 'Red, red krovvy.' Her stunned dizziness was, despite even odds of her being sick, only two points south of exhilaration. The jolted rational machinery of her brain slowly started to turn: she was alone in the house; she should summon medical assistance. An urgent corollary to the latter thought was the matter of her soapy nudity: twisting her head she glimpsed her pants and T-shirt dangling reassuringly on the edge of the basin. Everything was going to be alright. She applied herself more systematically to the conundrum of getting up by stretching a trembling foot towards the tap.

Now she lies in a comfortable annexe of the nothing-too-serious ward, after the nurses agreed to move her from Respiratory because, my God, the coughing! Breathing is painful, but the doctor says the lung damage from the puncture-wound on her back is not serious, and has opted to wait, see and prescribe painkillers. She has a jug of water, a button to call the nurse, and a slatted view of the Reading evening: garage rooftops like a Rio favela, the back of a pub where a dozen hardy patrons are sipping and puffing on damp garden furniture, and a sighting through clouds of the penny-hard edge of the full moon.

Mike Vickers stands at a pane of glass the size of a small house, watching a stubby short-haul plane taxi past from left to right, while a jumbo slides along a parallel lane in the opposite direction. It's like a screensaver, if you remember those. The programmer's whimsical signature is the unmistakeable silhouette of Windsor Castle upstage right, its tiny speck of a flag picked out by a spotlight, broadening the vista of both space and time.

Mike, thirty-three last week, feels he wears a faint halo of precociousness among the middle-aged gadget-toting veterans of the Executive Club. He turns away from the window to observe the one pretty waitress (this is BA) bend gorgeously to serve his G&T on a table whose lowness he silently appreciates. She might just fall for his habitual masque: the dot-com entrepreneur modestly eschewing First as part of some trendy web-ethos. He almost believes it himself.

Is one likely to obtain more pleasure, he wonders, letting the ice cubes nuzzle the fine Cupid's bow of his upper lip — or rather should one obtain more pleasure — from a luxury one chooses and pays for oneself out of hard-earned spondulicks, or a luxury that falls quite properly into one's lap? (We omit the phenomenon of theft, he notes.) The difference is surprisingly slight: in other words, these free G&Ts are tasting better and better.

Brenda Vickers zigs for another twenty yards, then starts her long zag up onto the dim bluish whaleback of the ridge. This is her favourite moment. The bite of her crampons is the only sound above the layered orchestra of the wind, which is winding up to its ridge-top crescendo. She prods her imagination to conjure the abyss of hard snow that the November darkness conceals, and smiles.

A vast white tentacle of moonlight slides up and over the mountain, and picks out in brilliant detail the tiny figure on the ridge, now walking fast. She is wearing a neat black windproof jacket, black leggings, and a headband to corral a wiry tumble of dark hair. You might want her to be a glamour-puss but she isn't, and the mountain doesn't care: her face is rather narrow, her forehead high, and her body lacking in curves, but, striding out onto a spiny outcrop of snow-plastered rocks, she moves like a wildcat.

It was somewhere just below here. She steps across a gap between two boulders, testing the footing of steel spikes on snowy rock before she commits, then leans to execute a delicate side-pull with a gloved hand, redirecting her nine stone of weight as she drops neatly into a sheltered hollow. Life feels precious up here. One false step.

Dan Mock has no friends in this unlovely tangle of a town. There is a chilly breeze but he feels quite calm, his own predicament merely comic when viewed beside that of his stricken wife. Limescale and the prong of a shower cradle: an unlikely conspiracy of violence, intruding on her well-ordered life. Undeserved. Not serious, the doctor said — but too close to serious, and his fault. What would he do or be without her?

His gaze alights with a flourish on his tarp-covered Yamaha steed: mile-devourer, freedom-giver. He'll hotwire it, hitch up his dressing gown, ride to Mark and Rachel's place along the Berkshire back-lanes — out of sight of the rozzas — and be tucked up on their sofa within half an hour. But hotwire with what? For a third time he fingers those balsa-woody tissues in his pockets. He mentally scans the bike for anything detachable. Nada: he keeps a tight ship. He will walk, and find a skip. Reading is well-supplied with skips, and skips are full of wire.

He passes a few lighted windows — should he knock at a door? These people will recognise him at least, if not know his name. Won't they? He plays through the possible outcomes and they are not encouraging — he doesn't even know Mark's phone number by heart — so he walks on. At the street corner he spies a beer can in the gutter: that will conduct, if he can cut a strip off. He scatters the dregs — Special Brew, no less — and puts it in his pocket to keep his options open.

Compared to his own shadowy street, the main road is lit

up like a film set. A man approaches, shelters behind his terrier and looks away. A young couple, students, cross to the other side before they pass him. He reaches the little parade of shops and sees his reflection in a darkened window: a shambling weirdo in a too-short dressing gown. A glimpse of somehow misshapen knees. He at last looks like he often secretly feels. Like everyone feels, for all he knows. The beer can protrudes shamelessly. He moves to throw it away but cannot bring himself to drop litter. He finds a rubbish bin, checks inside for any handy lengths of wire, shivers, blows on his hands, and wanders on.

James F. Saunders is awakened by the moist rustle of rain, or perhaps by its smell, which restores him instantly to the recumbent, unseeing alertness that the world's somniacs are spared. He imagines involuntarily the damp, tangled nest of limbs and hair beyond the wall; consciously stops grinding his teeth; extends an arm outside the duvet's warmth and explores the edge of his desk until his fingers close on a plastic cigarette lighter with no fuel left in it. He sits up suddenly and flicks the wheel. *Zhip*. There it is: this crappy little room, his whole dead-end life, in a flash. Chair desk lop-sided wardrobe dormer window tiny sink. None of it his. A mound of his clothes is heaped over the chair-back — this nightly balancing act unchanged since his student days — his jeans and long-johns half-covering the chunky laptop as though trying to delay the punch-line of a moderately good joke. Again: *zhip*.

He seems to smell something else, something rotten in that midnight rain. Yes indeed, he muses: why shouldn't the spectre of death loom large in one's early thirties? The ghosts of Byron, Mozart and Van Gogh, whose heavy-scented genius he both reveres and despises, all dwell hereabouts, flashing cold, brilliant eyes and whispering that it really doesn't matter whether or not you have a few decades left to live. You've had ample time to prove your worth, and from here on it's probably all just repetition. Who can blame old Rob and Trudy for moaning and slamming their headboard against the wall? Were they fucking or just having a breakdown?

James lets the lighter fall and sinks back onto his pillow. Without noticing what he is doing he begins to count — instead of sheep, and like the fool he undoubtedly is — all the great men and women who died when they were younger than he is now.

Nevertheless, tomorrow he will begin.

Natalie looks down at the little plastic socket they have stuck in the back of her hand, currently unattached to any tube. Her body is, of course, just a gadget to be charged up, and into which various branded gizmos must occasionally be downloaded.

How silly of her to forget this. It is, she supposes, a good thing to be reminded of the fragility of the body, that soggy bundle of offal without which all the rest, all the important stuff in your head, simply disappears. Every living adult is a miraculous soap opera of deaths averted, offal preserved — buses not walked in front of; infections heroically fought off by mechanisms she suspects nobody quite understands even today; railings on boats, bridges and balconies wistfully leaned against but not climbed over; cars impeccably, implausibly steered along miles of winding lanes — as well as a terrifyingly dense compress of experience: the bleak and brutal vastness of childhood somehow overcome. And yet, she observes, turning again to the sea of rooftops, here they are in their burgeoning thousands: the survivors. Adult specimens.

Mike strolls nonchalantly past the queuing mortals, waves his passport, springs jauntily down the walkway and is shown to his weird peapod of a seat. He changes from loafers to slippers and slides *The Economist* from his slim portfolio briefcase.

He settles into his seat and sighs: here in his hands are the troubles of the troubled world. As an accidental member of the so-called one per cent (his father would never believe it), he is duty bound at the very least to read, to understand.

Later. Wearing the same expression as Prince Hal trying out the burden of kingship, he crowns himself with a pair of noise-cancelling headphones, thumbs his way to something exquisite and closes his blond-lashed eyes.

Brenda shrugs off her rucksack and stands motionless for a few seconds, listening to wind singing gently over snow. She carefully backs out of the hollow and down onto the yawning slope, then turns to face the night and kicks in her spiked heels expertly. Hot piss burning through snow like an arc welder: always satisfying. The fifty blue-white peaks of Knoydart glow softly in the light of a clouded moon.

Back in the hollow she steps out of the crampons and boots and into a light sleeping bag, sits on her rucksack with her back nestled into a comfortable cleft and lights a tiny propane stove. Ten minutes after dropping into this remembered hollow just grazing three thousand feet and with the air temperature at minus six and falling, she has drunk a cup of hot soup, brushed her teeth, washed her face with a delicious gloveful of snow, pulled on a silk balaclava pre-warmed in her inside pocket, and is comfortably fast asleep. Her eyelashes, dark, carry a single fleck of wind-borne snow.

A hundred miles to the south, a 747 howls through space, heading for what was once the New World.

2. Life ring

'Do I feel her assaults? Indeed I do.'
Montaigne

Dan directs his steps towards the town centre: he recalls
building sites that seem the most promising wire-troves.
Reading is an obstacle-course town of underpasses, multi-
storey car-parks and complex pedestrian crossings. The River
Kennet somehow burrows its way through the concrete jungle
to join the larger Thames, which glides dismissively round the
leafier north side of the town.

There are youths on the Kennet's towpath, up to no good.
Youths — at the age of thirty-two, Dan already finds the word
on his lips. He stops for a moment on the footbridge. A girl
who ought to be cold is trying to hula the life-ring, and shrieks
when it lands on her foot with a thud. A boy laughs.

'Piece of shit,' she declares, and heaves the ring not very
impressively into the river. *Splosh*. A couple of half-hearted
cheers. Then the group wanders on down the towpath walkway.

Ripples glint as the life-ring begins to drift downstream,
accelerating silently. Two thoughts branch in Dan's mind. The
first is how the season of peak flow depends on the geography
of the region: while alpine rivers are super-charged by snowmelt
in the early summer and tropical waters are swelled by the

rainy season, here, in a temperate lowland with year-round rainfall, evaporation rates run the show and winter is the river's busy shift.

This thought snaps out automatically along synapses long trained to test observations against stores of knowledge. The second thought is more leisurely, and seems to reach away in the direction of the retreating teenagers: while these kids probably do suffer from a failure to imagine that something bad might happen to them, or to someone they love, the girl may have rightly estimated that the probability of any single life-ring ever being used to save a life is almost zero. He'll give her the benefit of the doubt.

He continues apprehensively into the boozy heart of the town. A glimpsed crane leads him down an unfamiliar street, and he is soon lost. Reading has a special gift for disorientation. After four years his mental map is still a bubble-chart of familiar fragments with no unifying structure. He does know the ring road — a crumpled triangle with each side a little under a mile — and so his last resort is always to proceed in a straight line until he hits this noisy and well-charted feature. Tonight he is in no hurry, so he allows himself to wander.

In a grimy side-street, more youths and plenty of not-so-youths stand outside a bar, and will have to be passed. Dan checks his dressing gown belt and tries to project a force-field of unremarkability. He receives stares and sniggers but no comments until his back is turned. Then a voice booms.

''ospital's the other way, mate!'

Guffaws. But this direction is helpful. If the hospital — and Natalie — are behind him, he is on course for the building sites near the station.

'Freak,' is the funny-man's final judgement. We are all freaks: we are all highly improbable. The crane looms nearer, and here is the last obstacle — the main shopping street, bustling with revellers. Dan strides out calmly. Involuntarily his mind sketches forces onto the crane's silhouette, delighting in the knowledge that all the pushing, pulling, weighing and hanging adds up beautifully according to simple geometric tricks.

As he steps briskly up onto the pavement, he feels the toe of his slipper catch on the kerb. Time slows as the slipper drags sideways along the vertical face of the kerbstone, deflected by some slight overhang and his oblique course, unable to clear the obstacle while his bodyweight pivots forward irresistibly. In free fall, he acquires for a moment the grace of an asteroid, all Newtonian mass and no weight, rolling silently through space. Then the earth intervenes, in the form of paving slabs and a low wall that eludes the defences of his groping hands and finds its mark glancingly on his cheekbone. To trip and almost fall is a commonplace, but to go the whole hog, to crash and burn, a rare honour. Somebody cheers. The more sober bystanders hesitate, noting the bare legs and dressing gown, but once Dan has hoisted himself into a sitting position a young woman approaches boldly.

'Are you okay?' she asks. 'There's an ambulance parked round that corner, if you need some help.'

Dan looks at his angel, his Samaritan. Mid-twenties, a little overweight but healthy-looking, probably donates blood and volunteers for the Guides. Now she's dressed for a night out but it doesn't come naturally. He can feel a trickling on his cheek, touches, looks, yes — blood, plenty, a dull darkish smear in the yellow lamplight.

'Thank you,' he says. 'I think perhaps I do.'

As a professional physicist who dabbles in chemistry and biology, Dan knows precisely why the lamplight is yellow and why the blood is red. But the presence of idle paramedics waiting to pick up drunks is genuine new information.

'Shall I go with you?' she offers. Her waiting friends, hot priests and Levites in short dresses, groan.

'I'll be fine. Thanks a lot, though. Have a good night.' Isn't that what you say to young people?

While the breezy but effective paramedic patches him up, a policewoman strolls over to find out whether he's a threat to himself or others. Apparently he is, because she offers to drive him to Mark and Rachel's place. Will somebody be at home, she keeps asking in the car. Yes, he repeats wearily, they're as old as me, they'll be home. And they are, with concerned faces quickly breaking into laughter, a slightly inferior glass of rosso and, best of all, a toothbrush in an unopened packet.

Lying on his friends' sofa in the faint, pointless glow of standby lights on various screens and boxes, Dan Mock briefly, guiltily entertains the thought that he subconsciously ignored the clogged showerhead because he likes being pummelled.

Mike Vickers has set his screen to display the flight path, and is disappointed to see that it won't, this time, commit the daring aeronautical transgression of cutting the nib of the giant Brie of Greenland. The glimpse across that desolation is pure geo-porn, inspiring a voluptuous shudder of horror at the vastness of the world. This time, sparsely twinkling Nova Scotia will have to suffice.

He likes the airlines' habit of labelling unexpected cities on the sprawling continents: not Paris, Moscow, Rome, but instead Vigo, Zagreb, Khartoum. They want you to feel there's more out there to explore — air tickets still worth buying. In Mike — a rare air-travel enthusiast — they're preaching to the converted. Even Heathrow for all its faults is a place, fittingly, of big and beautiful skies. And then there are the aeroplane skies, surpassing all comprehension: a sea of shining feathers; a shagpile combed by the gods — all humanity mere unseen underlay; a field of white cow-pats as far as the eye can see; a slash of scarlet bisected by a black spillage of rain; a billowing tower ten miles high, to which jets are meaningless flecks of aluminium to be swallowed, tossed about, spat into space; horizons banked in impossible precipices of mauve and gold.

Yes, even business travel is an adventure. As the right wing dipped after this evening's take-off, Mike ogled the M25 — those two competing funeral processions, the whites and the reds — and behind it the giant glowing organism of London. A god's-eye view of this triumph of civilization to make the heart sing, of peaceful, productive coexistence, orderly yet free, unparalleled in the history of humankind.

He again picks up his magazine. Unrest. Inequality. A lost generation. Apparently. A few weeks ago, in a European airport (he forgets which), there was a handwritten notice beside the immigrant cleaners' tips box: 'your money or we sing'. He dried his hands and slipped in twenty euros. Has he done his bit?

Brenda Vickers sleeps soundly until daybreak. This is a long time if you choose to measure it in hours, which she does not. The chill has crept into her arms and hands, and slows her movements as she retrieves her water bottle from her sleeping bag, lights the stove and makes tea. Speech would be difficult — her face is very cold — but is not necessary.

Boots are retrieved from the sleeping bag, crampons fitted, balaclava comes off, gloves go on, rucksack hoisted, ice axe gripped, and she steps out onto the slope of bullet-hard frozen snow. The sunrise picks out a thousand details of striation and patina whose beauty registers only peripherally as she monitors any implications for her own body's safe, steady passage, sideways across the great invisible arrow of gravity. Her mouth has warmed up now, and she begins to sing, quietly.

The slope softens at last into a frozen corrie, which in turn drops into a narrow glen where the snow peters out. The glen broadens and leads to a bay in a loch — a loch charged with the mystery and motion of the tide, somewhere joined to the unseen open sea. She half-walks, half-jogs along the shoreline path for five miles. The loch narrows and then terminates in a bleak, rocky beach. Behind the beach is the end, or the beginning, of a chaotic little road that leads to the rest of the world. Brenda's small green van stands meekly at the trailhead, the faded imprint of its effaced Forestry Commission insignia showing faintly under the frost. The windows are double-glazed with ice.

After teasing for a few seconds, it starts. She revs the engine hard, and then swaps her boots for a pair of grubby plimsolls. On the dashboard: gloves and socks frozen into odd shapes, malt loaf wrappers, empty box of Inderal (we are permitted to know that this is sometimes prescribed for anxiety and panic attacks). She opens the back of the van and tosses rucksack and boots in beside the chainsaw, petrol can, sun-lounger cushion used as a sleeping mat, multipacks of budget tinned spaghetti and other detritus. The door has to be slammed hard, and its report might have been heard for a mile or two up the glen, had there been anyone to hear.

The van tips and weaves playfully along the tiny rollercoaster road. Brenda hums the Postman Pat theme. Her mountain shock therapy has worked its usual magic: she's out of the woods.

'Oh, you have got to be joking.'

Dan is struck by a little wavelet of joy at seeing his wife her old self, and stoops to kiss her. A fringe of bruised skin extends beyond the dressing on her temple. He can hear her shallow breaths. 'Good morning, my love. How are you feeling?'

She smiles and whispers, 'Better, thank you, but seriously —' she raises a hand to his own dressing '— what the fuck?'

It is nearly ten o'clock, and the village is audibly going about its morning business. James F. Saunders, newly awakened from his eventual deep sleep, thinks of *Under Milk Wood*. This is an unoriginal opening salvo in the ridiculous cannonade of associations that habitually pounds away at his consciousness, but he isn't concerned. Not yet. This, no matter what, is the day he will begin.

He yanks back the flimsy curtain to reveal the sea view that supposedly makes up for his lodgings' lack of practical facilities. Fifty yards of sand, seaweed and slimy bedrock now lie exposed between the cobbled ramp and the breakers. A dozen gulls peck about. 'Attention,' declares a tinny voice somewhere up the too-narrow-to-turn-round street. 'This vehicle is reversing.'

James will today break out of his own creative cul-de-sac by a decisive forward plunge into perilous waters. He pulls on his clothes, fills a glass at the sink and clears his desk of everything except laptop, glass and a tattered paperback copy of the *Essays* of Montaigne, who is to be his maharishi. He has a notion that he will write better hungry. He closes his eyes and takes a slow breath, cold fingers poised over the keys.

Mediocrity in poets is not allowed by gods or men.

3. Crowded room

'... when they are grown men we find
them to excel in nothing.'
Montaigne

Rewind eight days. A man stands unsteady and unwashed in a carriage on the London Underground, staring in fascinated horror at his reflection in the curved window. He and his inverted Siamese twin are joined at the head. As he steps back, the heads are swallowed into the bodies, and then the bodies into the legs, until he is just two grotesque unconnected legs with feet at both ends. Becks' oft-repeated prediction has come true at last: he has literally disappeared up his own arse.

He sinks to the floor and slumps back against a seat, door, whatever. With his eyes closed, the speeding train sounds like the end of the world. There is a rumbling of thunder or guns or bombs, the rising howl of some tortured phantom, a sudden juddering scream. After hours, days, it all stops. For a single second there is perfect silence. He thinks he might have died. Then the door slides open, and he falls backwards into space.

'This station is Holborn,' says a female robot. He's alive. There is a dazzling light, and a jostling. He has fallen into the surprised arms of a man with pasty white skin and floppy hair.

'Well, hello,' the stooping man says, calmly checking that

nothing unpleasant is getting on his suit. 'Are you hopping off or staying on?'

'Change here for the Piccadilly line,' suggests the robot.

'I don't care,' mumbles our fallen hero.

'Alrighty, on we jump!' The man hoists him up and propels him into a seat. Sits next to him, unnecessarily as the carriage is sparsely peopled. Sound of doors flinging themselves together. A lurch into motion.

'Had a bad day, sir?' asks the man, cheerily. 'Me too, but it's about to get better. Walley.'

The man is proffering a white, long-fingered hand.

'Walley's the name,' he repeats. 'You?'

'James F. Saunders.'

'James. F. Saunders,' repeats Walley slowly, smirkingly. 'What does the F stand for?'

A whisper: 'Failure.'

Walley smirks again. What a wanker, thinks James, to laugh at a thing like that. Has never failed, I suppose. Goody two-shoes fucking banker or lawyer. Or an accountant. Never set a foot wrong or had an original thought. Thinks his floppy fucking hair is a mark of character. Tosser.

'Tell me, James F. Saunders — would you like to have an adventure?' He still has that smirk on his face.

'Leave me alone.'

'You'll be just the ticket. Vickers will adore you. Free drinks.' He leans and whispers: 'Free everything.'

James surrenders sullenly to this wanker's whim. Maybe he came to London in the hope that the city might do something to him, might abuse him in some way, and now it's doing it. Merryman's Bay is ineffectual: the only abuse he gets there is from the weather.

'Walley! Thank God. But who's this?'

A man of about James' age has opened the imposing door — five-nine, coiffed ginger hair, cocked ginger eyebrow, dinner jacket. Sort of carrot-top 007. Another goody two-shoes banker type. Or maybe worse — a salesman.

'*Monseigneur le comte de Vickers*,' pronounces Walley, bowing low with a flamboyant flopping of hair. 'May I present my undying felicitations.' He actually kisses the salesman's hand. 'This —' indicating James with a flourish '— is your big present. A deliciously authentic wastrel. Its name is James F. Saunders. Ask it what the F stands for.' As he crosses the threshold he taps his pocket and whispers, 'Don't worry — I brought you a little present, too.'

The host, Vickers, frowns. Or rather, he conjures a complex and masterful facial expression that simultaneously communicates puzzlement, amusement, tolerant disapproval toward his friend and cheery welcome to the newcomer. Definitely a salesman, and he's good.

'I've no idea what this is about, but do come in. Any friend of Pete's is very welcome. What *does* the F stand for?'

Another handshake. Always shaking hands, these people. Next he'll be giving me the wink and gun, thinks James.

'I'm not his friend. It stands for "Fuck fakes".'

Upstairs, Brenda Vickers peers between the vertical louvres of the ceiling-to-floor blind, along the canal with its lamp-lit concrete promenades and Paddington Basin's indecisive mix of office and apartment blocks, towards a narrow chink of horizon. There is of course no comforting glimpse of distant hills or fields — this city, its peculiar breed of self-satisfied desolation, sprawls away for miles in every direction.

She steps back and glances at a full-length mirror, which

frames her reflection as snugly as an open coffin. Boyish pants, a comfortable unwired bra that just barely escapes the category of sports bra, a physique not quite Jessica Ennis but unyielding, unforgiving and impossible to dress. Her body gives an impression of solid bigness, despite being neither broad nor especially tall. She can, after all — and frequently does as part of her on-off job — dead-lift a sizeable tree. She hates being in a crowded room.

The dress on the bed was last worn the last time she was told to wear a dress, perhaps at her graduation party. Her brother, who makes such choices effortlessly, has contributed an unshowy pendant that she doesn't hate. She picks it up. She seems to have stopped sweating.

Her gift to him — he's the birthday boy, after all — was a whittled sphere of scots pine the size of a tennis ball, with carved lines of latitude and longitude picked out in black, and a simple stand carved from the same wood. It had cost her one pound and ninety-five pence, for a fine-pointed pen.

'What can you give the man who already holds the world in the palm of his hand?' That was her prepared line, and it went down well. He frowned for an instant, but then twizzled the globe with delight and unhesitatingly put it on his mantelpiece beside a bronze knick-knack that he'd picked up in Marylebone for the price of a small car, after receiving his last bonus.

Brenda takes five deep breaths and reaches for the door. Her bedroom opens onto a mezzanine gallery above the double-height living space. A throng of about fifty people sips and babbles around a ridiculous ice sculpture, which depicts a naked muscleman wrestling a python. You are supposed to pour your drink into the man's grimacing mouth, and then collect it when it dribbles, well-chilled, out of the snake's mouth, or maybe out of the man's dick — she isn't sure whether Mike was joking about that and doesn't intend to embarrass herself by trying it out. A three-piece funk band is playing some gentle openers. She walks down the open-tread staircase with a white-knuckled grip on the handrail, and tries to ignore the two-dozen faces that glance upwards.

Mike Vickers has a birthday party every two years (on the even years, he lines up a date). He sips his Chablis and casts an approving eye over proceedings. Now that Pete Walley has arrived, the only really significant people missing are Dan (a cousin's wedding — who gets married in November?) and Mike's colleague Mij, whose stunning and oddly familiar-looking wife he will once again not meet. Sly bastard, is Mij.

Pete is already standing on a chair, force-feeding the Laocoön (a custom order from hotandicy.co.uk, donated by Mike's new boss, who tactfully declined his invitation) with a vivid red cocktail. There is a crackle of laughter. Brenda isn't talking to anyone, but looks calm. James, Pete's tramp, is behaving himself, sampling but not scoffing the nibbles and now eyeing up the place thoughtfully and sipping a bottle of beer.

He's a similar age to Mike, taller, with stooped shoulders and a week's untidy stubble. Kind of southern European complexion, but paler than he ought to be. You ain't seen the southern sun for a while, kiddo. Jeans with one knee ripped (not by design) and a shabby cardigan that proclaims arty type. Didn't get the memo about not being a student anymore. Mike feels an urge to talk to him, and meanders casually in his direction.

'Do you like my sculpture?' he asks, following James' sullen gaze.

'In a way.'

'In what way?'

'In that I'm glad the rich waste their money on tasteless, pointless crap. If they spent wisely I'd be more inclined to envy them.'

Nasal voice, well-spoken, hint of Brum. No doubt a disappointment to middle-class parents. Mike smiles. 'You envy their wealth precisely because you believe it would enable you to accomplish greater things, greater good, but you would struggle to elaborate. Anyway, it's not pointless: it's a tribute. Laocoön is one of my heroes.'

The wastrel shoots him a critical glance. For a moment it looks like there might be some substance to his arty charade, but then his face slackens and his puffy-looking eyes drift off. He needs a bath, a shave, a hot meal and a good night's sleep. Mike, on the other hand, needs to rescue Brenda, and politely excuses himself.

'We won't bite!'

It's Maurice, a university acquaintance, usually tiresome, occasionally sincere — Mike always invites him because he looks flamboyant (this evening, purple silk and mascara) and talks a lot. He doesn't know about Brenda, and his encouragements have a mocking edge.

'Oh, but you will, Maurice,' says Mike, feigning disapprobation and stepping between Brenda and the Oxford crowd. 'You're like an angler fish, dangling your little lamp.' Maurice, whose face has filled out alarmingly and looks more like a pink puffer fish, stares at him open-mouthed.

'That's the kindest thing anyone's ever said to me.' The others laugh, and Mike guides Brenda away.

'I'm going upstairs,' she declares, quietly. Mike gently takes her by the shoulders.

'Let's look at you. You're doing fine. Don't go yet. I want to introduce you to some friends I think you'll like. They run.

One's a triathlete.' Brenda shakes her head.

'I can't. My mouth's going weird. Just leave me alone.' Mike sighs.

'Alright. Just observe. I want a report on who's genuine and who's —' he emits a small cough '— fake.'

It's the very worst kind of party for an outsider — the kind with no other outsiders. These people, thinks James, punching out the *mots justes* in his mind, have harmonised their affluent conviviality to perfection. Nobody is even rude to him. As an opportunity to think bitter thoughts it could hardly be bettered, and he indulges.

The recent slow collapse of his self-belief, not from visible disappointments or external influences, but from an accumulation of internal failures — the insistent song of emptiness that plays in his mind — is neatly complemented by this evening's outward humiliation. An authentic wastrel — yes, he really is wasting his life trying to do something for which he has no talent.

There is, he notices, one woman standing on her own, devouring chips from a miniature cone of newspaper — the latest droll canapé offering. Her dress doesn't quite measure up to the general elegance: a plain navy number with a bit of lace on the upper arms that might be intended to conceal her formidable biceps, but only draws attention to them. She's another outsider.

James is beginning to overheat, but he hasn't washed for three days so the cardigan must stay on. As he goes for another cold beer, he catches the woman's eye and sees a refreshing hostility in it. That's more like it.

'Quite a party,' he says, momentarily revived by the slug of lager. 'You look like you don't know anyone either.'

A monotone is the best he can manage, but at least he's talking. The woman isn't wearing any make-up, and reminds James of the primary school teacher he yearned for at the age of seven. The pangs of love were sharpest when Miss Morley was vulnerable, when the class was out of control. The face now confronting him is the same.

'I'm Mike's sister,' she says, with a voice like a sulky teenager — sulky but real. 'Brenda. I live in Scotland.'

'Ah, that explains it. I'm James. I live up that way too. Well, Yorkshire. What do you do in Scotland?'

'Estate management.'

'What does that involve?' Words keep coming out of his mouth. He doesn't really care what her job involves, but a direct approach seems to come as standard with the jaded, robotic tone.

She hesitates. 'Well, I'm more of a — a chainsaw operator.'

The c-word cuts through the background babble of urban sophistication like, well, like a chainsaw. James feels this might be just a scene he's writing, and laughs. She's a chainsaw operator.

'So, your brother does — whatever it is that he does, to feel entitled to all this —' he waves a hand dismissively '— while you dismember the crap out of trees. Interesting. I'd like to hear your story.' He almost sounds like he means it.

'My story? What are you, a journalist?' No hint of a smile. He likes that.

'No — a novelist, actually.' Why make that absurd claim? The requisite embarrassment follows swiftly: a piggy-eyed androgyne in purple silk, cradling a trio of garnished highballs, has overheard him.

'Oh? Who's your publisher, Zadie?'

Again the sullen monotone: 'I'm not published yet.'

The interloper smirks, rolls his eyes at Brenda, mouths, 'Ah, one of those,' and waddles on his way.

'I don't much like the idea of being written about,' says Brenda. A trace of warmth creeps into her face.

'I'm glad to hear it.'

Brenda has endured an hour and a half of this hell. People keep trying to talk to her. The drugged-up homeless guy was the least hateful of them, but he slunk off. Probably nicked something — Mike can afford it. Now her decline is gathering pace — the familiar disengagement from her surroundings, the muffled voices, the hallucinations: arcs of blood suspended in the air, a thundering double bass, a keen soprano wail. Jeering eyes are on her sweat-soaked back as she climbs the stairs. It doesn't matter now. Just get into the room, turn the key. Lock them out. Five more steps. Three. Two. One.

The door has been locked from the inside. She hears a muffled giggling. So stupid. Not to have locked it herself. Didn't think it would be that sort of party. Can't knock, make a fuss — God knows who might answer and in what state. Nowhere to hide. Have to get out. She hurries back down the stairs and through the hideous gauntlet of bodies — one woman points, another laughs — snatches her proper shoes and coat from the hall, thuds down the echoing stairwell — no lifts for Brenda — and plunges outside.

A fine rain is now falling, and has softened the earlier etched glitter of the canal to an impressionistic glow. It's the sort of rain to dampen — rather than quicken with shrieks of laughter and running footsteps — the spirits of the Friday night crowd. Brenda glances back up at the looming apartment block, and thinks she can pick out her commandeered room, six floors up — dim lights behind the blind. Her one refuge in this nightmare city, now invaded.

She walks. The rain is balm. But bare legs make her feel naked, and this is not a place to be naked. The shadows slinking along the towpath are few enough to seem threatening. People are dangerous. On her return she follows the other side of the canal, which is busier and better lit. There's a figure slumped in the shadows under a road bridge, but room enough on the towpath to give it a wide berth. She walks faster and her body tenses, ready to run.

'Brenda?'

She starts, and James can see it takes her a moment to recognise him, wrapped as he is in a duffle-coat and a dirty woollen hat knitted by his landlady in Merryman's Bay.

'Oh. Hi.' She still looks angry, or scared. But relieved that it's him.

'Sorry if I scared you. Partied out too?'

'I suppose.'

'I'm not really homeless, you know.' He somehow manages to clamber to his feet. 'I'm just sheltering from the rain.'

'I'm glad.' For the first time, she actually smiles. His jaded heart skips.

'I was just thinking that it's a shame that I'll never see you again, and here you are.' Now she seems to nod and shrug at the same time, as though she both does and doesn't give a shit. He perseveres: 'Could I have your phone number?'

She looks him up and down. 'Okay,' she replies at last, vaguely.

He slips from his coat pocket the neglected writer's notebook and biro that he still keeps there as a kind of private joke, and hands them to her. She writes something, closes the book and hands it back.

'Are you heading back to your brother's place?'

'Aye.'

'It's a long way round.' The apartment block is almost opposite them, but there's no way up onto this road bridge. The canal glints. 'Unless you fancy a swim.'

She glances each way along the canal to confirm the truth of what he says, and then up at the apartment block. Then she peers up at the underside of the bridge. Huge steel I-beams. She runs a careful eye the whole length of one, wipes her rain-dampened hands carefully inside her coat, and rolls her shoulders.

'You're not serious.'

'Nice meeting you.' Suddenly, her voice is bolder. 'Look after yourself — I mean that. You look a mess.'

She jumps up and catches the beam neatly with a hand on each side, and then hefts herself out over the water. She doesn't waste energy kicking her legs about, but calmly swings her weight from one hand to the other — she's done this before. He glances down the towpath but nobody else seems to notice, and in about thirty seconds the thing is done. She drops lightly onto the opposite side.

'You're mad!' he shouts. 'I'll call you.' She is brushing something off her hands, and holds them up to display blackened fingers.

'Pigeon shit!' And she walks away.

James is buzzing. Without even trying, he has activated his long-abandoned Project Q. A case study. And a conduit, a wellhead for accessing buried treasure. If I have not love. He opens the notebook. What Brenda's written isn't a phone number. The letters 'NH' are followed by two sets of five digits: it looks like a grid reference.

4. Stacked fragments

'I speak the truth, not to the full, but as much as I dare.'
Montaigne

Dan Mock pours yesterday's glass of wine down the sink. It rankles that the television, the PC and several lights were switched on all night in the briefly impregnable house. With a couple of finger-taps he brings up the graph of the Mocks' past twenty-four hours' energy usage, overlaid on the daily profile averaged over the last three winters. There is a grotesque nocturnal overspend. He does a few quick sums in his head and, from the same virtual dashboard, tweaks the thermostat to make good: he'll wear an extra jumper until Nat comes home. It's not that they can't afford it — though bills do devour the lion's share of their salaries — and Dan is neither a raving environmentalist nor a miser. He just abhors waste.

With another finger-tap he summons a Sudoku puzzle. Sudoku doesn't count as waste, in Dan's book. At university he wrote one of the first programs to accurately grade any grid on a numerical scale, and he has now linked this to a scanner on his phone to create a handheld Sudoku Geiger counter. He usually focuses on puzzles graded from sixty-five to eighty-five on his scale, only stooping to the fifties (often described by newspapers as fiendish or devilish) if he's feeling lazy. He occasionally tracks down a ninety or a ninety-two just to prove that he's still got the Mock magic. He is happy to justify his hobby to the many detractors. No, it is not a narrow-minded obsession but an elegant means to appreciate the beauty of mathematics and human reason. And an allegory, perhaps: the basic components so few; the permutations, the possibilities, so many. It seems pointless only if you've missed the point.

After nailing three puzzles, he kills the screen and turns to a pile of small boxes delivered last week. He slits the tape on the first, and lifts out the bubble-wrapped treasure: an anemometer destined for his chimney pot. Then he pauses. This is how Natalie would expect him to spend the day — fiddling with his gadgets — but he'll surprise her and do something useful. His searching gaze falls on the cupboard where they keep their paperwork — Dan has had only partial success in his mission to eradicate paper — and into which an array of bric-a-brac has been crammed to keep it out of sight. It's a mess. He starts to pull the contents out onto the floor.

James F. Saunders was runner-up in the university poetry competition in his second year at York. His poem, 'Every hour, on the hour', about Becks and all the little associations that summoned her memory, evoked such fierce melancholy that readers assumed he was bereaved. It seemed a promising start. Becks, to his knowledge, never read it.

Disappointments followed, but another little gust of hope arrived two years later in the shape of his agent, Martin — the only person who has ever believed in him. Martin was not computer literate and struggled with electronic submissions, but nevertheless achieved some tantalising near misses with James' unfinished avant-garde novel, *The Cormorant*. So he said. Unfortunately, Martin died four years ago.

Suicide has always been a mere fantasy, a recurring frisson of dread, no more than a thought experiment for so many reasons. But recently James forgot what those reasons were, and became afraid of the sea, the long autumn nights and the voluptuously humped cliffs. London was a concentrated dose of humanity: cut with nasty chemicals, no doubt, and causing unknown side effects, but worth taking as a last resort. He did find grim satisfaction in its misspent riches, in its misery and filth, in lives even more wasted than his own — but grim satisfaction wasn't going to be enough. He vaguely remembers hearing the end of the world — or at least the end of his world — galloping towards him on a tube train. It was that self-satisfied wanker Walley who saved him, by leading him to Brenda. Chainsaw Brenda is only a connection — a human soul he doesn't instantly despise — but a connection was apparently all he needed to sidestep a crash that had seemed inevitable. And to invoke Project Q.

It wasn't difficult to track her down. He has no internet access in his room, but during the summer he successfully campaigned for the Merry Ladies' tearoom to install Wi-Fi. The proprietors ignored the suggestion when it came direct from him, but when he persuaded a few proper locals to ask for it, each separately and apparently unprompted, the old biddies surrendered. James' weekly trips to Whitby Library, by bus or occasionally on foot, are now solely for the quaint purpose of borrowing books.

The grid reference led him, on his return last week, to the village of Invergarry, right in the heart of the Highlands and adjacent to a large swathe of the National Forest Estate. A few phone calls later, he struck lucky and was told that Brenda Vickers was off sick — wearily, as though this was habitual — and would he like to leave a message? She hadn't seemed sick to him. Or maybe she had. 'Yes. Tell her James called. Do you mind if I leave a number?'

The following day, a cold, sunny Wednesday, two good things happened. Brenda called him back, and, later in the evening, he had the idea for the novel. Not exactly a new idea, but a new way to unite old ideas. He was surprised by the sudden urge to tell her about it, and the opposing intuition that he should keep these cards close and tell no one. Was this momentary sense of conflict the point of conception? Had it really come at last? He had been burnt out, a charred log in the grate, a hunk of inert material in a bed of ashes. Did meeting Brenda turn him over? Were ideas coming out of him like foretokening smoke, and was he about to burst into flames?

Now it is Saturday, the day of beginning. James F. Saunders, a bitter and solitary man who has never fallen in love — unless you count harried Miss Morley from Year 3, or the determined blue-haired chugger in Scarborough last summer with the smile calculated and destined to break his heart, or Becks, who finally finished with James when he announced his absolute disbelief in love at her twenty-first birthday dinner — is writing a great novel about it. About love, so-called.

Natalie, still in the hospital ward but now sitting in an enormous chair apparently designed for the morbidly obese, tries to read. 'Which books?' Dan asked, yesterday. 'Whichever ones you think I'll enjoy,' she replied, to his obvious annoyance. Their reading choices rarely overlap, so it was indeed a sort of test.

This morning he pulled a hefty tome from his rucksack and presented it with a flourish. '*A Hitchhiker's Guide to the Galaxy*. Omnibus edition.' She hadn't intended a tone quite so cutting.

'I thought maybe you'd like something funny,' he said defensively, 'to cheer you up.'

'Comedy sci-fi's not really my thing, is it?'

'Well, I brought you these as well.' An Iris Murdoch she'd read before — he'd no doubt thought a female author a good bet — and a grim-looking Zola. Parisian squalor. Bit of escapism.

'Quite a selection. How will I ever choose?'

Dan doesn't read fiction. Natalie, Dan would point out, doesn't read fact. 'I tried,' he muttered.

She smiled and squeezed his hand. 'I know — thanks. I think I will try the *Hitchhiker's*.'

She has now confirmed that it absolutely isn't her thing, and flops it heavily back onto the table. She listens to the hospital sounds: brisk sweep of a privacy curtain; bang of a trolley against a yielding door; steady, determined crutching down an unseen corridor; gentle medley of coughs and beeps. Ostensibly peaceful. But there is that faint aura of dread, a sense that dehumanising horrors are enacted here behind closed doors. She'll be glad to get out.

She and Dan have been together for ten years, and married for six. Should he be able to choose a book for her by now? Probably. But she has always thought of their personalities as complementary rather than two peas in a pod. Their first conversation, in a Sheffield University courtyard, was prompted by Dan overhearing her correct a friend's misidentification of a swift as a swallow. But while Dan knew about birds from studying his field guides with nerdish fascination, Nat knew because she'd grown up on a farm where such things were not of any special interest but merely taken for granted: Dan had not, after all, found a birding ally.

Nerdy is not the worst thing a husband can be, not by a

long chalk. And what's done is done — love the one you're with. They do like the same music, even though Dan sings like a donkey.

James F. Saunders has written an opening paragraph. He has tried to harness something of the daring, contradictory brilliance of Montaigne's opening, in which the essayist explains why his book is not worth reading and bids his misguided reader a friendly but abrupt farewell. James imagines a publisher encountering such a sentiment in the slush pile: 'Don't bother reading this self-indulgent mind-wank.' You'd have to read on, at least a page or two, wouldn't you?

Now he is walking along the cliff-top north of the village, fag angled into the windbreak of his cupped hand, feeling already blank and exhausted. The wind has turned easterly, and an early flurry of snow is sailing in from the sea and accumulating in wavering strands in the grass. He plods up to the top of the little headland, to a sheltering wall and stile.

He's often imagined his ashes being scattered at this spot, which, presumably, he loves as much as anybody else. Perhaps his erstwhile friends would even place an unobtrusive, guilt-assuaging memorial stone in the wall. His eyes wander along the stacked fragments of North Yorkshire shale, looking for a suitable nook. There, just in the place he would have chosen, he finds a memorial already staking its claim. He scoops a handful of snow from the little drift at the foot of the wall and rubs it across the weathered inscription. '*In loving ...*' Whatever.

Such a crowded world: crowded ideas, crowded schedules, crowded airwaves. He feels hemmed in, corralled by both his literary antecedents and his own smug generation into a hopelessly narrow realm of expression. He can't even find an original place to die. But he will carve out a territory: he'll fight for it, whatever the cost.

What, you might ask, does Montaigne have to do with love? In more than a hundred essays, the navel-gazing, ruff-toting Frenchman didn't think to give his wife more than a passing mention. But this patron saint of the self is, James has realised, his perfect guide through the landscape of the supposedly selfless emotion. Love is patient, love is kind, doesn't boast, keeps no ledger, is always home by nine, washes behind its ears, et cetera. Alternatively, *love is the flame life's Fury slings*. Either way, love is supposed to be a surrender of the self, but it isn't: love is an emanation. James feels he's glimpsed unexplored realms of possibility, and can tell his loved-out and lied-to readers — if he's destined to have any — something new and surprising. Love-affirming and self-affirming, is what the critics will say.

He doesn't reopen his laptop until late in the evening. That time of day — the sweet spot between blank, saturated daylight and the terrible desolation of the small hours, when everyone else is slumped in front of the telly or pissing away their wages in bars — has been a loyal friend to him. Take the fuckers by surprise.

He nervously reads through his opening gambit. Two memories from London have been bothering him: a tiny silhouette seated at a towering concert organ, ready to unleash the sublime; and a junkie tunelessly sucking and blowing a mouth organ with a paper cup between his feet. Which is he?

Dan pulls out a heavy box of unsorted papers, and begins to extract folders, loose papers and magazines that were saved for reasons now forgotten. Before chemistry (the calcium ions) and fluid mechanics (the water pressure) intervened, Natalie had ear-marked today for an early Christmas shopping sortie, unmoved by Dan's annual suggestion to do it all online. A cinema visit was to follow. Now, unexpected Natlessness and the troubling memory of her shallow, painful breaths keep turning his thoughts back to her.

Natalie. People talk of chemistry in relationships — the mere exchange of electrons — which naturally leads a physicist to a metaphor for something deeper, more fundamental and more potent: Natalie has turned out to be the nuclear reaction of his life.

A stranger seeing her for the first time might not describe her as beautiful. This is mostly irrelevant, though Dan has never been able to entirely ignore the discrepancy between his adolescent ideal of womankind — lithe, grave, dark-haired and ivory-skinned — and the red-headed reality of his wife: small, freckly and sardonic with a button-nose. Does this mismatch imply anything about the world's measure of his own worth? Perhaps they are both in the second or third tier of the selection game.

Yet outward beauty is mostly a cultural construct, whereas some of Natalie's qualities may be absolute. There are her character strengths, of course — her honesty, courage and kindness being instinctive (most of the time), while Dan's require a resolve that cannot always be relied upon — but there is something physical, too, something fascinating about the way her body is proportioned, and the way it moves, that doesn't wear out but grows with familiarity. A glimpsed memory: Nat swimming her strong breaststroke in the pool at his aunt's Spanish villa, fully submerged in that instant just after the kick, at once motionless and in surging motion. Yes, it is these subtler qualities that make her a desirable mate. Dan smiles at the idea that he had any choice in the matter: their courtship didn't feel at all like the Darwinian process that, biologically speaking, it was.

He frowns and drops a pile of *New Scientist* magazines into the recycling bin with a thump. Is it normal for a husband to subject his sick wife to an evaluation, to write her a spousal report card? Is he a calculating monster? And hasn't he overlooked the component of their relationship that cannot be rationalised: the mysterious ember at its core, dormant in the day-to-day but capable of sudden flares? He was, after all, not long ago, brought almost to tears by the sight of a mortal vein pulsing in the crook of her arm. He turns back to his labour with a resolve — yes, sadly it requires resolve — to be humbler, more generous and less questioning in his affection.

At the bottom of the box is an unmarked folder containing a thick bundle of letters, all written in the same hand, mostly on cheap lined paper and all in the same distinctive ink — fountain pen ink with a brownish hue. Dan has never seen them before.

5. Rocket Jesus

*'In one man's hand it is a sceptre, in another's
a fool's bauble. But let us proceed.'*
Montaigne

Monday morning. Mike's hotel sprawls nonchalantly along the prime real-estate beside Middlewich harbour, forty minutes' limo ride up the coast from New York and one of the priciest districts in America. The mega-yachts have by now all migrated to warmer climes, leaving only a few snugly-tarpaulined lesser boats to support the hotel's maritime pretensions. Inside, the decor is a muddle of mock Rococo and Provençal that Mike, to his initial surprise when he first stayed two years ago, finds rather charming.

Mike's big pitch — what colleagues call his magic show — begins in two hours. He'll poke his head into the regional office, slap a few backs, pick up his sales rep and then whizz back down the interstate to the prospective client's offices in the city.

The hotel's restaurant staff know his breakfast order: three poached eggs on brown toast (wheat toast, they call it here — what do Americans make white bread out of, then?) and half a pink grapefruit. The jazzy muzak has only just been awakened, and the remains of last night's log fire are still in the grate. One other table is occupied, by two men talking shop — an informal job interview, perhaps, or ex-colleagues catching up for a willy-waving contest, or to test the hiring waters.

'I can't change my stripes,' drawls one, a tanned walrus, shaking his head slowly, and Mike stops chewing to catch his words. 'In my heart —' the man lays a hand solemnly on his breast '— in my *heart*, I'm a portfolio manager.'

Mike finds himself coughing, a crumb tickling his throat. Is this a vision of his future? But then, after all, why not?

Whenever Dan Mock mentions that he goes to work by bike, most people assume he means a pedal bike: real bikes are out of fashion. Dan is not much of a biker — his 350cc machine is neither a muscle-bike nor a classic — but the thirty-minute blitz along the Thames Valley adds both pleasure and peril to his morning routine. He roars through the Goring Gap where the insistent Thames breaches the Chiltern hills, and then veers westward along the foot of the escarpment on the old London Road. Cornering on a bike is another glorious demonstration of mechanics: the terrible centrifugal heave that threatens to fling him into the hedgerow in either a slide, a spin or a roll depending on which mistake he makes, but that is — strictly speaking — only a consequence of his accelerating frame of reference, and the invisible, finely-tuned centripetal haul of his front tyre, imperceptibly rotated on the steering column, clawing against the indulgent road, dragging him round. The perfect corner is an exquisite joy.

Dan works his helmet gingerly over the dressing on his cheek, kicks back the stand, launches himself into the Reading rush hour and negotiates a few roundabouts and traffic lights. The open road beckons and his plucky twin-cylinder engine roars to greet it.

Of course he did know that Natalie had a meaningful boyfriend before he met her: they'd travelled a lot together, but the guy was at some other university and the long distance relationship hadn't worked out. That was about all he knew. He asked her about it a few times in the early days and she was dismissive, so he let it drop. He doesn't even know a name. He'll call him Chris.

And all this time she's kept Chris' letters. Why shouldn't she? Eighteen to twenty is an important chapter of any life. There was nothing in their marriage vows about erasing their browsing history, so to speak. Maybe, after all, she just wanted to remember what a loser the guy was.

The privacy of letters is, Dan felt instinctively, sacrosanct. Had it been a photo album, he could have looked. He'd have seen a teenage Natalie, with a bleached streak in her red hair, perhaps, and her man — Dan imagines him tall, dark and scruffy — happy and in love. There would have been lots of double selfies — a hit and miss composition in those days — their two faces pressed together (in one photo, kissing) with a wild landscape or ancient building in the background. There would probably have been photos of Chris looking relaxed and charismatic in exotic places: combat trousers, mirror shades, well-travelled rucksack. Perched daringly atop a rocky pinnacle; strumming a guitar on a beach; tearing up a blurry dance floor with unknown friends. And there would have been photos of the Nat he never knew: standing beside a waterfall, laughing, wearing not much and drenched by the spray; draped on the bonnet of a roofless car in the desert, relaxed in a short dress (she rarely wears dresses now, even on holiday). Carefree, fulfilled. So Dan imagines. As it happens, it wasn't a photo album — just some letters that he didn't read — but the effect is the same.

Now, with Dan, Nat has a mortgage, a Tesco Clubcard and office politics. However the relationship with Chris was broken off, are these letters likely to be anything other than a memento of profoundly happy times? How much of a problem is that?

'I think we'd all agree the markets aren't a hundred per cent rational,' Mike declares to the row of intent but sceptical faces. One wise old owl — white hair with that lurid yellow tinge, like tarnished silver, the CIO — three golfing family chaps in their forties, and a young woman power-dressed in vivid green. Mike has been carefully distributing his eye contact, giving Jade only her fair share even though a delicious little spark flies off her at each glance.

'They do reflect the fundamentals — growth, inflation, geopolitics, monetary policy —' he lingers wistfully over those ponderous syllables '— and it's hard enough forecasting those. But the markets mix in a lot of crazy shit.' Americans love hearing that in his plummy accent. There are nods and chuckles: he has them so far. 'Is that crazy shit easy to predict? No. But is it random? Absolutely not. It's the combined effect of a dozen behavioural biases clouding the judgement, tilting the decisions of thousands of market participants. Sure, each single investor might trade for any number of reasons, but those investor-specific motives average to zero. The biases, on the other hand, infect us all. So they're in the driving seat.'

No one argues. Mike flips open his laptop and two graphs appear on the giant screen behind him, one above the other. Like jagged rollercoasters, blue and red. The graphics are clean and spare: these graphs are more beautiful than any of the art on the walls.

'Here are two anonymous financial assets,' says Mike. He

hits a key and the graphs change. 'Here are two more.' He starts tapping the key and the graphs flex and bulge into a parade of different shapes. 'Here's a whole zoo of them. Now, just to prove I'm not cherry-picking to tell a good story, you get to tell me when to stop.' Tap, tap, tap, tap, tap —

'Stop.' It's the CIO.

'Done. Okay. Here are our two anonymous guinea pigs. Anyone like to guess what they are?'

No takers. Mike punches out a few more letters and hits enter. Five fainter lines, each in a different colour, slide onto both of the graphs from the left side of the screen. 'Here are your macroeconomic variables — the real, stick-your-fingers-in-it stuff.' He hits another key and the new lines slide off to the right. He pauses for effect.

'We don't care about those.'

The CIO raises an eyebrow. 'Economic forecasting isn't our game,' continues Mike. 'You hire other managers to do that. We only care about the price. Decades of research — by psychologists, not economists — has identified the key behavioural traits that drive prices. Our challenge is to model those traits, and then — this is a technical term — to scrunch the bejesus out of them until the story of our chosen investment starts to emerge. Let's see what happens.'

He hits enter, and a progress bar appears over the blue graph and begins smoothly to grow. Notifications appear beside it: '*Apply underreaction-to-news bias. Apply herding bias. Apply lottery bias. Apply disposition effect. Apply exuberance. Apply greed. Apply panic.*' With each new message, the graph flickers but doesn't change. After ten seconds, the progress bar completes and is replaced by message in bold text: '*MRI analysis effectuated. Model accounts for 0.0% of price variation. Signal: undefined.*'

'And we're done. Hold on — that doesn't look right. Signal undefined?'

Mike stares at the screen with a comical frown, and can sense that glances are being exchanged behind him. He catches the eye of his sales rep, an amiable Texan who only joined six months ago and who now smiles nervously.

'Gotcha,' declares Mike, turning to his audience with a grin. 'The blue line wasn't a financial asset — it was randomly generated. There's no signal, because there's no story.' Frowns all round. A chuckle. They're thinking: Is this guy wasting our time? Mike proceeds calmly. 'Let's try the red one.'

Again the progress bar, but progress is slower this time, and with each new message the line on the graph shifts — it's being dismantled, slowly collapsing, flattening onto the axis. After about thirty mesmerising seconds the bar completes. '*MRI analysis effectuated. Model accounts for 94.7% of price variation. Signal: long 56%.*'

'And there we have it. Long fifty-six per cent. This asset is, judging by the price profile, the Italian stock index.' His laptop tells him that discreetly.

'Your system wants to go long Italian stocks, as of today?' asks the CIO. He has an Italian name, Mike recalls. A lucky strike.

'That's correct. As of ten twenty-six this morning. Not full-throttle long, but decently long.'

'I'd better call my broker,' jokes the CIO, grinning.

Dan Mock loves cornering on his way to work, but his place of work itself, being circular, has no obvious corners. No, he's not a cricketer, a gladiator, an actor or a clown: he's a particle physicist. The synchrotron, a giant gleaming doughnut nestled in the downs, is all curves from the outside — but, as it happens, corners are what make it tick.

This accelerator isn't used for incomprehensible (to most) particle physics research like its more famous big sister at CERN: here, the particle physics is just a means to more practical ends. 'I make electrons dizzy,' is how Dan describes it to the laity. He and his colleagues have to keep their little flock together and chivvy them up to about 99.9999% of the speed of light. At this rate they do half a million laps of the stadium-sized doughnut every second, which understandably makes them queasy. At each breakneck corner (the track is not actually a circle but a forty-eight sided polygon), the queasy electrons, which don't like cornering as much as Dan does, spew out high-energy photons — these are what the synchrotron's customers channel into their experiments. Dan's official job is just to keep that dazzling photon-spew coming, in many shades and flavours, but he usually finds an excuse to poke around in the experiments too.

He parks the bike, swipes his pass at several sets of sliding doors and descends into his windowless lab just as dawn begins to break. Natalie is coming home today. He'll have to wait a while, until she's feeling better — just as he'll have to wait before tentatively trying to initiate some sort of sexual contact, which in further evidence of his uncaring nature he has been missing — but when the time is right, he's going to ask Natalie to tell him more about her life before they met.

Curiosity of the jealous kind — Dan acknowledges a trace of that hazardous element, uncharacteristic in him — is as unlikely to fade as desire.

'I have a question.' It's the young woman: a rising star. Even her ambition is ambitious. Mike senses both danger and opportunity.

'Sure — fire away.'

'I've run a few numbers based on the data that you kindly sent over last week. I was surprised to find that your so-called supercomputer is eighty per cent correlated to a naive strategy of buying what went up over the past year, and going short what went down.' *So-called*, she said. The atmosphere in the room is drawn taut. 'I'm talking about the most basic trend-following. Any high school geek could code it up in half an hour. So my question is: why should we pay two-and-twenty for that, when we can get it in a more transparent product for half that fee?'

The sales rep glances at him uneasily. The CIO's smile has gone; he frowns and nods as if he'd been thinking that all along.

'You're absolutely right,' says Mike, making full frontal eye contact. 'Just about eighty per cent.' Now the sales rep is frowning, too. Mike leaves a dramatic pause. 'If only you could eat correlations,' he says at last. 'But what you and, more importantly, your beneficiaries get to eat is returns. Do you know which twenty per cent of naive trend-following the MRI strategy is *not* correlated to?'

His challenger looks slightly sick. She can already guess that her little gambit is going to backfire. Nobody answers.

'We're *not* correlated to the twenty per cent that throws away most of your gains. The whipsaws. The bolts from the blue. The head-in-hands disasters. MRI can see those coming. Let's throw a comparison up on the screen. Don't worry — it won't take me half an hour.' He flashes her a smile and bangs away on the keyboard for about ten seconds. Two jagged lines appear — a black one relentlessly rising and a green one following similar contours but lagging far behind.

'Now let's adjust for different fees. One and ten, you said?' He types again and the gap narrows infinitesimally: the black line is still streets ahead. 'It was a great point,' he says, magnanimously but using the past tense, 'but I hope I've allayed that concern. Alpha is measured in returns, not correlations. This strategy delivers the real deal.'

As they all shake hands at the end of the meeting, Mike saves his earnest 'Thanks for taking the time' for the CIO, who responds with glowing compliments. The young woman offers a curt and dismissive 'thanks' — she hasn't forgiven him for making the naive, underperforming line on the graph green to match her outfit. Some things can't be helped.

In the lift, the sales rep grins and slaps him on the back. 'God damn Rocket Jesus. Now I get why they call you that.'

6. Empty space

*'The most manifest sign of wisdom
is a constant happiness.'*
Montaigne

Brenda Vickers is on a restocking team this week, which suits the sense of stubborn regeneration that often follows the passing of her darker episodes. The clear-felled swathe of mountain has lain fallow and unsightly for two years, and is now ready to nourish ten thousand new saplings — beams and rafters for the houses of 2050. A mild weather system has conveniently thawed the ground.

What was it James called the saw-work? Dismembering the crap out of trees. Sometimes that's all she's good for. Taking revenge. Other times she's almost normal, an outdoorsy girl in her element. Most of the estate boys like her, even the two or three she's slept with. You might expect these Highlanders to bear grudges, but they don't.

Her rented house, a two-bed pebble-dashed semi in a modern outgrowth of the village of Invergarry, is one of many called The Shieling. From her bedroom window she can watch the copious waters of the Garry swirling towards Loch Ness. In the kitchen, a PG Tips magnet secures a *Scotsman* cutting to the fridge: 'Mountain race abandoned after "mindless sabotage".' Brenda doesn't take kindly to litter on the mountains, whatever its purpose — she kept the stack of fluorescent flags as a souvenir. A second clipping hangs from a Nessie magnet: 'Paisley Nurse Smashes Highland Way Record.' This article is a source of private amusement because Brenda ran the ninety-five-mile trail twenty minutes faster with a couple of lads from the *Monarcan a' Ghlinne*, an elite climbers' club whose membership criteria are 'Drink hard, get up early and prove you're neither feart nor bamstick.' The *Monarcan*, who invited her to join, don't know about the Inderal.

Brenda's violent aversion to social appearances covers parties, dates, family gatherings, job interviews, ceilidh night at the Lock, and even simple photographs: since the age of twelve she has been physically incapable of smiling on demand, though that's the least of her problems. Mike's hideous party did to her exactly what she told him it would, and the aftermath of self-loathing festered. James' message was a jolt, an invasion both thrilling and unwelcome. She surprised herself by calling him back; she found she wasn't afraid to — after all, he was even more of a mess than her. But it made no difference to her urgent, gathering need to be alone, which was only finally satisfied by making herself, for one night, the most isolated person in the country. Over the mountain she went, to see what she could see. And all that she could see, thank god, was empty space.

She feels better now. She wouldn't even mind if James called her again, but he hasn't. These Sitka saplings must be planted densely, to slow down the juvenile growth and produce stronger timber. Too much space is bad for them. He'll call again.

A simile trips off James' cursor: *like a man left sitting in the bath after the water has run out*. He smiles with satisfaction and then suddenly frowns. Did he read that somewhere? Lowry, or one of the American masters? He can't be sure he didn't. These bastards are still jostling him, crowding him out. He hammers the backspace furiously, then sits for a moment with fingers poised. It's no good: he's lost the flow. He's the man sitting in that fucking bath.

When did he last have a bath, anyway? It was last Christmas Eve, on his annual visit to the Old Enemy, his parents. His mother offered him one as though he were a vagabond they had received in an act of charity. He shaved out of consideration for her bourgeois feelings.

His father is an accountant, now approaching retirement. His Portuguese mother was one too, but retrained as a teacher. They are conscientious people, who moved into the catchment of the right school and asked him gently challenging questions about his schoolwork. His father in particular, whose parents 'came from nothing' (it was writ large in Saunders lore that James' grandmother wore clogs in the winter and went barefoot in the summer), values hard work and financial security and takes nothing for granted.

Shortly after James told his father he wanted to be a writer and would not even complete his degree, a magazine was left prominently open on the kitchen table, showing grainy photographs of evicted tenant farmers in Ireland — Nanna's ancestors. The intended message: spoilt brat.

That was ten years ago.

Mike Vickers is back in London, pounding the treadmill. The good news is that the prospective client has agreed to invest a cool two hundred million dollars in his system, subject to final board approval which is virtually assured. The bad news is that the very same system is down almost five per cent on the week.

It could bounce back, of course — it has before — but as of now, both a chunk of his existing investors' gains and a slab of his own end-of-year haul have gone up in smoke. He has effectively donated it to the dopey chumps on the other side of his trades — for every buyer there is a seller, for every loser a winner. This time their irrational phobias and foibles have paid off.

A tall woman is interval training on the treadmill in front of his: she runs hard for a minute or two, leaps off, straddling the machine as the belt whips round beneath her for thirty seconds, then hits the belt running for another burst. During one of her rests, Mike studies the lycra-clad outline of her thighs. If there were such thing as a perfect body, it would soon pall. But a woman's beauty presents infinite variations: he has never seen these miraculous thighs before.

The walls of the gym are covered in mirrors, and where two walls meet he sees his own labouring reflection: the aspect not head-on but oblique; the image not reversed but true. Who is this sweaty, lecherous man in the corner, no longer in the first flush of youth, and how did he get here?

The careers questionnaire at school prophesied 'marine biologist' as his destiny, and 'astrophysicist' as Dan's. Dan's misdirection from galaxies to dizzy electrons was only a matter of scale, but Mike's own path has gone more fundamentally astray. He won a place to study mathematics at Oxford — getting one over on Dan, whom Cambridge foolishly rejected — but his first term was a disaster. The simple, memorised recipes for A-level success were useless here, where maths was taught quite differently by real mathematicians who were baffled by his lack of ability. During the second term, though, he began to get the measure of his situation — not as a scholar but as a fraud and a bluffer. He spent four years polishing his act, his veneer of competence, so that even the supposedly fearsome scrutiny of Oxford's Examination Schools merely bounced off it. After the last exam, he remembers quaffing champagne with the bewildered relief of a criminal who has just pulled off an outrageous heist and got clean away with it. Master of Mathematics. Master of anything. First Class.

The little mathematics he did grasp is all forgotten now: he'd probably fail a GSCE paper. He has come to realise that at the very core of his mind, where the weightiest and most precious substance should be concealed, there is a void. At the same time, he has come to realise that it doesn't seem to matter.

It was from a rare satisfied client of his father's that he first heard the words *hedge* and *fund* linked together. The man was a ferocious maths nerd who, learning of Mike's academic triumph, mistook him for a kindred spirit. After a few cosy chats in his Vickers-built extension — triple-glazed, climate-controlled and mood-lit — the ferocious nerd offered him a job. 'We're one of the big fish, but you won't have heard of us — and don't bother looking for a website. We call ourselves traders, not portfolio managers. We don't sit around managing. We make money by trading the right stuff at the right time: it's a zero-sum game.'

So, instead of becoming a marine biologist, Mike became a trader's assistant at a large and secretive hedge fund that had figured out how to turn the zero-sum game into a dead cert. The genius, he discovered, was only partly in the timing of the trades: it was also in the marketing and the fee structure. There was nothing illegal or dishonest. 'We're just giving the investors what they want,' one Ferrari-owning cynic told him with a shrug. 'Heads we both win, tails they lose. We call it the money valve.'

The traders weren't all cynics. But Mike felt uneasy in those early days, and told himself the mystifying job was only temporary: a way to pay off a chunk of student debt while he thought about what he really wanted to do. What he really wanted to be.

That was ten years ago.

Glancing again at his reflection he dimly remembers fearing that he might become accustomed to a mean, material existence — fearing it, but never really believing it could happen. This is how it happens. The gentle reclassification of aspirations and ideals from noble to naive, the fading of frustrations as the heart accommodates. *All will return later*, he suddenly realises. He grasps at the thought and then hastily flings it away: all will return later in the terrible, terminal form of regrets.

Natalie Mock is back at home. The doctor has signed her off work for a week, but the team meeting is tomorrow and she's going to try to attend. Dan has been brilliant: the house looks eerily spick and span as though on the market, the laundry has been done and her clothes folded the way she likes them, and the fridge is full. The showerhead has been replaced with a comforting, plasticky one with big holes that delivers a gentle but drenching rain; the cradle is no more. She keeps telling him the accident wasn't his fault.

Natalie doesn't like being off sick. Her salary is paid out of money that would otherwise be helping the most desperate people in the world, in countries where thirty-two thousand pounds goes a long way. '100% of your donation goes towards helping people like Mirembe,' say the posters that she helps to design. It's sort of true — some colluding donor has agreed to cover staff costs, to make it sort of true — but it's sort of untrue. Unless you consider Natalie Mock to be a person like Mirembe.

Which in some ways she is. Both of them grew up without a father (Natalie's died of a brain tumour when she was twelve), both are intelligent and kind-hearted — if Mirembe's photo is anything to go by — and both have been unable to follow their dreams: Natalie was supposed to be an architect.

There the similarities end. She lives a comfortable life with a loving and reliable husband, a robust health that even a stab in the back can't impair for long, free access to world-class healthcare, and the indescribable pleasure of catch-up TV.

Natalie knows that SmartAid's expensive national fundraising campaigns peddle a subtler untruth than merely disguising their own cost. They represent each problem with a photogenic individual, vulnerable, desperate and yet so easy to help. Text MIREMBE to give her three pounds right now. Who wouldn't? The true magnitude of the world's suffering, its harrowing, godless injustice, its sheer bewildering self-inflicted self-perpetuating incurable fucked-up-ness, is vaguely understood by all but a subject better avoided. Feelings of helplessness and resignation are evoked; a need to escape, not engage.

Natalie knows this from personal experience: she prescribes herself the same deception every day. As she searches guiltily for the remote control, it occurs to her that Dan never feels helpless about anything. He doesn't ignore difficulties, but simply works with what he's got. This is both admirable and infuriating.

In the early evening, James F. Saunders receives a text message on his ancient Nokia: '*James. Good to meet u the other week. I believe u may have borrowed one of my books, and wanted to make sure u have the correct address to return it to. Take ur time tho. Mike.*' Then a postal address and an email address.

James reads it again, and frowns. Brenda must have given the carrot-top 007 his number, which he considers a breach of trust. She's not the only guilty one, though: on his desk, beside the creased paperback Montaigne, is another book. Not just a book — a thing of beauty: a 1759 edition of Charles Cotton's translation in the original leather binding. Volume Two was all James could smuggle under his cardigan that night, but it contains three of his favourite essays. It turns out Mike doesn't only spend his money on tasteless, pointless crap.

He'll have it out with Brenda. Or perhaps not — has she just given him two connections for the price of one? Could the smarmy salesman brother be a useful offshoot of Project Q?

7. Mad things

'I undervalue the things that I possess.'
Montaigne

'You worked a miracle on this cupboard,' says Natalie on Saturday morning, as she bends stiffly and files away some hospital paperwork that she'll never need again. Dan immediately recognises this as his moment.

'All part of the service. By the way,' he adds casually, 'I found some letters of yours in there.' She glances enquiringly; has no idea. 'From before we met. In a bundle.' Her face adjusts slowly: the sparkle fades out of it.

'Oh, them.'

'I didn't read them, obviously. You never talk about that guy.'

'Why would I?'

'Well, it was two years of your life. I'm interested in any two years of your life.'

'You're saying you actually want to hear about my ex-boyfriend from ten years ago.' Then she adds, with sarcastic brightness, 'Which bits shall I tell you about?'

Dan shoots her a reproving glance. 'I just wondered. I'm always interested in how you became the person you are.' He crosses the room to her, remembers at the last moment not to put his hand on her bandaged back, kisses her hair. 'The person I love.'

She looks up at him and her face softens, then hardens again. 'It was just a wrong turning, a dead end — it didn't lead me here. It's better forgotten about. I didn't even know those letters still existed.'

'I'll throw them in the recycling, then.'

'Sure.' They both know he won't.

Dan survives lunch, but as he dries the soup pan he finds he can't quite let the subject drop. There's a fine line between dismissiveness and touchiness and he wants a positive ID.

'The guy who wrote those letters — was he your first?'

'Oh, for Christ's sake.'

'What?' Dan spreads his hands in protest, pan in one, towel in the other. 'It's just a question.'

'No, he wasn't. As it happens.' Dan's mind quietly boggles: how much history doesn't he know?

'Who was, then?' Nat is about to snap, but gives him a pitying smile instead.

'Just some pimply boy. Not all of us went to repressed single-sex schools, you know.'

'We had girls in the sixth form.'

'The school did, but you didn't, did you, my love?' That hurts.

James gets up too late for a coffee from his landlady, so heads to the tearoom. One of the proprietors gives a little smile of pride as he flips open his laptop, while the other looks suspicious — she's heard all about the internet.

He awoke with a sense of purpose. Mike's text message has been niggling him for two days: the slimy, hand-shaking, wink-and-gun spiv is so rich, so superior, so infuriatingly *charmant* that he doesn't give a damn about losing his book. If James had managed to snaffle all three volumes, he'd have sold them online and made enough to write for months uninterrupted by the need to earn his daily bread. Volume Two on its own isn't worth selling.

James dislikes text messages, ugly and ephemeral abasers of his beloved language, crushing it to fit a tiny screen. Email he considers an acceptable medium for correspondence (he used to correspond with friends, before 'How's the book going?' became intolerable). Without giving his objective a moment's thought, he begins typing.

> Dear Mike,
> I have the book: it is necessary for my work. If you are looking for something pretty to replace it, might I suggest a jewel-encrusted tortoise?
> Sincerely,
> James F. Saunders
>
> P.S. My intention is to marry your sister and thereby inherit your ill-gotten wealth when your chopper crashes mysteriously in the Carpathians. I hope this plan has your blessing.

Send. He hasn't felt so good for weeks. Does he have enough change for a parkin square?

Natalie has to pay attention to her breathing: normal, shallow breaths are fine now, but anything deeper still hurts. She's surprised by how often she sighs, while awake and, apparently, while asleep too. Every sleepy sigh wakes her with an unpleasant start. She stares up into the darkness and waits for sleep to come creeping back.

She hasn't thought about him, Dan's predecessor, for years: used to, perhaps, occasionally, but not anymore. Time heals. Or conceals. Or just obliterates. Outside, a jet scores a murmuring line across the sky.

She curtails another sigh. She met him in Laos, on her gap year: they had both joined a loose-knit group of backpackers to tackle a hiking trail. The two of them got ahead of the group, and she had hiccups that wouldn't go away. 'You need to surprise me,' she said, as they paused on an outcrop and looked out across the bejungled hills — a pristine realm at their feet. He kissed her (the best kiss of her life); the hiccups stopped; they stayed together for two years, despite going to different universities; they split up. Now, a decade later, she finds that she doesn't quite like to say his name even in her head.

Unlike Dan, he seemed to know her by instinct. There — she's committed the thought-crime of comparing them. It didn't stop him being a knob, of course, and the fact that he always knew when his behaviour was knobbish made it less excusable. Dan's occasional knobbishness tends to be accidental.

The comparisons come easily now. Unlike Dan, he was spontaneous. He persuaded her to do mad things — hitching a lift with Mexican gangsters — while Dan, fearsome logician, can rarely persuade her to do sane things. Why is that? After all, Dan usually turns out to be right.

Unlike Dan the walking encyclopaedia, her ex experienced the world with a childlike wonder. 'Look at that!' she can hear him saying. 'Feel this!' Facts were unimportant; guidebooks were shunned — sensation was everything. He ignored, subverted the obvious to delight in the peripheral and the overlooked. 'Weird!' he would pronounce, turning to look at her, his eyes flashing with joy. Odd, the tricks of memory: those times seem so expansive, so luxurious, while the years with Dan have flown.

Natalie remembers the feeling of being eighteen, the taste of it. 'Let's do it right here,' he would whisper, usually as part of a running joke, sometimes for real. How silly and selfish life was then, and yet ... She shifts a little closer to Dan, whose back is turned to her. Presses her face gently against the nape of his neck to smell him, feels that little stab in her lungs again and cuts short her inhalation. Slides a hand onto his chest, where he has an off-centre straggle of hair. He grunts and sleepily reaches an answering hand back onto her hip. The hand stops, surprised to find no T-shirt or pants, and he gives a murmur of pleasure.

'Hi,' she breathes into his ear. 'Be gentle.'

Stocks are down, bonds are up, copper is tanking. Mike is short copper. He sits quietly and surveys the markets. He double-clicks a chart of the copper price so that it fills one of his four screens: a jagged white path on a black map, a quiet trail of destruction that is twitching and probing as he watches.

A gobbet of economic news emerged from China this morning. Mike is hazy on the details — Rocket Jesus he may be, but he doesn't know the first thing about investing or economics (okay, perhaps the first thing, but not the second). As far as he can tell, he's not alone. The pundits paraded on the financial news channels are the new astrologers, aren't they? Spouting shameless, ambiguous crap designed to seem like a bold prediction while keeping all options open. As for the other traders around him, Mike wouldn't be able distinguish luck from skill. There might be a bit of both.

Anyway, impelled by a divine mystery, the Box, a.k.a the MRI, Mike's trading system, is raging back from last week's wobble. He raises his coffee to his lips, eyes still fixed on the copper chart. The white line jolts down to a new low, and he glances across at his live profit-and-loss dashboard. Where last week it was covered in red, now he sees black numbers multiplying. Someone has hit their stops and is dumping copper, and nobody's buying: it's free money.

His desk has a window on one side, looking into a vertiginous atrium. A translucent film has been applied to the lower half of the glass to frustrate any prying eyes from two floors below, where another large hedge fund is working its proprietary magic. On Mike's other side sits Mij, a developer working on electronic trade execution. This is in some ways an old-fashioned shop, where many of the traders still murmur or snap into their double-handset phones to trade — Mij is on the team tasked with dragging it into the electronic age. Since April, Mij, softly spoken, shrewd, somehow always in the know, has been Mike's closest confidant. Mij's name suits him well, in the manner of Little John's — he's built like a fridge — but his other colleagues, apparently lacking a sense of irony, call him that — Fridge — instead. The photograph of him and his pouting wife, for whom Mike feels that troubling sense of recognition as well as covetous attraction, stands inches from Mike's mouse hand.

It was in April that Mike's former boss, Crispin, ferocious nerd and architect of the Box, stormed out of the office, never to return. Mike later learned that Crispin's boss, one of the big-shots, a tall, stooped, reptilian man with heavy-lidded eyes, had been heard saying to Crispin, with his office door wide open, 'What was it David Ricardo said? Let your profits run and cut your losses. I think we both know which you are.' Crispin had replied, 'And we both know what you are, too,' and that was that. Once you're out, you're out of the building.

But Mike and the Box remained. It wasn't actually losing

money, just not making much, and as well as personality clashes there had been a few unfortunate breaches of trading mandates and risk limits. Crispin, who had designed a rules-based trading system of devilish complexity, didn't much like obeying rules himself.

The lizard summoned Mike to his office the same afternoon. 'Can you operate it?' he snapped. His eyes have a habit of wandering up and down, and Mike always thinks his flies must be undone, but they never are. 'Yes,' he said, feeling flattered. '*He'll ask if you can operate it,*' Crispin wrote in a text, which Mike read three minutes later. '*He'll flatter you, say you're promoted and then keep all the profits. You must DEMAND a trading contract in your name with the same $$$, and threaten to resign if you don't get it. If he calls your bluff I'll look after you. If he doesn't, good luck. Crispin.*'

That, a few months of good performance, a decision to spin off the strategy as a new product, and Mike's unexpected gift of the gab is how he's ascended rapidly from the position of assistant trader to that of Rocket Jesus. The big money is coming in next week. Since Mike's bonus — his first as a trader in his own right — will be based on his strategy's raw dollars of profit, the last month of the year will be decisive.

Mike's bank of screens is designed to dominate the real-estate of his visual field. He pushes his chair back a few inches and looks around at the office, the white-and-glass-walled cultural desert quietly humming with transactions that has gradually become his natural habitat.

To be fair, love is here, remotely. 'The wife' and 'the kids' are common topics for vapid banter, alongside sport and financial markets, but a different tone, hushed, charged, is produced for the telephone when 'HOME' flashes up on the screen. Love and its expensive offshoots are, after all, why most of the mere mortals — the underclass of facilitators of which Mike was until recently a member — are here (the megastars, seated a few desks away in the centre of the trading floor, toil for other, stranger masters).

And death is here, of course — the security guards, ex-Gurkhas with kukris, it is said, in their suit pockets, cannot keep him out. He poisons the icing on birthday doughnuts — one year closer — and drapes his mocking pall over the partners' private gym, the only defence money can buy.

As for beauty, well, there are those silly token plants that look fake — their leaves glossy as vinyl — but are in fact real, and alive, and furtively watered.

James F. Saunders needs to expedite Project Q. He has written five thousand words and hit a wall: introduced his themes but not explored them — produced an unresolved short story, not a great novel.

There is no credit on his phone, so he calls Brenda from the payphone in the Bay Hotel. *On answer press A*. The coin clatters down.

'Hi.'

'Hello Brenda — it's James.' Silence. The seconds are ticking on the display.

'Oh. Hi.'

'How's the chainsaw?' More seconds.

'Fine. Noisy bugger. How's the typewriter, or whatever you have?'

'Pretty quiet, actually.'

'Writer's block?' She's picked up a sporadic Highland twang, and it sounds like 'bollock'. That's his affliction: he's suffering from writer's bollock.

'I'd like to see you.' More seconds of silence.

'I don't know.' James holds his nerve, says nothing. 'I'll be in Edinburgh this weekend,' she says at last, the tone reluctant. 'Staying with a friend. We could meet.'

'It's a date.'

'It's not a date.'

He's elated. It was so easy. Getting to Edinburgh will be expensive, but not nearly as expensive as getting to NH 30253 00930.

'I'll wear my lucky pants anyway,' he says.

8. Unruly trail

'... whoever calls to his mind ... the great image
of our mother nature ... whoever sees himself in it,
and not only himself but a whole kingdom, like a dot
made by a very fine pencil; he alone estimates
things according to their true proportions.'
Montaigne

Let's talk about electrons. Wait, don't skip this bit! Not because Dan's dizzy little flock might take offence, but because there is magic here. Electrons, as most of us vaguely know and little care, govern chemistry and bind atoms into molecules, and so explain why everything around us — including this page, the air in your lungs and the front tyre of Dan's motorbike — looks, feels and works the way it does. Most of us could also guess that electrons are what electricity is made of: when you switch on your kettle, electrons in the copper cable start to sway backward and forward, like weeds on the seabed. The electric current shuttles through at the speed of light, but the electrons themselves just sway gently: the current is not them flowing, but them passing on the nudge, like the clicking balls in a Newton's cradle. Similes drawn from scales we can comprehend.

But what are electrons, really? Are they, really and truly,

little shiny balls whirling around in orbits, and occasionally drifting off as though caught in a breeze? Like any other balls, but smaller? Or are they mere eddies of the breeze itself, or ripples in a flowing stream? Or are they, in the end, just equations on a page, mathematical constructs designed to embody a fundamental constant — a suspiciously arbitrary number, the elementary charge, that we are told possesses a profound and magical significance — that it is better not to try visualising at all?

Dan Mock is happy to think of his electrons as all of these things simultaneously. When he first encountered the wave-particle duality, reading ahead of the GCSE syllabus at school, the concept elbowed its way into his tidy brain and started a riot. Not waves, not particles, but both! At the same time. Wow! Everything I — we, everyone — had assumed about the world is fucked! When, soon afterwards, he read about relativity and its consequences, his mouth hung open. Even more fucked. It had been years earlier, at a parents' evening when he was just eleven, that his science teacher had confidently predicted, 'Natural Sciences at Cambridge' (overconfidently, as it turned out — Dan spilled a glass of water down his trousers while waiting to be called for his interview at Peterhouse, and fluffed it). But it was then, at sixteen, learning of these mind-bending wonders, that the passion, the thrill, took root.

Since then his vision of the universe — yes, Dan carries in his mind a vision of the universe — has matured and expanded, but the thrill has remained. His vision encompasses not only observable reality, which is peculiar enough, but also the hinterland of conjecture, of interpretation, at the fringes of science. You can, for example, make the wave-particle duality go away, if it troubles you — but at the cost of accepting countless parallel universes. His job at the synchrotron combines the fantastical — electrons going so fast that time itself runs slow — and the tangible — oversized fridge magnets. Magnets are the tools of his trade. It's magnets that accelerate the electrons to their barely conceivable, take-it-on-trust speed, magnets that steer and focus them, and magnets that hurl them around those vomit-inducing corners. Dan's father — another gadget-lover, but one fitted with a pacemaker — isn't allowed on the guided tour.

Dan didn't end up at this particular synchrotron by accident. Ever since he specialised it has been his ambition to defy the critics of his arcane field — particle physics — by helping to solve real problems. In recent months he has been working with a team of pharmacologists, interrogating a protein in the DNA of *Mycobacterium tuberculosis*, seeking a vulnerable spot on which to focus future attacks.

Come on, he urges, as the electrons shine their blinding X-ray torch on the miscreant. Strike a blow for all the consumptive scientists who died before they could make their discoveries, and whose names we have therefore forgotten — and for the million human hosts TB works through every year in its own mindless, pointless battle for survival. It has a ferocious armoury of adaptations, but we, the human species, are the more ingenious.

Are we the more deserving? Dan briefly ponders interspecies ethics as he skips through diffraction images of blurry dots — TB's Enigma code. Yes: the vicious little monsters have to die.

James F. Saunders thinks about his impending rendezvous with Brenda, and speculates furiously. He hasn't had sex for seven years. After Becks commanded him, in front of all their friends, to walk out of her life (he pushed back his chair, stood up, strolled out of the restaurant forgetting his jacket and never saw Becks or the jacket again), he had a couple of drunken one-nighters. Then there was a two-month thing with Kate, the librarian with big glasses, who was a decade older and didn't really want a loser like James. He shudders to think of it.

Cowed by the failure and embarrassment of these ill-matched unions, he became for a while a sullen slave to internet porn. He was living in a shabby house-share in York, supposedly writing his debut novel behind a locked door, but actually clicking through an endless, lonely anatomical slideshow, trying to escape or conjure memories of Becks, perhaps, or just wallowing without intention. *The Cormorant*, at first so imperious, so electrifying, his paean to mortality, died itself there among the computer viruses and bog roll.

This is one reason he is happy to have no internet connection in his room in Merryman's Bay. Over the past five years the sexual impulse, which transforms an intelligent man into a slavering beast but which is, ironically, essential to his identity, has slowly faded. He has written about it, read about it, abstracted it, and finally starved and sublimated it almost out of existence. Almost: arousal revisits occasionally at odd or inconvenient times, like a bad back. He usually tries to ignore it.

Now he's going to meet Brenda. It's not a date. But he can't stop thinking about those biceps under the lace — that physicality — and a knowingness, a sexual presence that moved behind the screen of her shyness. He pushes aside his chair to make a space on the floor and attempts a few press-ups. To his surprise, he can do ten. Later, in the bathroom, he examines his stooped reflection, forces his shoulders back, tries to look like a sound specimen. Should he clean-shave, or just tidy up? Should he trim the unruly trail of hair below his navel? Should he splurge eight pounds fifty on a haircut in Whitby?

Love is an emanation. Love is a mirror. Bring the notebook.

When Natalie Mock describes her accident, representing the shower cradle with two up-curled fingers of her right hand and her falling body with her left, her colleagues' faces wrinkle with fascinated horror. The bruises and the breathing discomfort are fading and various scabs are itching and flaking over vivid new skin.

She has, of course, skimmed through the letters. The girl they're addressed to isn't her — no longer exists. Could it have been otherwise? Is it possible to ride so carefully through life, push so smoothly and confidently over obstacles and traumas, that your identity is preserved more or less intact at thirty, forty, eighty? Would you want to? Or does time itself enforce reinvention, repurposing, rebranding? Are she and Dan the same people who agreed to marry each other? Back then, she was going to be an architect (a nettling postscript: Dan was going to be a particle physicist, and is one).

> Such silence here without you. You are my voice, my music, my rowan parting the wind. Rain falls, my heart beats without a sound until you return. Come back to me soon.

While her nearest colleagues are out for lunch, Natalie opens a browser and types her ex-boyfriend's name. Thousands of hits. She skims down a few pages of images of smiling men, young and old: suited Californian surgeons, bloggers in arty monochrome, a police mugshot. Strange to think of all these insignificant men casually flaunting the same name — *his* name.

She adds 'UK' to narrow the search. Tries his middle name, the name of his university, a couple of likely professions, remembered hobbies, the city where he lived. Nothing. She'll need more to go on.

Or she would need more to go on, if she actually cared. Making himself untraceable is somehow characteristic of his arrogance. She remembers the gathering whispers of suspicion that he might not be the generous, dependable soulmate she wanted. His endless intellectualisation of their relationship was, she acknowledged to herself at last, his way of preparing the ground for future selfishness. She was certain, back then — had no regrets. But now a mischievous little hand of doubt tugs at her. All she wants is a glimpse of who he has become. To make sure. She hears the approaching chatter of colleagues and closes the browser.

Mike Vickers graciously admits to himself that his job sometimes makes him happy. The Box has recovered last week's losses, and his firm's colossal main fund is doing well enough to soothe touchy egos. He thumbs the key in his pocket and is mildly surprised to see the lights flash not on a battered Volvo estate that looks very much like the car his father passed down to him when he was eighteen (the old man had bought a Jag during a brief spell of prosperity), but on the sleek, black Audi S5 behind it. Maybe he'll gift it to his dad when he trades up.

As he drives, he dictates to his hands-free phone. 'Email. Compose. To. James Fuck Fakes Saunders. Subject. Execution. Dear James comma new line. Thank you for your frank reply, but I think we can do better. We both have doubts about our place in the cosmos.' He slows, waves a group of students across the road, beneficent behind the embossed leather wheel. 'I am succeeding at an enterprise of questionable value to mankind, while you have a calling you think noble, but have failed to execute. The problem is, your calling is only noble if you do execute — otherwise it's merely self-indulgence of the most contemptible kind.' A set of traffic lights turns green as he approaches, as though by arrangement. 'Have you at least tried to diversify? Journalism, perhaps, or tutoring? I make these suggestions for your own good, and that of the welfare state. New line. Sincerely comma new line. Mike Vickers. New line. P.S. Brenda can look after herself, as you may soon discover. Send.'

That evening, while taking a satisfied stroll along the canal, hands in pockets, quite by accident but with deific precision, he steps on a snail.

James F. Saunders is taking his mind off Brenda's physicality with some composition exercises. He's a stylist. Not in the hairdressing sense, although he did try that once, briefly, with the idea that a secular confessor might gather a rich crop of material from his customers. No, James is a prose stylist — his novel is never going to be described as rollicking.

King Edward's was rare among state schools in offering Latin through to A-Level. James relishes the dead language spoken, for its precise, merciless exertion of tongue, teeth and lips, but even more he delights in its glinting density on the page. A conventional English paragraph, by comparison, is spattered with ugly little words that say nothing much — pronouns, conjunctions, articles. If English could be rendered down to a comparable density, might it not answer Latin's mineral glint with something glistening, urgent, wet with life?

It's not only the little words that have to go. Punctuation is like a disease on the skin of the language, a nasty, nannying obsession of amateurs and minnow-minded school-teachers.

On this point James agrees with his great Irish namesake, the writer he calls the Exile and whose faded bespectacled photograph, cut from the *TLS* a decade ago, is still tacked to his wardrobe door: perverted commas can have no place in his dialogue.

Then there is the question of voice, of seamlessly reconciling authorial omniscience and the immediacy of character; his whole armoury of means and devices must be smoothly confluent with the course of the narrative, the whole sliding inexorably towards its crisis as a river to the sea.

Flawed world, James types, *flawless apple. Glossy anomaly, turn you over yes unblemished skin a Monet sky, spotless bruiseless, flesh like crisp snow: temptation to believe in fated love. Minutes later, acid taste lingering, exposed core browning. True love: false love.*

The cursor blinks. He nods. Adds a mark to a long tally he's made on a library ticket. Deletes. Tries again.

'I have a story for you. Just to remind a married man what he's missing.'

Dan Mock rolls his eyes. 'Go on, then.' He looks forward to these meetings, which alternate between London and Reading. This cosy pub in Little Venice, a short walk from Mike's flat, is a favourite rendezvous.

'So it's like this,' begins Mike, in a low, conspiratorial voice. 'I have a date, name of Victoria, who's a friend of a friend of Pete's. I've got tickets for *Betrayal,* and we're supposed to meet in the foyer, and then have dinner afterwards. Problem is, she doesn't show. Doesn't answer her phone. These are great tickets, and I don't want to waste them. What do I do?'

'Phone a friend?' suggests Dan.

'No time for that — it starts in five minutes. So I go outside and call out, "One free ticket for the performance starting now! Best seat in the house! Only catch is that you have to sit next to me!" It takes a few goes, but eventually there's a taker. She's an older woman, forty, maybe, but —'

'— strangely attractive,' contributes Dan, setting down his pint.

'Not only that, but she's the kind of woman I'm drawn to. Spirited. Says her name is Carmen. Intense, spirited women are, as you know, my passion. So we're watching the play, and just before the interval I get a text from Victoria: *Mike, so sorry, bath overflowed, disaster, missed your calls on the tube. At the theatre now. Hope we can still hook up. Call me.*'

'For a minute I'm flummoxed, thinking of Victoria in the bath and not much else, but then the way ahead emerges with perfect clarity. At the interval, Carmen and I battle our way to the foyer and find her — Victoria — looking contrite and stunning. I explain the whole situation to both of them, and insist they watch the second half together while I wait in the bar.' Dan frowns.

'It's the only way you could fulfil your obligations as a gentleman.'

'Precisely. Anyway, it turns out the two girls get on like a theatre on fire. Afterwards, Carmen thanks us graciously and wishes us a good evening, but Vic's having none of that, and invites her along to dinner. Of course, I've already changed the booking to three.'

'I must be a mind-reader, because I can see where this is going.'

'It is going there, but wait for the punch-line. Carmen turns out to be a sculptor, and I mention that I own a few pieces myself, and somehow we all agree to go back to my flat for a drink. We've already worked through a couple of bottles by now.'

'I've definitely seen this one,' says Dan. 'While you're making the drinks, the girls start getting friendly on the sofa. There's a close-up shot of the glasses filling, and then the camera focus shifts to nascent frolics in the background.'

'I kid you not,' protests Mike. 'That's how it is. I guess they're fired up by the play and the wine, impressed by my pad, whatever. Things are progressing pretty rapidly and I'm just rolling with it. We're more than halfway around the bases, and I'm like this —' he gestures with both his hands '— and they're like this and like this, when the doorbell rings.'

'You ignore it.'

'Of course I do. But then I hear a key in the door.'

'Who's got a key?'

'My fucking mother, that's who! I'd left a set at her house months ago, when I was on holiday and she wanted a stopover in town. "Michael," she calls softly. "Are you still up?" I'm up, alright. We all start to tidy ourselves sharpish, but within seconds there she is. I make introductions. The girls think it's hilarious, of course. "I'm afraid I've been out on a jolly," Mum says. "I would have called ahead but my phone died." Her phone is always dying. She might guess the lie of the land but doesn't let on, and before I know it the three of them are hooting with laughter.'

'And then what?'

'I went to bed. The sight of my dolled-up mother meant I wasn't even capable of having a wank to let off steam.'

'And now?'

'We're all Facebook friends. I don't think I could see either of them without thinking of Mum. I've moved on to new pastures.' He wags a finger at Dan's tolerant smile. 'Don't even think of disapproving.'

He rises, clothes-pegging the empty glasses with finger

and thumb, then leans and adds in a murmur, 'Here's a paradox of sorts. I savour each new girl, each conquest if you want to call them that, the act itself, its — its unique aesthetic details, for weeks or months afterwards. Years, in some cases. I'm a savourer, an appreciator, a connoisseur. And yet at the same time, I struggle to muster enthusiasm for a repeat performance with a girl I've been seeing for a month. God knows how you play the game to your rules. When I get back, you can tell me.'

Dan, watching his friend saunter to the bar, feels a blend of pity and envy characteristic of their alliance. Town mouse and country mouse. Fox and hedgehog. Tortoise and hare. Perhaps it's just as well Mike keeps his liaisons short and shallow. As far as Dan can tell, he's always respected his philandering and hapless father more than the formidable mother who funded his education. An appreciator? Of X, yes — of half of what life has to offer — but not of Y, not of the whole equation.

Dan feels comfortable defending his own position. His marriage is not a whirlwind of passion, and he has the potential Achilles heel that Natalie was his first and only. But he's considered this many times: his reward is something finer, a complex, maturing bond of which Mike, for all his japes, knows nothing. Not X, not Mike's territory, but Y. Right?

'Well?' prompts the japer, returning from the bar. 'Playing the lurrve game?'

'I suppose the main difference is that I'm not playing a game.'

Mike mouths the last five words in time with him — he considers his answer trite. Dan shrugs.

Later: he has cut it fine, and jogs along the foot tunnel towards the mainline station. As he takes the stairs two at a time, he misses his footing, plunges forward, and is one inch from knocking out his front teeth on the top step.

He stands up carefully, tests his jarred back and climbs into the vast chill of the station as though from an airlock into outer space, fingertips on his surprisingly intact teeth. Can he blame the beers this time and the slippers last time? Or does he need to slow down? Is he getting old already?

On the platform, two people he took to be strangers suddenly kiss. The world is full of possibility.

9. Honour codes

'Every day I hear fools saying things that are not foolish.'
Montaigne

Nobody could call Brenda the black sheep of her family: her father, Vincent Vickers, builder, property developer, solar panel supplier and serial bankrupt, is hardly fleecy white. Her mother has proved a devoted wife — Vince's third, the one retainer of his unlikely loyalty — as well as a big-hearted mother to two children, but the formative years of Brenda and her younger brother Austin were not a well-considered project. Mike's mother, on the other hand — Elizabeth, never shortened — was organised, exacting and, until recently, unforgiving. While Mike may have grown up wondering why his parents couldn't have stayed together, for Brenda the mystery was what could possibly have attracted her dad and Elizabeth to each other and sustained their five-year marriage.

Brenda is driving as far as Dalwhinnie, the nearest village on the Edinburgh railway line (road miles are precious because her van's cam belt is ready to snap). Yes, she's feeling sick at the prospect of her non-date with James, but no sicker than she would before meeting a new doctor or work associate: her social phobia is not sexual. Men are implicated in the world's hostility, in its sneering rejection of her, but they are not the ringleaders. During her darker episodes men seem merely a different species, stupid and dangerous but without malice. In happier moods she is positively drawn to their simple honour codes and their exaltation of the physical. But there is something particular about James. She has a feeling they're on the same side.

He's there before her, standing beside the station Christmas tree as arranged, reading a free paper folded over in one hand. He's ditched the shabby coat and woolly hat, and is sporting a sort of bomber jacket over a roll-neck jumper. He's made an effort. Her nerves are, for once, the better sort of nerves. She takes a deep breath.

'Hey.'

He starts. 'Brenda! Hi.' His jaw is smooth, a hint of tobacco. He looks happy to see her, and suggests they climb the Seat before it gets dark. Another breath. No trace of the usual horrors. This might just work out.

Natalie Mock has her bare feet on Dan's lap. He can't keep his hands off them, and the tickling is a distraction.

'Can't you just —' She pulls them away, reads for a while, and then adds, reflectively, 'Perverts always have a thing about feet, don't they? I've never understood that. Feet are just feet.'

'Mmm,' answers Dan distantly, still reading the tablet balanced on the arm of the sofa, taking hold of her feet again, pushing his thumb along her instep as though scooping ice cream and ignoring her evasive twitches. 'I hereby confess that I have a thing about your feet. I can't get enough of them. Being trampled to death by your feet would be my ideal way to go.'

'Careful,' she says, kicking him. 'What. You. Wish. For.' The tablet falls on the rug with a thump, and Dan looks up.

'I've been thinking,' he says, in his serious voice. 'Is it time?'

'For?'

'Is it time we had a baby?' Christ. Here we go.

'I don't want a baby, Dan. You know I don't. I'm not a having-a-baby kind of girl. Woman. Whatever.'

'I know. But think about what that means. It means this is it. The story ends here with us sitting on the sofa.'

'What story? The human race isn't about to die out. Four babies are born every second.'

'But not our babies.'

'And every ten seconds, a child dies of hunger.'

Dan frowns, suddenly discomposed. When he hears a statistic like that, he actually thinks about what it means. Doesn't jump up and down or become a vegan, but thinks about it and — in an instant — understands its moral enormity. Nat does love him for that.

'Just think about it,' he says, quietly. 'That's all I'm asking.' He's trying to look philosophical, but was clearly hoping for a more encouraging reaction. Too bad. Natalie has already thought about it. The idea of pushing a buggy is absurd; insulting, even. She thinks of women with ravaged bodies, stunted careers, dulled brains, cheerfully blaming it all on those ravenous little bundles of selfishness, the children. A fate not for her.

'I'm not having a baby, Dan. You knew that when you married me.'

He nods slowly, and then adds, 'You weren't a big fan of getting married either, I seem to remember. At first.' He loves bringing that up — that she didn't say yes on the spot and faint away into his arms. Tells it to all and sundry as a self-deprecating anecdote. That she said she had to think about it.

'No, Dan. The answer is no.'

'I hope this is okay,' says James, as they take their seats in a modest little bistro, after descending Arthur's Seat in drizzle and dying light. 'If you want to be taken to posh restaurants, I'm the wrong guy.'

'I loathe posh restaurants,' says Brenda. 'You can't imagine how much I loathe them.' James could shout for joy: Project Q at a bargain price. Once settled, their eyes meet across the table. They smile, and nobody speaks. Two introverts on a first date, and there's no awkwardness. Just energy. Charge.

'You were going to tell me your story,' suggests James at last. Brenda shrugs.

'I'm not brainy. I'm not a people person. I like the outdoors — cold, rain, snow, whatever. I enjoy what I do. That's it, really.'

'Tell me something you like about being outdoors,' says James, as the young waiter, sensing romance, pours house red with a flourish.

'Something I like. Hmm. Well, yesterday I was thinking about the wind.' She laughs. 'Yes, that's my world. How it doesn't just slide smoothly over you. It has invisible fingers. It strokes you and tickles you and bumps against you. If you could see it, it would be all swirls and feathers, but you have to feel it instead.' As she speaks, her eyes shine. Maybe she should be the writer.

'Did you always want to work outdoors?'

'I was never a girly girl, if that's what you mean. My brother — not Mike, I mean my younger brother, Austin — we like all the same things. He lives in Australia now. Works on a farm.'

'And Mike?'

'He's my half-brother. He's a fund manager, or something. Earns megabucks. Prances about. Plays the field. We went to different schools, had different friends — we have nothing in common but he's always been there for me.'

James feels a waft of possessiveness: Mike be damned — he wants to be the one who's there for her now. At the same time he detects an echo of past emotion, of Becks' ghost. Fascinating.

Natalie and Dan are still on the sofa. Natalie is writing an email to an old school friend, Lisa, whom she hasn't seen for, what, five years? Could it really be ten? She has heard that Lisa is now both a teacher at a snazzy boarding school and a mother. Hard to imagine. At any of a dozen parties, Lisa was the one who drank too much or smoked too much and had to be carried home. Not in a wild-child way, but in an annoying, embarrassing way.

Lisa was in Laos, on that hike. Afterwards, she followed them around half of Asia, ignoring hints. When they finally shook her off, leaving her with some wacko Americans on Phuket, Natalie was struck by remorse. But annoying Lisa has done just fine.

Lisa kept in touch with the backpacker crowd, Natalie recalls, and always knew who was doing what with whom. She'll put the crucial enquiry in a casual, gossipy postscript. She glances at Dan but he's miles away, poring over a complicated diagram on his tablet. She and Dan don't read each other's emails: it's a privacy thing, a respect thing, like not using the toilet while the other person's in the shower. Or it's a trust thing.

As she types, her heart flutters. But the involvement of that organ is incidental biology.

May God bless Brenda, who has the key to a friend's empty flat, and who, without asking where James was planning to stay, positively encouraged their evening towards that destination. His booking at the youth hostel won't be needed.

In her friend's grubby kitchen, which is miraculously provisioned with booze, fruit and ice, they make cocktails that would have cost him dear at a bar.

After a raid on the kitchen cupboards, he returns to the sofa to find her lying on the floor on her front, eyes closed. Surely she hasn't passed out on him?

'Brenda?'

'When I was little,' she says, wide awake, her eyes still closed, 'if my dad was riding his luck, we'd go on holiday to Spain. The Costa Brava. I remember lying exactly like this on the beach, eyes closed, head on my arms, listening to the waves breaking — that slow, irregular rhythm, sometimes a big wave, sometimes a small one — and feeling the hot sand between my toes, the breeze coming and going, nothing to do but soak it all in, thinking, "This is now. You wanted this, you waited for months for this, and here it is. Soon it will be over and you'll be home, with lessons and homework and people you hate, remembering this moment and wishing you were back here. But this is now, right now." I was just thinking the same thing: "This is now."'

Not much later, they're in Brenda's friend's bed. James is in the stupor of any starved man presented with a feast, and content to follow Brenda's lead. She won't stay underneath him, but rolls him this way and that, laughing, until they lie side by side in an awkward tangle.

The laughing troubles him. To James, sex is about as funny as appendicitis or the Cuban Missile Crisis. He has a vivid memory of Becks once laughing in his face. There he was, desperate, defenceless — ethereal, you might say, flush'd and like a throbbing star — and she laughed. Couldn't help it, she said. The look on his face. She apologised lovingly but he never quite forgave her. Anything but that. Brenda's laughter isn't so bad: she isn't laughing at him. Is she?

Gradually, these thoughts fade as his mental field collapses into a point. He unthinkingly takes hold of her hip, tries to turn her to better direct his efforts. She disengages. Did he go too far? 'If you want it that way,' she says in a matter-of-fact voice, rising onto hands and widely-planted knees, 'we might as well do it properly.' Her eyes flash a friendly challenge. Christ, this woman means business, after all. How long will he last? He finds his gaze fixed on the knotted contours of her upper back, the deep valley between muscles drawn together over her spine. For a brief, weird instant he's fucking a guy, not a girl. This distracting notion helps to delay his moment of crisis, which nevertheless rushes upon him all too soon.

The sheet splits loudly, right between his knees. A few stunned seconds follow — deep, slowing exhalations — before they both dissolve in laughter.

Brenda wakes before James. The flat is cold. She pees, brushes her teeth, and then lies back down to watch him for a while. Every morning after every social interaction, her impulsive habit is to pick over each mortifying episode — the wrong things she said, the people who laughed at her or ignored her, the witnesses to her freakish symptoms — and work herself into a delicious agony of shame. But this morning is different — she casts her mind back over the previous day and doesn't feel any trace of her signature emotion.

James doesn't snore. He's dead to the world. These writers get up late. He probably has a cheap ticket only valid on one train.

'Hey. Morning. When's your train?'

'Hmm.' He sighs, moistens his mouth, opens his eyes. They wander down over the small breasts that for some reason she isn't ashamed of, the washboard stomach, then back up to meet hers. 'Love is pleasin',' he sings, in a soft, Irish lilt. 'Love is teasin'. Ten fifteen.'

She wants him again. Didn't expect to. She throws back the duvet, and when he reaches for it, pushes him down.

'We have ten minutes,' she says, then adds, 'Invergarry and Merryman's Bay — this isn't really going to work, is it?'

Mike arrives at his desk early on Monday morning. He looks through the bar charts showing the Box's new signals, and then opens the window where inflows and outflows are specified. He slowly punches out the zeroes of two hundred million dollars and hits enter to calculate the new target positions. The Box uses a ton of leverage, meaning he'll have to do nearly a billion dollars of trades to regain his risk target. He opens all the trading platforms and arranges them across his screens. Markets are calm, and he'll trickle the orders throughout the morning. The first trade sitting in the holding pen, waiting for him to authorize it, is to buy seventy-six million US dollars against Japanese yen. Here goes.

At two the next morning, Mike finds himself awake and can't help checking his phone to see if anything is going on. He reads: 'YEN DOWN 6% ON BOJ INTERVENTION STATEMENT'. What the. He's short yen, right? He's definitely short. The trend has been up, but Crispin's eccentric bells and whistles are outweighing it. A gift from the gods.

But. These big shocks often reverse on a sixpence. Especially if they happen with Europe and America sleeping, on thin volumes. It could just be a flash-crash. His instincts scream that he should lock in the profits. He flips open his laptop to access his work computer remotely.

Crispin would tell him to let it be. Ad hoc interventions are a big no-no: let others be greedy and fearful, he'd say. But surely this is a special case. Mike opens the dashboard: the Box is up ten million dollars. He can't update the signals from here, but they'd probably tell him to cut the position — the risk controls would see to that, wouldn't they? Might as well do it now, secure the gains. It's not supposed to be possible to trade remotely, but Mij once showed him a trick to get round the barrier, just in case he ever needed to make a one-off adjustment out of hours. His position is one hundred and sixty-seven million, so he could sell, say, a hundred — a little more than half. Make it one twenty. He opens the currency platform and punches it in: 'SELL $120M JPY vs. USD'. Quote. Execute. Filled. He feels a surge of relief — he's locked in the winnings — and goes to back to bed.

He has a dream in which he did the trade the wrong way round — sold yen instead of bought — but bluffers like him are used to such anxiety dreams and he rides it calmly. It's okay, he reminds himself during moments of wakefulness. I'm up big, and I'm safe. It's not until he's sitting on the tube on the way to the office that realisation hits him in the stomach: he really did sell, not buy. He loaded the boat. He's short about thirty billion yen. He's probably blown his risk limits. Rogue trader. Fuck. Shitting fuck.

The crowded escalator, the pedestrian crossing, the lift — they all take an eternity. So. An ignominious end to ten wasted years. Sacked for unauthorised trading. Criminal investigation. Car-crash CV. Tabloid mockery. At last, with sinking heart but maintaining an appearance of calm, Mike walks to his desk and logs on. The screaming headline has changed — now it says, 'YEN DOWN 10% ON BOJ INTERVENTION STATEMENT'. His eyes swivel across to the tracker. His accidental trade has sent the Box up another twelve million.

Breathe. Get it right this time. 'BUY $200 MILLION JPY vs.

USD'. Buy. Not sell. Actually, let's make it a hundred and ninety-one point five. Looks more like a real MRI trade. The bid-ask is wide but who cares. Quote. Execute. Filled. Confirmed. Done.

As soon as the new trade feeds into his spreadsheet, the yo-yoing numbers settle down. He freezes the live data-feed for a moment, to savour their fat blackness. For reasons unknown, copper has moved in his favour too. Month-to-date profit: +$27,744,550. Year-to-date profit: +$33,030,898. Not bad for a night's work.

'Who's got a yen position?' snaps the big boss, the Generalissimo, as the trading floor begins to fill. Some traders look smug, some vaguely disappointed to have missed the action, a few pale and staring at their screens. 'Rocket?'

'The MRI was short,' says Mike, brightly but without betraying any of the post-traumatic elation he feels. 'It's decently up.'

'Good. Now you're going to tell me it wants to double up. Underreaction effect, right? You seriously think this market's underreacted? Underreacted, my arse.'

'No — it's cutting the position. I've already worked over a hundred bucks at seventy-eight fifty. It's the risk model kicking in.'

The Generalissimo, whose largest positions are measured not in millions of dollars but billions, looks momentarily impressed. 'For once your Crispin-o-matic contraption is actually thinking like a trader.' Then the spotlight of his attention swings off elsewhere.

Mike slowly, stealthily opens the MRI's virtual bonnet, tweaks a few well-buried risk parameters and hits a re-calc. Fancy that: the black-box supercomputer wants to trim positions across the board. Very sensible, this system of his. His contract entitles him to a twelve per cent cut of profits, which, as even he can calculate, currently amounts to more than two million pounds for the year.

A ray of autumn sunshine, having entered the atrium's pinball machine of architectural glass somewhere high above, lays its hand miraculously on his arm. He's the Rocket Jesus: the chosen one.

10. Explicit response

'Strong diseases require strong remedies.'
Montaigne

By eleven, the Japanese dust has begun to settle and Mike takes a break, dodging the cabs to cross Park Lane. His daily constitutional is mocked by market-obsessed colleagues, but contributes to the semblance of self-assurance, of trusting the Box, on which his act depends. He shields his phone from the low sun and checks for personal emails. There is one.

> Dear Mike,
> At least I have hope. What hope do you have? You'll always be a parasite. A gambler who doesn't even have the guts to gamble with his own money. You invent nothing, you produce nothing, you inspire nothing, you facilitate sweet nothing. Your industry is specifically designed to contribute nothing positive to the world. You already know this.
> Sincerely,
> James

Mike frowns, then smiles blandly. He wouldn't expect a waster like James to understand concepts like price discovery, liquidity provision and market efficiency. Should he try to explain? Could he? Something about peaceful civilisations being built on systems of fair exchange? The challenge does not appeal. He pockets his phone and walks on.

Dan Mock is getting cold hands on his morning ride. His heavy gloves have seen him comfortably through the last few winters, but maybe the insulation has become compressed, or air is leaking through the stitching. Or maybe the vibration is doing something to his circulation. Working the throttle and brake has become hard work, and when he gets to work his hands feel weak for the next hour or two. One morning, he tries to help his technician disassemble a shielding rig but the nuts won't budge. 'Which gorilla tightened these?' he asks, straining on the spanner. 'You did,' is the amused reply. Dan sighs and returns to the beam-modeller on his computer. He's not employed for his spanner skills, after all.

The next morning, on the bike, he becomes aware that not only his hands but his toes are playing up. Definitely a circulation problem. The cold, posture and vibration might all be playing a part. He decides to make a few changes, as an experiment: extra liner gloves and socks; no coffee or alcohol and keep hydrated; stretch before and after each ride and at a halfway rest. If this basket of changes does the trick, he'll withdraw them one by one to identify the true remedy.

But the changes don't seem to help. After a week, Dan reinstates the much-missed glass of rosso and puts up with the uncomfortable ride. He lets the technicians deal with nuts and bolts, and works instead on some calculations in six-dimensional phase space, and his strategy for changing Nat's mind about having a baby.

She described Chris as a dead end. She won't settle for another dead end in her life — she'll come round.

At the age of thirty, James F. Saunders has discovered the art of sexting. Brenda is less enthusiastic and often sends dismissive replies like, *Glad to hear it, thinking of u too, sleep well xxx*, but once in a while she humours him with a single explicit response (his persistent follow-ups are patiently ignored). One favourite, which he saved in his phone's tiny memory, was: *wetter than a scottish summer right now, got all 4 fingers in there but its not the same. ps. ur a writer, dont get rsi xx*

When he's not risking RSI — so much for the sublimation of desire — James is making progress on the novel. He thinks constantly of the great writers who have trodden this love-path before him. Sappho, by all accounts. Catullus, Ovid, Chaucer. The fair youth and dark lady. The Metaphysicals, Emily B., Tolstoy. La Moustache had a few fine moments in his *fleuveroo* but got hung up on jealousy — universality lost. The Exile, faithful married man branded a perv the world over, made heroic attempts culminating in Molly's heavenly rant. Colonial love-merchants like E. M., Larry Durrell and the bondage queen. And of course, the Americans: Miller, Mailer (those two sound the same here in the north-east), the Bellower, the Upstart. A parade of masters, but they all missed the mark. Thank god.

Yes, James shares Montaigne's tendency to write — or at least think — like a dictionary of quotations. Adrift in a sea of these prophets' words. The essayist notes wistfully that Epicurus *did not introduce a single quotation into any of the three hundred volumes he left behind him.* Bully for the old glutton. In 300 B.C. you could read everything there was in a couple of weeks — Homer and whatnot — and then forget about it. Twenty-three centuries later, the human race is drowning in its written excreta. But this time, somehow, James must build an outcrop of words he can claim as his own.

If he sexts Brenda on her lunchbreak, will she respond?

Unlikely. Brenda is running. While her brother hits the Mayfair treadmill, and again ogles, and again contemplates his oblique reflection, Brenda jogs up to the unmarked deer path that does a lap of Ben Tee, just below the snowline. Four hilly miles is just right to sharpen the dinner appetite, and with Brenda's job no shower is required — a quick vest-and-sock change in the van will suffice.

She jogs lightly over the rough, wet ground. Above her, a dozen deer hinds race a cloud-shadow across the mountainside. The low sun lights up a puddled morass in dazzling monochrome, and later, as she ducks and blinks in a gloomy stand of spruce, a single, soft beam drapes itself over a bough.

Brenda was six years old when she challenged her grandfather, Old Vickers, to chase her round the bandstand in the local park. He was a big, red-faced man, like her father, and he worshipped her. 'Alright, Brennie,' he gasped after a token lap. 'That's enough for Grandad.'

'But I'm only a little girl,' she complained, 'and you're a man. You have to run faster than that.' She pulled him by the hand, broke away with a mocking laugh, and when she next looked back he was staggering, his mouth gaping in a kind of yawn and his arm flopping about. Then he fell over.

She ran to him, asked him what the matter was. But he just stared up at her, looking sad and strange. She shouted for help but nobody was near enough. She didn't want to leave him, but when she sat on the ground and said she'd look after him, he pushed her away and seemed to be angry with her. She kept begging him to say something, but he didn't. Not a word. It was a long time until a passer-by saw them and called an ambulance, and Old Vickers died a few hours later.

In a shocked stupor of guilt, Brenda told the paramedic, 'We were walking and he just fell over. We were walking really slowly. He just yawned and fell over.' This was the version of events that the Vickers family first heard, and Brenda has never corrected it.

She feels her ankle begin to turn on a loose rock, and catches it just in time. The deer, traumatised survivors of a recent cull, have completed a lap of the mountain too.

James F. Saunders does not write to a weekly schedule or observe weekends; all days begin alike. Some few turn into good writing days, the others bad. Saturday opens promisingly: the indignant sea tosses spray against his window, dawn hardly bothers to break, and James, having taken nothing stronger than an instant coffee, is having visions. Creative visions. More specifically, he's losing the ability to distinguish between fact and fiction. Was Gaddafi really real? With those sunglasses, that curling lip? Or was he just another fictional bad guy like Sauron, the Kaiser and Darth Vader? Was James' aborted English degree a very disappointing novel? His keyboard rattles.

'Oi, James!'

The *deus ex machina*. Is that you, Samuel Beckett? Or is it Dmitri Karamazov? Not Mephisto, surely — that would be hackneyed.

'James, are you up there? Is he up there, Mrs Peacock? James, want to earn a few more quid?'

At the mention of money, reality and fiction begin to disengage. Earn a few quid. Yes. Need to do that. James opens the creaking casement and a gust of salty air rolls in, banishing Muammar and Mephisto from the room.

'Hello! Rob? Sure. How long for?'

The deal is made swiftly. Once upstairs, James' charge, a boy named Hugo, follows his every move with huge, tragic eyes.

'So. What shall we do? Would you like to look in the rock pools? The tide's dropped.'

Hugo looks disappointed. 'Actually, I've done that several times before,' he says in a tiny voice, his enunciation much better than his father's. Then he adds, respectfully, 'Though it is very interesting.'

'The museum?' The disappointed expression remains; it is a very small museum. 'How about exploring the secret passages in the village? Have you done that? Have you seen where the smugglers hid their cargo?'

A complicated frown spreads like a vine across Hugo's enormous forehead. His head is far too big for his body, and not quite the right shape.

'Actually, I don't think so,' he replies, carefully.

'Get your coat on, then. And take some paper so we can draw a map. If we don't draw a map, we'll get lost and starve to death.'

James glances back ruefully at the laptop as they leave. Cyril Connolly, the failed writer's writer, asserted that the only treatment for a writer's envy of successful and distracted peers is to write. 'By working,' goes the line that old Cyril relegated to a footnote, but that jingles so often in James' head, 'you are doing what they would most envy you.' By working — writing — not by babysitting creepy children.

But maybe there's some material here. Hugo, aged six, is the son of Rob, who rents the adjoining house in the heart of

Merryman's Bay. This house, originally intended by Rob as a base for family fun, became instead the venue for his extramarital assignations with Trudy, a work associate. He has now separated from his wife and lives with Trudy semi-legitimately in Leeds, but the crooked little house, with its bouncy bed and naughty associations, apparently remains useful for rekindling the flames. Rob has his son every other weekend, but makes liberal use of the childcare services of his mother — who lives further up the coast and can often be persuaded to take the boy overnight — as well as various cash-strapped locals.

This much James has inferred from his own observations and the barbed comments of his landlady. Rob doesn't say much to the Bay locals, though he did wax philosophical yesterday evening, leaning on his BMW, watching Hugo labour up James' steep stairs with a pile of beloved books and toys. 'Life, man — it happens to you.'

Rob is not back when he promised, so James takes the boy to the chippie. The weather has brightened and they carry their warm, greasy bundles up a flight of steps and along a path to a bench contemplating the village from the south. A ray of sun catches the red roofs tumbling down towards the sea.

'This is the fish and chips bench,' says the boy.

'It is.' The boy stares out at the cloud-scuffed horizon.

'James?'

'Yes?'

'Have you got any brothers or sisters?'

'No. When I was a baby, I cried so much that my parents called it a day. Have you?'

'Actually, I had a sister. But Mummy said that God wanted her to live in Heaven.' The boy folds a chip into his small mouth and chews it, frowning. 'Daddy said that means she came out dead.' James finds he has no words to answer this abridged family tragedy. 'Daddy says life goes on,' the boy adds, with his mouth still full. 'Mummy says that's wrong, and she says Daddy's a callous. But life does go on, doesn't it?'

James' sense of adult authority has drained away in the presence of this sorrowful, big-headed boy. It's not a child but a little man, a philosopher, whose minuscule bottom is perched on the front plank of the bench, feet swinging.

'Well,' he replies, 'I suppose it does and it doesn't.'

11. Unspoken meaning

'This is a backward step, but hardly perceptible.'
Montaigne

Dan Mock considers himself a feminist. In other words, he doesn't just believe in equality of the sexes, but also that society — even the most enlightened, liberal society — isn't quite there yet. Of all the campaigns Natalie helps to design, the ones for girls' education and women's rights strike him as the most laudable. He rates the empowerment of women in western and other cultures as their greatest achievement of the past century.

In spite of this, sex in the Mock marriage is not a cat-and-cat game, or a mouse-and-mouse game: it's a cat-and-mouse game, and Dan is nearly always the cat. Today, a Sunday, is day six since they last had sex. Dan is counting, Natalie is not: that's the difference between them.

Natalie swam a kilometre this morning, which both demonstrated her substantial recovery from the accident and denied Dan his habitual stratagem of pouncing as she comes out of the shower (a moment, he reasons, that might just supply the requisite combination of relaxation and invigoration — though a woman armed with hairdryer and straighteners is no pushover). This coming week he's working the night shift at the synchrotron — his seniority ensures this happens rarely, but he has to show willing — so their paths will rarely intersect in the bedroom. Six plus another five equals eleven. Dan has factored this in. Natalie, apparently, has not.

In Natalie's world, sex seems to occupy a place beside going for a walk by the river. Something to consider when more pressing tasks are out of the way; enjoyable, once it gets going; afterwards she might say, 'We should do that more often.' But peripheral. Dan envies her this absolute freedom from the sex curse. He suspects, however, that in its place in her mind are mostly mundane concerns — a mental grocery list, what to wear tomorrow, whose birthday is coming up. Is the demon crouching in his own mind better or worse than these?

Their marriage has brought Dan oscillating phases of satiety and gnawing hunger. During the sexual droughts his mind fixates on foolish, repetitive fantasies, destined to be swept away by the glorious saving fuck, which, when it finally arrives, offers richer, subtler pleasures that the demon had completely overlooked. For a few days or weeks of plenty, sex is not an obsession. Then the cycle begins again.

Like any quantum physicist, he thinks in distributions and not generalisations: there are outliers as well as averages. But he guesses most marriages are in more or less the same boat as the Mocks — the quantities of desire not merely dissimilar but plotted on different axes. Man's anxiety about Woman's sexual indifference is, after all, almost as entrenched in human culture as His paranoia about Her ungovernable lust. The poor woman can't win, it seems.

'Shall we get an early night?' Dan suggests lightly, after dinner.

'I promised Mum I'd give her a call.'

He presses his lips together and nods, stoically. These calls tend to be long. 'Okay. Come up soon, though.'

How would Natalie tell her side of the sex story? After ten

years together, Dan isn't sure. Presumably, she feels mildly pestered (though on rare, unforeseen occasions she's gone at him so hard he thought he'd suffer an injury). When he asks, she says defensively that yes, of course it's important to her. That's about it. The defining characteristic of sexual desire is its appalling selfishness: the dark heart of any marriage.

Mike Vickers commutes by car, cab, bus or tube as the whim takes him. On cool summer mornings he likes to walk to work through Hyde Park. He doesn't do bicycles. Today, the Friday morning after the office Christmas party, he stumbles onto a bus. It stops in traffic near Edgware Road tube station, next to a roadside sculpture of a window cleaner holding a short ladder and looking up at a ten-storey building — symbolising resolve in adversity, Mike supposes, or work that's never done, or following ambitious dreams. What's his ten-storey building — his noble aim? He doesn't have one. The bus moves on, passes a gap between buildings: a soft strike of sunlight on his eyes knocks down the lids — a touch of the divine. The world is full of blessings, and what is his response? To invent nothing, inspire nothing, contribute nothing. Whatever else James accused him of. It doesn't need to be factually correct — it feels true enough.

He misses his stop, and as the bus trundles onward down baubled Oxford Street and Regent Street, he watches the grotesque theatre of shop workers preparing their windows for the day ahead — smoothing, straightening, dusting, tip-toeing reverently around plastic idols in their glass tanks. Nothing important, nothing good, nothing true.

Mike begins his descent from the top deck just as the driver accelerates into the Regent Street bend. He lets his body swing wildly into the gaping stairwell and imagines himself flying through trees on a liana. Then he stumbles out onto the chill grey pavement, and it's over. All for one pound thirty.

The plastic women are far too skinny in the waist and legs, but have fabulous breasts.

Natalie Mock was thirty-one today. She and Dan hosted a little Christmassy party. They were expecting about ten guests, but only five showed. People have lots on at this time of year, and Reading is just a little too far from London — such a pain to get home. Rachel and Mark are dependable, but Mike was a no-show (payback for them missing his bash last month?), as was Dan's flighty sister, Laura.

It was a nice evening, though. Natalie jostles unopened bottles of wine into a cupboard and consolidates unfinished plates of nibbles. She made a quiche that nobody touched. 'Oh well,' is how she verbalises a crushing, disproportionate pang of sadness. She carries back upstairs the first of two chairs that nobody sat on. This would normally be Dan's job, but he went straight from the party to his last night shift. He's been looking exhausted. Last weekend at the shopping centre he seemed to be limping but said it was nothing, and this evening he couldn't pull the cork from a bottle of wine. Have to feed him up, go for some winter walks.

Annoying Lisa replied to the email. Ed — whoever he is — is taking her to the Canaries. Charlie's an early talker. Six of her pupils had interviews at Oxbridge this week. Smug bitch. No, she hasn't heard anything about Natalie's ex for years:

> He was trying to be a DJ or something — guess it
> never came to anything LOL. He was gorgeous though,
> wasn't he. Intense. I used to be so jealous LOL. TTFN.

Gorgeous, intense — yes, he was. Natalie pours the dregs of a bottle of Cava into her glass and plants her bum against the table. Party music is still playing softly. His university was barely an hour's bus or train ride from hers, and at first they met almost every weekend, comparing canteens, shower facilities, narrow beds — and work. Natalie worked hard: the studio was her passion and devoured huge tracts of time, late into the evenings, but she also had to keep up with modules on IT, construction principles, history and, worst of all, contract law. She needed support and encouragement from him, and was disappointed: he sneered when she wanted to attend lectures, skipped his own, and would sneak into the studio and distract her — it's not easy to assemble tiny model components with UHU and tweezers while a guy is feeling you up.

His passion in those days was clubbing — he considered himself a techno music connoisseur, but he'd settle for anywhere with drinks, pills, dancing, a hedonistic vibe. He wanted Natalie to be there, but he would go without her and, when she had deadlines looming, often did. He was charismatic, of course, and attracted a ragtag of disciples. He had ideas. He passed his first year exams without effort. But he had a problem with authority, and with responsibility, and with commitment.

Back then. People change.

'We did the nativity this week,' says Hugo. 'I was a wise man.'

'Very apt.'

Again the fish and chips bench. James is earning another twenty pounds, which will help to cover his bus fare home for Christmas. The annual charade.

'What's does yapt mean?'

'It means very suitable.'

Hugo has got ketchup on his scarf, and bows his big head to

suck it off. James is surprised that he doesn't topple forward. 'I had to kneel down,' adds the boy, sounding puzzled, 'worship the baby Jesus and give him a bottle.'

'I always think it's worth remembering, even at Christmas, that when the baby Jesus grew up to be my age, they nailed him to a tree.'

'No they didn't — they nailed him to a cross.'

'Oh yes, a cross. You're right. He had to carry it himself. Shall I tell you something to make you even wiser?'

'Yes.'

'When Jesus had to carry his cross, that was a symbol. A kind of message. It means that we all have to carry difficult things.'

'Like Trudy's suitcase.'

'No — things we have to carry in our heads.'

'What things?' James hesitates. Is the boy too young? No — he deserves the truth.

'Cross number one: you are alone. Even if someone else is with you, you're still alone inside — nothing can change that.' Hugo frowns his huge, sorrowful frown, but he doesn't argue. 'Cross number two: you must die. You don't know when, but you know it won't be long. When someone says forever, they're lying.' The little man fishes out his last, soggy chip and stares at it with wide eyes. 'That brings us to cross number three, the heaviest of them all.' A look of dread creeps over the odd-shaped face, and James attempts a consoling smile.

'What's cross number three?' A voice to break your heart. James scans the dirty grey horizon. A few ships, precise number immaterial.

'There's nothing new under the sun.'

Five minutes after signing off the day's trade blotter and taking a last glance at his screen to observe that the Box's year-to-date profit has crept above forty million dollars for the first time, Mike Vickers is approached in the street by a deranged-looking African man in ragged clothes. 'You got to hep me,' the man says, waving a crutch. The whites of his eyes catch the Christmas lights hanging above. 'You got to hep me.'

'Sorry,' says Mike, trying to look sympathetic as he neatly swerves round the moving obstacle. Damn. Damn horrible world. Seconds later, his snap judgement — that this was just another supply-demand beggar who shouldn't be encouraged — seems off the mark. The guy asked for help, not spare change. Mike could have told him about St. Martin's, or some other shelter that would know what to do with him. Could have bought him a burger and walked him there. Could have shown a bit of humanity.

But it isn't only Mike's mind that has a void at its core. Apparently, his heart does too. His good intentions are repeatedly caught out by the little moral tests that life sets him. These tests can't be crammed for like a maths exam or a sales pitch — they come in disguise when you're not expecting them, each different from the last. Presumably, all you need to pass these tests is a measure of human decency.

Damn horrible world. Mike takes a breath, resets his face and hails a cab with a presumptuous flick of his hand.

Dear James,
I have suspended judgement on the question of benefitting my fellow man. I have means, but it is not yet clear to me how to proceed. I shall begin by attempting to do no harm and looking after myself. I don't believe your own position is any better.

We've both a spent a long time doing what we're
doing. Today on the side of a bus I saw the slogan, 'time
is precious' — meaningless unless you know what to
do with your life, which of course these fuckers won't
tell you. May I take this opportunity to wish you a
Merry Christmas.
Mike

He's not sure whether that was a defence or a concession,
but it makes him feel better.

Dan Mock has become vaguely aware that his right shoe keeps
scuffing the ground, and that he's subconsciously adjusted his
walking pattern to stop it happening — as you might if you
had a flapping sole. It was Natalie who first referred to this
adjustment as a limp. Strictly speaking, it is a limp. And his
fingers still feel weak and strange — sort of distant. After riding
the bike, but not only after riding the bike.

Dan has no medical training beyond biology GCSE and
twenty years of the *New Scientist*, but he is not, like many men,
blind to his body's messages. Something isn't right. Natalie
thinks a rest will cure him, but he has enough data to predict it
won't. He makes an appointment.

The GP, a woman in her fifties whom he hasn't seen before,
listens to his story attentively. She asks if he has any family
history of neurological problems, paralysis, muscle wasting or
tremors. He doesn't think so. His father has arrhythmia, his
maternal grandmother had arthritis. 'It may be nothing,' says
the GP. 'But I think you should see a neurologist, just to rule
some things out.'

'What could it be, in the worst case scenario?' asks Dan.
You have to get right to the point in these ten-minute visits.

'In the worst case, it could be a neurological condition such as a form of multiple sclerosis. Or a genetic wasting condition that your family members have just been lucky not to develop.' Great choice, thinks Dan. 'On the other hand, it could just be a coincidence of several minor or not-so-minor health problems, possibly stress-related. The neurologist will have some very clever tests to figure out exactly what it is and isn't. You'll receive a letter with details of your appointment.'

The letter comes two days later: Dan's appointment is in mid-January, three weeks away. These neurologists need their Christmas break, like anyone else.

After the poetry and before the novels, James F. Saunders wrote short stories. These usually described everyday events, but were supposed to be loaded with unspoken meaning and import like the stories of his hero, the Upstart. He sent them off to competitions and won nothing. Even the university magazine couldn't find space for one. He made the mistake of reading a few last month, and they induced only bafflement and horror.

When he embarked on the now-abandoned *Cormorant*, his ambition, and indeed his sworn obligation, was to create a concise and concentrated gem with not one superfluous word (the bespectacled Exile taught him that). A sprawling, self-indulgent book was, he believed, an unforgivable arrogance, a spit in the eye of art and humanity. That belief hasn't changed.

He nurses a cold coffee in the tearoom and silently admits that Mike's emails score highly for conciseness. Tailored for an attention-deficit world. The patronising, conciliatory tone of the last deserves an abrupt and violent reply, but James finds he wants to keep the exchange rolling.

Dear Mike,

Let me educate you a little on the subject of literature. Literature can shine a light on our most secret and intimate thoughts, feelings and motives. It can pose moral puzzles of great complexity, explore the implications of social or technological change, engender empathy and understanding for those in different circumstances, and expose bullshit. Since literature spread beyond a privileged elite and trickled its way deep into the living matter of civilisation, the human race has become wiser, more sympathetic and more generous, and people have lived richer, more fulfilling lives. There is further to go. That's the business I'm in. Merry Christmas.

Sincerely,

James

P.S. As for your bus — *ars longa*: developing genuine skill and expertise takes time. I've spent ten years learning to write. What have you learned to do?

The Merry Ladies are ready to close for Christmas, and encourage James out the door. He tucks the precious laptop under his arm.

12. Family history

'I never the see the whole of anything;
nor do those who promise to show it to us.'
Montaigne

If all goes well, Invergarry to Basildon is a ten-hour journey: an hour's drive in the van, train to Edinburgh, train to London, tube, train again. All does go well. As the Intercity races down the Vale of Mowbray, Brenda looks east towards the bleak rampart of the Moors and thinks of James. Is he thinking of her too? (In fact he is in York, duffle-coated, waiting for the bus to Coventry, pondering Henry Miller's admiration for Hamsun; her train passes within a hundred yards.) At Basildon station, she throws her rucksack into the boot of the ageing Jag.

'Is that whisky I hear clinking?' her dad calls through the open window. He leans across and gives her a beery bear-hug. 'Brennie.' He's looking more and more like Grandad.

'Hi Dad.'

Mike's Audi is already in the driveway — thank god. Mum has thrown the front door open, letting all the heat out. The TV is blaring. The flashing Father Christmas is climbing the drainpipe.

Brenda's mum is smiling so broadly that she seems about to cry. They embrace silently and a tear is indeed transferred from mother's cheek to daughter's. Brenda sighs.

'Mum, what are you crying for? You saw me six weeks ago.'

'I'll cry if I want to.'

'Let's get inside and close the door.'

'You look well, Brennie.' Then she adds, with a sudden, inspired gasp, 'You haven't met someone, have you?'

Natalie is well aware that Dan finds staying with her mum awkward. It's a small house with thin walls, and Mum isn't very good at giving them space. Last year, she forgot to lock the bathroom door and Dan walked in on her perched on the loo, wearing nothing but a towel turban. Barnstaple is a three-hour drive from Reading and she insists they stay at least one night. Dan insists they stay at most one night, so one night it is.

Dan looks tired in the car — they share the driving — but he's on good form when they arrive. They've decided not to mention his appointment. They'll tell her if she notices anything and asks, but she doesn't. Nor does she mention the dreaded having of babies. In fact, she seems to forget Nat and Dan's circumstances and the lives they lead in Reading, and talks instead about the local gossip, about family overseas, and about the past. She's put on another few pounds, and her arms are going flabby. Her parsnips are still heavenly, though.

Poor Mum. Who would she be, what life would she be leading, if Dad hadn't died? She reminds Natalie of a child in a playground game who's 'out' right at the start, and just waits glumly by the wall while the other girls play on. She's mis-interpreted the rules: she could have rejoined if she wanted to.

Several glasses of wine later, Natalie closes the flimsy door silently but firmly and lowers herself onto the sofa bed that takes up most of the tiny spare room.

'Thanks, love,' she whispers in the darkness.

'For what?'

They hear her mum cough, and the stairs creak. Natalie snuggles up to Dan, slides a hand down his stomach and onto his boxers.

'What are you doing?' he breathes.

'Nothing.' His dick swells — poor thing can't help it.

'Nat. Your mum?'

'We can be quiet.'

Her mum is still moving around in the next room. But Natalie is thirty-one years old and has every right to fuck her husband. If Mum has a problem with it, she should finally see about getting herself a boyfriend. A dance class. The internet. Life goes on.

They have sex with the volume switched off. She gets a bit carried away, but the sofa bed doesn't creak. It's like being a teenager again.

'Shit doesn't just happen, actually,' preaches Richard Saunders, father of James F. This is one of his most infuriating catchphrases. He's arguing with his cousin, Joe, visiting from Cork.

'Jaysus, Richard, what made you such a hard-hearted man?' These disagreements on the interpretation of the family history are an annual tradition. As are the childhood reminiscences which Richard intends as a lesson for his no-hoper son.

'In the fifties,' he begins, as always, 'one of our favourite games was to take a paper bag — we didn't have polythene ones — and catch as many wasps as we could, one by one, until they were roaring like a jet engine. Then you'd twist the top and hide it in someone's desk at the start of a lesson —'

'Or how about the chickens' feet?' suggests Uncle Joe, playing along. 'When you came to stay with us on the farm, if my mother killed a chicken she'd give us boys the feet to play with. You could make them open and close by pulling the tendons, like little wires.'

'We did a lot with a little in those days, didn't we?' says Richard. 'Now it's all video games and iPods.' They both look at James.

'Is it?' says James. Who, apart from Dad, calls them polythene bags? 'I wouldn't know. I don't have kids.'

'Fortunate,' retorts his father under his breath, 'given the circumstances.'

Later, Uncle Joe brings out his fiddle. James has a hard English heart of his own, but it melts at the bouncing, tripping tones, timeless as birdsong, butter-knifing down the sad, swift decades. 'I wish, I wish,' sings Joe, in a cracked voice that suits the song perfectly, 'I wish in vain, I wish, I wish, I was a youth again.'

James, slumped awkwardly on the same sofa that hosted his first kiss fifteen years earlier — Emma was her name — and on which he and Becks many times sat and talked and once made love, and on which he read Virginia Woolf's *The Waves* in one spellbound sitting, and on which, fuming after a family row, he first formed his decade-old resolution never to compromise, never to submit, and never to take his father's advice, now with a glass of the old man's Jameson in his hand, feels the pang of mortality.

This song nails crosses one and two. But it's well-worn and trite, and affecting only when you're drunk — and there is cross three. Nothing new: incitement and curse.

'So. Mikey. How's work? Good year?'

Big Vince, Mike's dad, has litmus lips — blue when sober, they flush to a more conventional pink after a couple of pints. His blotchy skin seems half obscured under a permanent thin dusting of builders' plaster. Yet despite questionable health he is immensely strong. A memory: Dad teaching him to saw timber when he was about twelve. Mike would do ten hard thrusts, and then his dad would bite through the same distance with a single smooth stroke. 'One day, I'll be able to do that,' he thought then, marvelling at the mystery of manhood. He was wrong: at thirty-three, with as much manliness as he's likely to acquire, he's still a child. A crafty child, but a child nonetheless.

'It was a pretty good year for me.' On the coffee table is a dish filled with gold and silver: chocolate money.

'How does it feel to be a big, swinging plonker? Isn't that what you are now?'

'I'm a trader. But I still just run Crispin's system — I don't make trading decisions myself.'

'Funny bloke, that Crispin,' muses Vince. 'Drove a TVR but didn't know how to change a tyre. Sold up and buggered off to Hong Kong. Who'd have thought my son's entire career would come down to him?' Mike doesn't like the sound of that. Entire career. It's early days.

'I owe him a lot.'

'How much? I mean, how much are they paying you these days? I'm your father — you can tell me.'

'I'm doing well. I haven't got my bonus yet.'

'But you must have a *sense*.' He stresses that word, showing big, sound, yellow teeth. For one Oedipal moment, Mike imagines his father's enormous skull. The timber-sawing anecdote told at the funeral. He smiles nervously.

'Dad, if you want to know whether I'm earning more than you, yes I am. So if you're ever in trouble, let me know.' He stands up. 'Can I get you a mince pie?'

'Insolent little shit,' says his dad, perhaps half joking. 'Never built so much as a Lego tower.' Too true.

In a closed system, disorder must increase. Even Dan Mock's father's garage, Exhibit A, would, if locked up for long enough — a few centuries — exhibit some traces of disorder. A drip from a leaking roof, perhaps, scudding down the tiny drawer-fronts and causing their handwritten labels to run; or a draught rolling the well-sharpened pencil off the workbench and shattering the lead; or a mouse eating through the homemade pulley-based ceiling storage to bring a pressure washer or pair of trestles crashing down. Exhibit B is the human body: immeasurably higher pinnacle of order; same laws. The universe does not permit such anomalies to endure. Et cetera.

Dan did not expect the outriders of disorder to be already at his door, though his limp has, he thinks, improved. That doesn't stop his dad noticing it immediately — Dan says he isn't sure what it is but has an appointment to get it checked out. 'Good,' is Dad's reply, with a concerned pat on the shoulder. He considers Dan to be a chip off the sensible old block.

Dan takes a walnut from the bowl on the sideboard and fits it into the nutcracker. He has a delicious premonition of the nut's stout resistance, its sudden yielding to ruthless mechanics, the mysterious, brain-like kernel — its feel in the fingers and in the mouth — and the dry-mouth aftertaste. Then he remembers the weakness in his hands, quietly replaces nut and nutcracker in the bowl, and takes a foil-wrapped chocolate instead.

He can hear Natalie in the kitchen with his mum, attempting with a light, unobtrusive touch to prevent the usual culinary disaster. If he does have MS or Parkinson's, her life will change too — he's told her this. But she doesn't seem worried.

There is one possibility he hasn't discussed with Natalie: a disease his GP chose to omit from her list. Much worse than MS. Dan has looked up what the first symptoms are.

Just after four, lunch is served. God bless us, every one.

13. Lifetime allowance

'I wish for no misunderstandings,
either in my favour or my disfavour.'
Montaigne

James F. Saunders fell in love on the bus last week — he's now comfortable using that phrase: fell in love — but is recovering. It's New Year's Eve, and he's back in Bay; Coventry has nothing for him. He sits on the chill concrete of the sea wall, back against a bollard, legs dangling.

The girl seated behind him on the bus, whose face he never saw and who was probably only fifteen or sixteen, told her friend that she didn't consider her parents to be fully human, because they didn't feel as intensely as she did. They were more like fish, she suggested. The friend giggled; the girl didn't. It was an unexceptional thing for an adolescent to say. But then she added, 'And the worst thing is, they know it's true, because they were our age themselves once, so they know they've like slowly become subhuman, but they won't admit it. Not even to themselves. I feel sorry for them.'

This girl will, in time, discover her assertion to be precisely correct. Adults are indeed subhuman. Burned out bureaucrats of the species. Of course by then, she'll be one too. Won't care to remember her youthful insight. For a writer, emotion is an engine of ideas and not vice versa. If James experiences fewer and feebler emotions as he grows older, inhabits a barren, worked-out emotional field, is it any wonder he has fewer ideas?

He throws a pebble into the sea, with a vague notion that it's the right thing, the emotional thing to do. The act resounds with emptiness. A single gull flies high above, following the line of the coast, making steady progress towards an unstated but certain goal: another reproach.

It doesn't matter. There are methods, workarounds, by which old men can write great books. James walks slowly back to his lodgings. Flexes his fingers. For a subhuman to whom nothing comes naturally anymore, the novel is a test of intellect, guile, mettle; above all, memory. Bringing old emotion to mind. Project Q. *Auld lang syne.*

As Brenda's train rushes northward past the snow-dusted Moors, she again watches for James. They did not avail themselves of the opportunity to meet up over Christmas. James' texts have been petering out. Absence makes the heart grow cold, in Brenda's experience.

Mike did the older brother thing, told her to be careful. A guy like Mike is never likely to understand a guy like James. She braced herself for more, especially as James pinched his fancy book, but that was it — be careful. The cocked ginger eyebrow. Thanks, Mike, but I'm twenty-eight.

She spots a kestrel, a quivering fan of feathers fixed in space. Last summer she visited a birds of prey centre near Loch Lomond, and afterwards wished she hadn't. Lots of chit-chat about conservation but ultimately birds in cages and birds tethered to posts. There's no such thing as a cage big enough for an eagle. Now James is no eagle, but he could be, say, a

Harris hawk — perched in a cage of his own devising. It used to have big ideas; now it blinks and fidgets on a well-soiled perch looking a bit foolish. But still handsome: the noble soul undefeated.

Brenda, on the other hand, is a hooded crow soaring free: the Highlands are calling. Will her van start? And is James on her side, or not?

Mike Vickers doesn't have his money yet. His unauthorised nocturnal trade was probably a breach of contract and could, in theory, give the bastards an excuse not to pay him. But, he keeps telling himself, it made money: whoever heard of a rogue trader who made money? Nobody. Anyway, the trade seems to have gone unnoticed. Too small to matter. Mike just has to sit tight for another three weeks, and not get fired.

Every January an email goes round offering tax planning advice. Every year Mike, one of the small fry, embarrassed enough by his net pay, ignores it and takes the near-fifty-per cent PAYE hit like a gentleman. This year, Mij persuades him to make an appointment. If Mike has always felt like an imposter in this business, an inside man, now he feels like a double agent. He's always hated spy thrillers — can never follow who's working for whom.

'Mr Vickers. Please take a seat.' The accountant is an amphibian — small, moist and astonishingly ugly. Isn't the devil supposed to wear fine raiment? His wife, in her silver frame, presents a stoical smile to the camera; the gurning children have their father's looks.

Apparently Mike can whack some of his bonus into his pension, but not all of it because he'd blow his lifetime allowance. Or he can invest in some shady-but-safe scheme that attracts tax relief. Attracts it, just like that. Or he can keep the money offshore and withdraw a small amount each year, tax-free. A small amount, in his case, means over a hundred grand.

As he listens to these choices, Mike understands perfectly why the wealthy are so despised. Offshore bank account: here is the irrevocable fork in the road, the decisive plunge into Macbeth's bloody river, the final, unambiguous breach of another, more important contract: the social contract.

But. For ten years this job has been a fat, obscuring blob of self-deception stuck fast in the middle of his life. Important things — beauty, truth, perhaps love — have peeped and curled at the margins, always just out of reach or sight. He could have been someone else, someone real, but he's been this instead. He wants payback.

'I'll take the offshore option,' he says, decisively. Stepped in so far.

The neurologist is younger than Dan. Sporty sort of chap — triathlon finisher's medal, bicycle helmet hanging on the back of his door. He's called Dan too.

During the past few family-filled and friend-filled weeks, our Dan's apprehension has been a lonely burden. He said nothing more to his parents. His mum has always been a worrier, which of course means her children — usually Laura, but this time Dan — have always been less likely to tell her the things she so desperately wants to know. As for his dad, ten years ago Dan might have talked it all through with him in the pub, or more likely in the garage. But one of the subtle changes age has engineered in his dad's mind is to make him a worrier too. The pair of them are now as bad as each other. And Dan might not be horribly ill, or might be only moderately horribly ill.

Finally, Natalie: he has told *her* everything the GP told him.

Every last detail. He's wanted to go further, to fling his worst fear on the table, but something has stopped him. He doesn't want to touch that worst fear, to utter it, to justify it. Natalie's matter-of-fact optimism — she may not be a doctor, but she's no fool — is all he's had to hold on to.

Now he needs answers. As he describes his symptoms again and the other Dan nods thoughtfully, he's struck by the towering asymmetry between doctor and patient. No other human interaction is quite like it. Little wonder doctors have been revered and reviled over the millennia — setting themselves up as God. Dan himself, trained to a comparable level of specialised knowledge and skill, is a god only to his electrons; if he loses a batch, nobody weeps. Here, he might as well be on his knees.

The young doctor looks grave, but otherwise gives little away. He wants tests. As an experimentalist Dan is no stranger to the process of diagnosis, and tries to read between the lines. What he reads is not good.

'Can you give me some possibilities, in order of likelihood?'

'I'd rather not. I know it's frustrating. We'll get these tests arranged as quickly as possible — next week, hopefully. What I want you to do in the meantime is just ...'

Something about wellbeing, relaxation and living his normal life.

Brenda rubs a little Swarfega into her palms to work out the grease, then cranks up the gas fire and changes into a fleece and jeans. While she's eating her supper of tinned soup and half a pack of stale crackers, Callum, her neighbour, knocks on the door to tell her that another neighbour, Mrs McCready, had a turn after Christmas and died last week. Peacefully, he says. The funeral is on Friday.

Brenda drifts back to the kitchen, frowning. Old Mrs

McCready led an uncomfortable life; her only pleasure, probably, came in cheerfully chronicling her many discomforts to anyone within earshot — usually Brenda. 'Och, don't worry about me,' she would reply to any words of sympathy. 'I'm no good to anyone.' Which was true. A dark, tangled forest of memories, connections and secret foibles now clear-cut. Pulped. Peacefully pulped. Gone. Poor Mrs M.

Mike bought Brenda a laptop for Christmas — this is so that she can take an online self-help course which her therapist recommended after she missed three appointments in a row. 'You will develop alternative, more helpful core beliefs,' the programme confidently declares. 'Fear extinction is achievable.' She and Mike refer to it light-heartedly as her re-education course, a term her therapist gently rejects.

The first session explains the difference between agoraphobia, which as a solo mountaineer, fell-runner and expert in wilderness self-sufficiency she presumably doesn't have, and social phobia, which sounds more like it. There are video clips of other messed-up people telling their stories. I'd like to hear your story, James said, but he's not going to hear this story. Sweating seems to be a common symptom, but nobody in the videos says anything about their mouth going funny, or being unable to smile, or suspended arcs of blood.

Mike gave her cash as well, as usual. Always in fifties, always slipped into her bag without a word — it's meant to be for the therapy. She fetches the envelope, rolls the stack of notes into a tight, red-and-white cigar and pushes it into an empty whisky miniature. Screws the lid tight. She appreciates his love and concern — even if they carry a faint, selfish odour of penance for crimes unknown — but she doesn't need his money. This time, Mrs McCready doesn't either. Someone else might — someone noble and undefeated.

The annual comp letters — yes, *compensation* is the euphemism of choice — always come in heavy white envelopes. Super opaque. Mij pretends to lick his enormous finger, reaches over to Mike's envelope and makes a sizzling sound. Mike slides it silently into an inside pocket. He opens it later, in the park. It's a short letter, and the number is in the first sentence. 'Your total gross compensation for the year 2011 is £3,145,966.' Then some blah blah. Finally: 'We thank you for your ongoing contribution to the firm.'

So, here it is. Freedom to do anything. Of course, he could blow the lot in a few weeks. Move from the canal to an exquisite little flat here in Mayfair. Buy a more appropriate car, a few knick-knacks from these dimly-lit boutiques that stink of more money than sense.

Will they make him invest some of it in the Box? Alignment of interests. He'd rather not. Perhaps a token hundred k. He tucks the letter back in his pocket and looks around. The naff winter fairground rides have been taken down and the enclosures cleared away, leaving a few roped-off acres of mud. Above a smokescreen of bare trees, the naff London skyline, just as perfunctory, remains.

Yes, he could spend it easily here. Waste it. But out there in the world beyond — out there, it's a fortune, and he could do anything.

Anywhere. Anything. Absolutely anything. But what?

Round one is electric shocks, round two is needles. If Dan didn't have a serious neurological condition when he walked in here, he will by the time these inquisitors have finished with him. He really shouldn't be squeamish about needles. He recognises that a conflict arises between the instinct to defend the territory demarcated by his skin, ancient and unthinking, and the judicious invasions of medicine: the surgical strike. But old instincts die hard, and there are a lot of needles, and these ones hurt. He focuses his gaze on the intersection of walls and ceiling, and takes slow breaths.

Round three is a blood sample, and round four — he did ask to have all the tests at once — is the MRI scan. Dan and the radiographer recognise each other at once.

'You're the man who tripped over on Friar Street.'

'Wearing a dressing gown, yes — not unlike this. And you're my Samaritan. Thanks for helping me that night.' Dan can see that she's trying to figure out whether the fall and this scan are related in some way, and is about to conclude that they aren't. 'I'd locked myself out,' he explains. 'That trip was — well — they think I might have a neurological condition.'

'Right. Yes.' She smiles, nods, very professional. But she grasps his meaning: she was there at the very beginning. Of whatever this is. A disconcerting note of intimacy chimes.

'Three Tesla,' says Dan, to change the subject, peering at the controls of the giant glossy polo mint. 'That's a strong magnet.'

'This is the strongest magnet you're ever likely to meet,' she proclaims, brightly. 'Any metal objects in this room have to be bolted down.' The pen in her breast pocket is a plastic felt-tip. 'But don't worry, it won't hurt you. It's just a bit noisy. Let me explain how it works —'

'It's okay,' says Dan, with a modest smile, 'I know how it works.' His mind's eye peers into the moist, fibrous internal structure of his body, zooms in to its fabulous, soaring architecture of cells, zooms in again to its molecular frogspawn, again to a single atom of hydrogen, and again, past his little familiar, the orbiting electron, to the spinning proton at the atom's core. Not really spinning, of course — spin is just a parameter in the elegant magic of the maths of Pauli and Dirac

— but it's an effective visual metaphor. 'I've worked with superconducting magnets up to twelve T,' he adds, 'but I don't usually lie inside them.'

The scan's nightmare symphony is performed by an orchestra of monstrous sirens, frenzied ringtones and frantic assembly-line machinery. Dan stares at the blank casing inches from his face and thinks of mashers and slashers and bone-pulverisers, of barbed wire and searchlights, of Pink Floyd and late Radiohead, and of every alarm clock that ever snatched him from a beautiful dream.

14. Blank page

'These are not matters about which
it is wrong to be ignorant.'
Montaigne

James F. Saunders had a job delivering pizzas before he came to Merryman's Bay. Logistics, he told his father. Menial jobs a long-established literary tradition, of course. It was always on the scooter that his flashes of self-confidence struck — glimpses of the unrevealed truth that would be his raw material, of the glittering style that would be his vehicle, of the fame and prizes that would be his inevitable destiny. Back at the keyboard, at the blank page, this intricate tissue of hope disintegrated in his hands, dissolved, drained into the gaps between the keys, only to rear up again, shimmering, on his next ride.

It was partly to break the cycle of delusion and despair that James moved to Bay. That, and the lure, the quickening influence, the fecund promise of the elements: the sea, the sea. His lodgings are in an ancient cottage called The End House, named after something he has never yet reached in his many abandoned novels. This time, this novel, will be different.

Mrs Peacock has given James a vase of cheap flowers to brighten his desk, and he is sitting staring at these, tonguing a mouth ulcer and recalling Lawrence's 'Odour of

Chrysanthemums', when his phone buzzes and makes him jump. It's Brenda. *Hi. I have a computer now. Connection is slow but maybe we could catch up by video? Might be fun xxx*

James is submerged in a reverie so deep and viscous that he has to read this through several times, but as he finally surfaces his heart burns for those three little xs. He has, of course, no internet in his room or on his phone. He imagines sitting in a quiet corner of Whitby library, angling his laptop screen away from the toddlers and grannies, sound switched off, while Brenda teases him, stripping to that lycra underwear of hers that looks like a running outfit, sticking her sporadically-pixelated arse in the camera. Oh god, it would be torture — furtively hunched with his trousers like a tee-pee. He has to see her.

He's been putting it off. He can't decide whether Project Q has run its course or whether it has more to give. But after this message arrives he surprises himself by writing a paragraph of unsurpassed elegance. Heaving with intensity, yet technically flawless. Lawrencian.

Over Christmas, Natalie Mock's curiosity regarding her ex-boyfriend was dimmed by worries about Dan's health. But he seems almost back to normal. He's lost a little weight, perhaps, and still has that odd limp. But it's hardly a limp — just a slight stiffness in his leg. He doesn't have any family history of those horrible illnesses. She has a hunch he's just overworked, and is going to be fine.

So curiosity about her ex was dimmed, but not extinguished. She remembers the moment when their two futures, previously assumed — by her, at least — to be indivisible matter, revealed themselves as distinct. He'd borrowed some money — eighty pounds, to be precise — and she'd asked for it back. He explained at length why money isn't real. She said, that's fascinating, but I'd still like it back. He talked, but no wallet emerged. Nowhere, she realised at that moment, was it decreed that she must spend her life with a man disinclined to grow up. This man, she thought, will hinder my dreams.

Ah, yes: her dreams. She teamed up with Dan instead — older, more reliable, more supportive. She got her degree. Before her master's she needed a year in industry, but struggled to find a job — the jobs were in London, and Dan was in Sheffield. She got some short placements, then answered a graphic design ad just to pay the rent. Then Dan turned down his postdoc offer in Sheffield to accept one in Bristol. Just like that. More relevant, he said. She made a late application to Bristol, was advised to get more professional experience. Somehow, Plan A retreated behind blurry obstacles, and Plan B presented itself: a large aid organisation. A steady job with the feel-good factor.

She has one life, one chance, and for reasons she cannot precisely recall she's following Plan B.

'Mr Mock. Please take a seat.' The phone call came at work this afternoon. Would he be able to come right over. Dan sits silently, but can feel his heart thumping. He folds his shaking fingers decisively in his lap. Here it comes.

'I have the results of your tests here, and I've discussed them with several colleagues.' Not just young Doctor Dan's word on this. 'We all agree they are conclusive. I'm afraid you are going to have to make very serious adjustments to your expectations of your future life.' Before he even finishes the sentence, Dan has begun to make exactly those adjustments. Reductions. Everything must go. 'The tests indicate that you have amyotrophic lateral sclerosis.' He silently extracts the acronym from this heavy bundle of syllables. 'This is more commonly known as motor neurone disease. Have you heard of motor neurone disease?'

'Yes.'

'Do you understand what this means?'

It means I'll talk like a satnav. Head tipped forward, moist lower lip projecting. Commanding rapt attention. It means I'll have to become a theorist if I want to keep working. Inhabit a world of mathematics. I could write books. I might live for decades. I might have a cameo in *The Simpsons*.

'It means I'm going to die.'

'Yes. I'm afraid so. It's a terminal condition for which there is currently no cure. I'm very sorry. But we don't know how long it will take. You could live for many years. Or just a year or two.' A year. Or two. As though it doesn't matter which. Perhaps it doesn't.

'This will take some time to sink in,' adds Doctor Dan, his voice the voice of God. He's rehearsed. Dan might even be his first. There's a half-drunk mug of coffee on a shelf beside his desk, its slogan discreetly turned away. 'There is no rush. I would advise you not to make any major decisions or life changes immediately. Take some time. Try to be open with family and friends and seek their support. We'll schedule two follow-up appointments, and I'll give you the details of some excellent organisations.'

Take some time. Time just became a scarcer resource. But in these first scarcer minutes Dan feels an unexpected lightness of spirit. Now that his future has been taken away from him, he realises what an insubstantial thing it was. A question mark. A blank sheet of paper now tossed in the flames. He was going to die anyway.

'If there are any experimental drugs,' he says, coolly, 'blind trials, that sort of thing, I want to be on them. Even if I get the placebo.' The doctor looks surprised.

'Yes. Of course.' His eyes fall on Dan's helmet and gloves. 'You'll be alright riding home?'

'Why wouldn't I be?'

In the hospital car park he passes a young family — harried mum in charge, useless-looking, well-intentioned dad, sleeping baby in a pushchair, solemn toddler riding on the back. Children. Not for him, after all. Probably for the best, that he and Nat haven't got round to it. A clean break. For them both.

He climbs into the saddle, still calm. Checks his watch. He should go straight home — Nat will be home before him — but he doesn't want to go straight home. He wants to ride. Be alone with this thing. Talk to it. Get to know it. Alone, he's not afraid of it.

But he imagines Nat at this precise moment, perhaps waiting at the pedestrian crossing and chatting to an old lady she recognises, or just home, skimming through the junk mail she found on the doormat. Optimistic, unaware. This vision conjures a sadness more crushing than any other he's felt. A parade of images follow: Nat helping him out of a chair; Nat — his proud, beautiful Nat — spooning food into his mouth; Nat unable to make out what he's trying to say. It's now that he feels his face twitch, his eyes prickle with tears. He has to go home.

On the twenty-minute rush-hour journey, he sees laughing children everywhere. Dads. Grandads. Old men. The world has changed.

'Alumni office. Martha speaking.' Natalie takes a breath.

'Hi. I wonder if you can help me. I'm trying to trace one of your alumni. I'm an old friend but we've lost touch. I thought you might be able to look him up on your system.'

'I'm afraid that wouldn't be possible,' says Martha, with exaggerated sympathy. 'We can't give out any personal information.'

'Right. I thought you might say that.' Stupid idea in the first place. *Finito*.

'Have you tried social media — mutual friends, that sort of thing? You can find almost anyone these days.'

'Yes, I've tried. Oh well. Thanks for your time.'

'Wait a moment.' Martha is the sort of girl who wants to help — a problem-solver. 'This is a little off-piste, but if you give me your own name and contact details, and your friend's name and their graduation year, I could try to contact your friend, and ask if he wants to be put in touch. You did say he was a he, didn't you? That's the best I can offer you.'

Natalie wasn't expecting this. It's too much, too fast. Too direct, too suggestive. Too downright unfaithful. Or is it?

'Um. That's very kind of you. Let me just think a moment.'

Suddenly, Dan's key scrapes in the lock. He's home early.

'I'll think about it thanks again bye.'

Dan closes the front door, turns slowly and looks at her with a rather solemn, disappointed smile. He overheard and is going to confront her. No. Something else.

'Hi. Dan? What is it?'

He puts his helmet down on the side table and lays his gloves on top. Eases off his heavy jacket.

'I've just come from the hospital,' he says calmly, his back to her as he hangs up the jacket. 'My results came.'

Something isn't quite right, so Natalie says nothing. Waits. The boots come off. Slim under all that armour. He pads over to her in his socks, still with the calm, solemn smile. The usual kiss.

'It's bad news.' Natalie's heart lurches. He was right, she was wrong. Doubly wrong. A needle of shame.

'Oh, love. What is it? What did they say?' She reaches a hand up to his face. His eyes are bloodshot. The shame is forgotten.

'I'm sorry,' he whispers, no longer calm, no longer himself. 'You don't deserve this.'

'Me? What do you mean?' He stares down at her. 'Dan?' At last the words come choking out of him.

'Everything's going to be completely fucked.'

15. Nervous system

*'We sweat, we tremble, we turn pale, we flush,
beneath our imagination's impact.'*
Montaigne

Brenda surveys her bedroom. James says he's coming to visit
— he's going to hire a car for the weekend. Four hundred miles,
just to see her.

The main thing wrong with her bedroom, she decides, is
that there are too many sticks in it. Brenda collects forked
sticks — Y for Yggdrasil, the world tree. Or V for Vickers. Fir
cones, too, and bark. She makes a large artistic arrangement in
the corner of the main downstairs room, obscuring the stolen
race flags, then rejumbles her clothes until all the drawers
close; drags her capacious laundry basket into the spare room.
Much better. Presumably she should change the sheets, shave
her legs.

She does a careful visual sweep downstairs and spots a
couple of books and leaflets that must be hidden away in the
drawer now heavy with what she calls her loony library. What
about food? Maybe she can order a Tesco delivery on her
computer, since James probably expects more than malt loaf
and PG Tips. Venison is cheap at this time of year, but how do
you cook it? What's a good wine?

As Brenda works through this checklist, she can't help feeling that James probably doesn't much care whether she has an untamed bikini line or a bedroom full of forked sticks. He's on her side.

But after a seven-hour drive he still deserves a decent meal. And he still mustn't find the loony library.

The Mocks spent their evening in a rotation of mutual weeping, calm conversation, laughter, detached silence and eloquent, bone-bending embraces. They argued when Dan refused to eat any dinner. Finally, they had sex. '*Now* you take pity,' he joked.

When Dan wakes, his first sensation is of sharp hunger; the reason for it breaks into his consciousness shortly afterwards. Ah yes, that was it: he's going to die. He eats an enormous breakfast, persuades Natalie to go to work as normal, and does likewise.

When someone actually dies, the first thing you do is tell people. The conventions reject those expediencies of not knowing or not telling that are permissible — even encouraged — for mere illness. The conventions recognise the urgency of disseminating the absolute, the unalterable fact. Ring around the immediates, perhaps send a short, sombre group email to the rest. Get it out there.

Dan's new status is both absolute and ongoing. He examines his dazed conscience and finds that he must tell his parents and sister at once. Friends, colleagues — perhaps not yet. Reasons for the distinction unclear.

He calls his dad from the synchrotron car park, asks to be put on speaker so his parents hear it together. He doesn't start by saying he has something to tell them. He tries to get to the point quickly but with some warning context. A sense of role reversal. It is now they who must one day survive in the world without him, and not the other way round.

'You need to get a second opinion,' says his dad, in the trough following the first wave of shock. Even his voice, high, wavering, has shrunk to that of a child.

'I don't think so. There isn't a single box I don't tick. Some people get it in their upper neurons first — the ones that go down the spine from the brain — and some in the their lower neurons, the ones that go out to the muscles. Some people get it in their arms first, some in their legs. I've got the lot, all at once. I'm sorry.'

An indecipherable sob from his mum. She doesn't ask the peevish, pleading question he expected — why he didn't tell them about his tests. He feels a pang of guilt about that, and about the reassurance, the protection that he cannot give them. But when she declares that they're coming to see him today, right now, he encounters within himself an unexpected bedrock of resolve that this is his trial, his journey, and he wants to set his thoughts in order.

'Mum, I'm at work. And anyway, I'll need some time on my own. I'll call again at the weekend.'

His parents have each other, they have their long lives behind them, and they have another child to carry their hopes of the future. By comparison, they are immortals.

The call to Laura is unedifying. 'No,' she declares, without turning off the background music. 'I don't believe it for a moment. Absolutely not.'

'I'm not going to argue,' he says, lowering his voice as a colleague approaches. 'I just thought you should know.'

'But it's ridiculous.'

Dan sympathises. But when it's you, ridiculous isn't the right word.

In the Highlands, there's never a petrol station when you need one, and there's never a road leading in the direction you want to go — instead you follow the giant geological trellis of the glens and hope for the best. The meeting of two glens is not always obvious from the pine-blinkered road, and critical junctions, appearing suddenly without much fuss, send you to destinations on opposite sides of the country. James is a poor navigator, and his hired Micra traces out more of the trellis than he intended. He's late.

A genuine Scotch mist glitters in the headlights as he finally noses into Brenda's little cul-de-sac. She's at the door before him, wearing the same jeans, a knee-length cardigan, bare feet.

'Hey.'

'I told you I'd find it.' She looks him up and down, and grins.

'You've got crumbs on your jumper. What *is* that? Cake? Hedging your bets, eh?'

Everything is as it should be: the reassuring smallness and simplicity of Brenda's house, the cosy gas fire, and between them the palpable, happy charge that works such miracles on James' shrivelled heart. If I have not love. She has a few books whose titles and quaint covers are soothing balm — simple memoirs of shepherds, naturalists, a lighthouse keeper. These people have no anger in them, no violence, no ambition.

Brenda doesn't ask him about his own book — she really is a marvel. Instead she asks about the Moors, and about living by the sea. She grew up near Southend with its ridiculous folly of a pier, and James grew up as far from the sea as you can get. So they've swapped. The casserole is burned on top and a little salty, and they laugh about it. James enjoys the proximity of that moment when he'll walk kisses across her astonishing stomach, peel down her jeans, but he feels no need to hasten it.

Enough just to watch her bare feet padding the threadbare carpet and to sense, leaning innocuously against the other side of the PVC windows, an enormous, untamed night.

Later he stands behind her at the sink, hands reaching round into the scalding water, pretending to help. He can't see her face but her words are said through a smile. Greasy fingers interlacing; love in the washing-up bowl. She's still holding his hand as she leads him up the stairs. He feels a euphoric blend of discovery and rediscovery. A mirror: the rediscovery of his own buried soul.

'Have you seen tomorrow's weather forecast?' she asks.

James wants to laugh at the nonchalant timing of this question and all it signifies. He silently acknowledges the element pouring into his heart with luxurious abundance.

It's material. Love doesn't lie.

'Cheers, old man. Belated Happy New Year.'

A clink of glasses. How many more times will Dan's oldest friend wish him that? Once more? Twice, perhaps? It's a home fixture for Dan this time, in Reading, the date agreed last week. Before. Just as well he doesn't have to go far: the limp is worse, right foot clearly dropping, drooping, not every step, but now and then. Old man, yes.

'I'm having a bit of weird one, so far,' says Mike, oblivious of the pall of death that hangs over them.

'Go on,' invites Dan, setting aside his own intended opener. Mike glances around, checking that no one's listening in, and begins in a low voice.

'This isn't something I'd normally talk about.'

'It can't be your sex life then. It must be money.' Mike nods and grimaces.

'It is money.'

'Trouble at work?'

'Not exactly — not at all. That's just it.' He looks genuinely nervous. His voice sinks to a whisper. 'The thing is, I've made a lot of it. Money.'

Dan gives a short laugh. The distance between them has never felt so great as in this instant. He feels culpable, but he's missed his moment.

'That's your problem?'

'I know. I'm not complaining about it. I struck lucky. It all happened quickly at the end of the year. The thing is, I haven't told anyone else.'

'Am I allowed to ask how much?'

'Enough to retire on, if I don't buy a yacht.' He makes a calculating frown. 'Actually, I could probably buy a modest yacht, too.'

'Vickers, you jammy dodger. Well. That's the business you're in, isn't it?'

'I don't know what to do with it. And I don't know what do with myself. I never wanted to be — you know — one of those people.'

'Well, you are one. Relax. Give a little away, if it'll make you feel better. Give some to your college — establish the Vickers bursary for ginger students.'

'People talk about good causes, but I don't know which causes are good. And if I just give it away, I'm back where I started — scrabbling for more.'

'Then quit. Start your own business.'

'Doing what?'

'Jesus, Mike. Show a bit of initiative. What are you passionate about?'

Mike frowns, as though he's never considered that question — or rather as though he has, but doesn't know the answer.

He's always been like this. The world rewards grace, polish and a harmony of elements — attributes Mike has in spades — while Dan's substantive passion leaves it indifferent, has to fight for recognition. Not that it matters now.

Mike asks him about work, about his family, about Nat, but not about his health — not a simple, 'How are you?' that would demand an honest answer. Dan finds himself preferring not to volunteer his news. It will pollute everything it touches, including friendships.

'Regards to Nat,' says Mike as they part. 'Funnily enough, I had a dream about her the other night.' Dan turns, and he and Mike stand looking at each other, five yards apart. 'It was absolutely filthy.' The years, the light years, fall away and then pile back up swiftly. 'That was a joke,' adds Mike, with a frown and a parting wave.

Dan must have forgotten to smile.

'EAT DA RICH.' Mike, homeward bound, notices the enormous lamp-lit graffito on the approach to Paddington. His eyebrow twitches. Boarding the train earlier this evening, on his way out to Reading with the commuter hordes, he observed the righteous anger of the passengers unable to board — raving, knocking on the glass — and the sulking, incremental accommodation of those standing in the aisle. Shuffle a few steps to gift a stranger the chance to say goodnight to his kids — but the gift isn't given. A microcosm of haves and have-nots. Factions at war forever, like the young and the old, the sick and well, perhaps the lover and the beloved.

Mike, with his sculptures and his Audi, was already a have. What does that make him now? With freedom comes responsibility. So said Spiderman, maybe. Now that the central excuse, the central apology of Mike's life — the necessity to earn his crust — has effectively expired, he feels moral obligations pressing down on him unsupported, inescapable: obligations to the fellow man who didn't strike it so lucky, obligations to his family and friends, and, above all, obligations to himself.

He owes something to his past self, that accomplished, popular schoolboy — Ginger Knickers, they called him, but they admired him nonetheless — patiently expectant and expected-of; and he owes something to his future self, the bent old man looking back on his life, a cup of dread in his hands, searching for traces of worth. He even feels like he owes something to his as-yet unimaginable children — some achievement, some narrative to earn their respect. His life so far would set an incoherent example.

He can't ignore a sneaking feeling of being hard done by. His very privilege and good fortune have given him no material with which to build his character. Is that his fault? He might, after all, have battled adversity or injustice as lustily as the next man. (The last time he suffered severe physical discomfort? He fell out of an overloaded hammock five years ago and fractured his kneecap. The girl, a curvy Spanish siren, fell on top of him.) He never asked for all this. Does he deserve to be judged?

You might think luck would even out — for every serendipitous swing an eventual roundabout — but even Mike is hazily aware that randomness doesn't work like that. That's the gambler's fallacy. The truth is that unevenness persists. Those honest plodders at Oxford, whose tutorial work he copied religiously before outscoring them in the final exams — they'll never see a payback.

So there it is: no misfortune, no adversity, no character (being thirty-three, in the absolute prime of life, is the crowning insult). What is he passionate about? Women, obviously — sculpted contours of a woman's crossed legs, exquisite interplay of muscle and bone — but what else? Air travel. Chablis. Civilisation. Beautiful things. In days gone by, one could simply be a collector. Today, that doesn't wash.

His train slides into the snug, curved holster of the station. Dan was in a peculiar mood. He looked overworked and underpaid. Should meet him again to get to the bottom of it. Can't have miserable friends. Mike swings the door open and contemplates Bruncl's iron cathedral as he treads the long, gum-pocked aisle of Platform Four.

Dear James, he taps swiftly from the back of his cab.

> Sorry it's taken me so long to reply to your heartfelt, ego-felt defence of literature. I get all that. The problem, as I thought we had established, is that you haven't produced any. What makes you think your ideas are better than everyone else's? You're like a crackpot evangelist, stubbornly traipsing from door to slammed door. Nobody cares.

He's about to sign off, but then adds a second paragraph, not so swiftly:

> Here's a question for you. What would you do if you had absolute freedom? If money was no object? And don't say you'd write — money can't buy you your masterpiece, so you'd be in the same predicament there. What would you do if, say, you inherited a fortune? I'm sure literature has explored that plotline pretty thoroughly, so as a beneficiary of those insights, you ought to have a good answer.
> Sincerely,
> Mike

Natalie Mock grasps the handle of the rumbling kettle, stares out of the window at the neighbour's fence and surrenders for a moment to selfish thoughts. She can't believe this is happening again. For twenty years she's constructed something original and resilient on the rubble of her father's death. She can still remember asking him what the word *diagnosis* meant. Horrible long-legged insect of a word, now crawling back into her life. Did she ignore Dan's symptoms because of scar tissue in her brain blocking out any thoughts of a re-run? Will it be harder this time? Slower? Lonelier?

She looks down at the two waiting mugs and feels an upwelling of love that inhabits, recolours her anger. Dan is sitting quietly, waiting. Is he ready for what's going to happen?

She sets the mugs down and takes her usual place, half facing him on the adjacent side of the old table they bought in Sheffield for twenty pounds. Winter sun charms the twin snakes of steam and makes a dissection puzzle of the tabletop, belying, offending the overwhelming atmosphere of gloom. When Natalie speaks, her voice is barely audible even to herself.

'It's all those particles you work with.' Dan says nothing. When he lifts his mug, he uses both hands. 'Radiation. Magnetic fields. It must be. It's scrambled your nervous system. That place you work is so — so unnatural.'

'I don't think it was my work.'

'But that other physicist — whatshisname — Stephen Hawkins. He got the same thing.'

'Hawking. He's a theorist,' replies Dan, wearily. 'He wasn't exposed to anything more hazardous than a stick of chalk.'

Natalie is powerless. 'Then why?' she whispers. 'Why you?'

'I don't know. For years I've felt like there's — something not quite right with me. Getting old before my time.' This is the first Natalie's heard of it.

'Why didn't you say something earlier?'

'I told myself it was just paranoia. It probably was. We all feel a bit feeble inside, a bit achy and creaky, a bit twitchy — don't we?'

Natalie shakes her head. Feeble in her mind, yes — ignorant, peevish, yes — but she's always trusted her body. Firm, reliable, downright miraculous little body. If you look after it, your body isn't supposed to just give up on you at thirty-three.

'If living organisms weren't unstable, imperfect systems,' says Dan, staring down into his tea, 'there could be no evolution. Some of us are not born to be ancestors. We're just sketches for the main project. Defective specimens. Off-cuts. Dead ends.'

'Stop. Don't talk like that.'

He looks up. Reaches out a sun-striped hand. Natalie can see what he's doing, even feels a rush of pride for her serene, nerdy husband with his unshakable foundation of self-knowledge — no snivelling, no wallowing for him, no denial, no anger, no bargaining (whatever the hell that means). At the same time, she feels a desperate frustration that they can't face this together and in the same way. The normal, bewildered way.

This — the thing they have to face — being the prospect of Dan, husband, lover, best friend, disintegrating before her eyes and then vanishing altogether. She watched some films on the internet about other sufferers of the disease. Men with young kids, mostly — she's read that more older people get it, but maybe they don't have the same urge to record, to preserve. One young dad read bedtime stories into a tape recorder, for when his voice went. Another made video messages for his kids to watch when they were old enough to understand. For these men, the knowledge they would never be the father they should have been for their kids and wouldn't see them grow up was the deepest of their many sorrows.

But they had kids. A legacy. The saintly wives had a reason to be strong. What if you have no kids to listen to your video messages after you're gone? To one day stand your pre-disease, pre-dribble picture on their bedside table in their unimaginable student digs? To remind your wife of the man you once were?

What if you're going to simply disappear and leave the world — and your wife — as you found them?

16. Rich tapestry

'I am as doubtful of myself as of anything else.'
Montaigne

The gents' at Mike's office has two urinals side by side — not one or three, but a snug pair — and is notorious among junior employees for awkward encounters with their superiors. Stagefright; remarkable farts that can't be remarked on; expectoration and misdirected spitting ditto; the garrulous, the weirdly intent, the human firehose. Some cowards pee in the cubicles, but their ungentlemanly behaviour is noted.

Mike is relaxed unless his pee-buddy is the Generalissimo — a highly strung introvert-turned-billionaire, a genius of sorts — or his immediate boss, with those wandering, basilisk eyes. Today it's George, a friendly, tubby bigshot who trades commodities, wears a Rolex, and has a prestigious desk near the gravitational centre of the floor. He's known as the Gas Man — natural gas futures were his big ticket.

'I heard you had a good year,' George says, with a glance round to see that the cubicles are empty. 'Feeling pretty flush.' Mike nods. 'I bet you haven't spent any of it yet.'

'Nope.'

'We all started with a year like you've just had. We all felt the way you're feeling — out of our depth. But if you hold your nerve, you could earn twice, three times as much this year. Ten times as much, within a few years.' Mike follows him to the washbasins. 'Here's a word of advice,' continues George. 'That dubious theory about money not buying happiness — you can only test it if you spend a little. You probably still feel like a student of life, or something. Forget that now. You've graduated. Go out there, stand tall, and purchase life's rich tapestry by the yard.'

'I'll bear that in mind,' says Mike, in the corridor. 'Thanks.' He walks slowly back to his desk. Maybe the Gas Man's right. Does it matter that he made his money from an erroneous trade? In this business, how do you distinguish the deliberate from the accidental anyway? He could start by blasting his way through twenty or thirty grand and just see what happens. Perhaps doors will open. He is, after all, the goddamn Rocket Jesus.

That night he calls Victoria. She's seeing someone now, she says. That's a shame, says Mike, because I've got a table at Hibiscus and tickets for the *Hunger Games* premiere and after-party. You'd need a dress, of course — my treat. Carmen's not invited this time. Didn't you hear me, says Victoria. I'm seeing someone. Pity, says Mike. Let me know if you change your mind. The next day, she does change her mind. Rich tapestry, here I come.

Dan Mock stands on the towpath at dusk, looking out across Father Thames. The river's surface is flat calm but dimpled by the rain, and distinctly marbled in the fading light by meandering lanes of gloss and matt. This giant endpaper in monochrome is, he decides, a conspicuous manifestation of some subtle physics. It could be floating deposits — diesel, perhaps — interfering with the surface tension, or it could be thermal circulation caused by the entry of colder water from above. He'd like to find out for sure, one day. This unthinking invocation of the future brings the disease crashing into his thoughts: if he wants to find out anything about anything, he'd better get onto it pronto.

The disease will, at least, leave his mind untouched until the end. This is a relief not only because his greatest (or rather his loftiest) pleasures are cerebral, but also because he'll be able to decide, in principle at least, when enough is enough. Dementia would be a more terrifying, a more degrading prospect for him: the world becoming senseless. But his mind will only get him so far. How do you take an overdose when your hands won't move? Arrangements will have to be made carefully and in good time.

He'll keep eyesight, hearing, touch. Movement is his rare earth: this coming summer might be his last as a locomotive organism. Last chance to take the perfect corner on his bike. Dance badly and not care. Play an instrument (he's never learned one). Row a boat, kick a ball (when did he last do that?). Fix things. Adjust a dial. Shake hands, perhaps. Hold Nat, stroke her hair — but he diverts his train of thought from that too-painful track.

A small launch appears from behind the island and turns into the main channel, casting a fan of ripples. These advance across the marbled river, reflect off its banks, intersect their fellows, superpose, cohere and decohere in a silent, mathematical dance. Dan smiles at the sheer beauty of it. In the time he has left it's more of this he wants, but you can't buy it, you can't add it to a list and tick it off. You just have to keep your eyes and your mind open as long as you can.

The streetlights on the bridge go on, lighting a world of possibilities that is no longer his. This world, down here, the exquisite ripples in the dusk — this is his world. He already feels reborn.

Brenda Vickers has reached Section Six of her online course. It's telling her about SMART goals. She begins to grasp the intention: to bore her out of her phobia. To make it ridiculous — paint a moustache on it, balance a traffic cone of self-help jargon on its head. Maybe it will work. When her mouth goes weird, she can't smile or express herself or engage with humanity, but presumably she can still yawn.

Outside lie two feet of fresh snow. Work is cancelled until the access boys have cleared the tracks. Her skis were stolen last winter, so she needs a brief thaw cycle — a moist breeze or a sunny afternoon — to bake the mountain snow into a giant, firm meringue for her crampons to devour.

She and James exchanged half a dozen texts this morning. When he was here she could feel his high spirits, a kind of exhilaration in him that was infectious. She's never felt it with a guy before. He genuinely likes her — likes being around her, likes everything about her (*likes* is the word she hears in her head, but her heart hears the other). In Edinburgh she told him it wouldn't work, but it has to work.

Her boss mentioned a vacancy on the Galloway estate, which is much closer to James. There are even some pretty seaside towns nearby — not Bay pretty, maybe, but pretty for Scotland. There's that town with all the bookshops. He might like that. She hasn't mentioned this idea yet — there's no rush. But she has a goal: somehow James and Brenda has to work.

Specific, measurable, achievable.

Natalie Mock has trained her swimming thoughts to occupy a territory as narrow as the lane, the furrow her body ploughs and reploughs: her stroke, her breathing, her time and distance, the status of her muscles, or by default a pleasant sensual trance. But today her thoughts are a marble too heavy to stay in its groove.

Diagnosis. The same thing happening again, but not the same. Everywhere Natalie sees the unconditional love of kin: parents for children, children for parents, sisters for brothers, wives for the fathers of their children. She and Dan have a different sort of tie. A work in progress. Even after six years of marriage, if she has to state 'next of kin' she begins to write her moping mother's name, and inserts Dan's only with some confusion.

She thinks back to their marriage vows — something about respecting and cherishing, throughout our lives together. Neither of them wanted anything too soppy. She dragged him out for a run on the morning of the wedding. Her thumb feels for the ring, which is not there, of course, but in her locker. There are days when she forgets to put it on. Dan always wears his.

Less than two weeks ago, she was searching for news of her ex-boyfriend with a vague, mutinous sense that Dan didn't understand her. Life without him was vaguely, mutinously imaginable. And now? She tests that shady mental water, while the pool's bubbles course brightly over her skin.

Now, life without Dan is an unimaginable horror. An injustice. Get ill if you must, but stay with me. She urges her body towards the wall and ducks into her turn. Stay with me, my love.

James F. Saunders takes a triumphant sip of his first homemade cup of espresso. A bitter, clinging swamp in the mouth: superb. The machine arrived yesterday, a birthday present from his parents. From his mother — though his father did sign the card this year.

James' relationship with his mother was collateral damage in the just war of following his vocation. When he fell out with his father she patiently negotiated, tried to make peace. Blessed are that bunch.

'Whose side are you on?' James asked her, bluntly.

'I'm on both your sides.'

'Sorry, Mum, that's not possible. Either you believe in me, support me, or you don't.'

'Of course I believe in you, James. But I also know your father is only thinking of you and your future.'

'I can't be entangled in that stuff. Goodbye.'

'What do you mean, goodbye?' There was a note of anger in her voice that she would afterwards regret. Too bad.

'I'll visit at Christmas. That's it. Goodbye, Mum.'

He can still remember the triumphant rush as he hung up on the woman who had more or less dedicated her life to his happiness. A sacrificial offering has to be something precious, and the best writers have to be bastards.

He takes another sip and opens his laptop. The coffee is good; the novel, splendid and precarious like an unfinished bridge. The anxiety attendant on committing to a project of uncertain worth is nothing new, but the weight of ten years' commitment and ten years' anxiety now rests on this one trail of words. Doubts are inevitable. For instance: his story takes place over a calendar year — his aim to harness the deep, biological rhythm of the seasons — but perhaps a single day would have better suited his purpose. One voyage from wife to lover, or lover to wife. A day is nearly eternity for the mind, as the Exile demonstrated.

But he's learned his lesson: to hesitate now would be to

invite disaster. He has to see it through. Fifty thousand words down. Just keep writing.

One distraction that needs eliminating is Mike. A barren connection, after all, though it is doubly gratifying to James that the ginger spiv both allowed himself to be goaded back into an exchange of insults, and saw fit, in the same email, to ask for advice. What a prize pillock: but James will answer his question.

Dear Mike,
You ask what I would do if I had absolute freedom.
Ah, freedom: that great divider of what it means to
be human. So much of the human story, and the art
reflecting it, is concerned with the struggles of
individuals in the face of hostile external forces —
war, tyranny, penury. In such circumstances, the goal
is clear — simple freedom to live and to love. Even
Montaigne's self-examination was, in a sense —
as of course you know — a private quest for freedom
in barbarous times.

Then there are the rest of us — the lucky few
already free and whose freedom is not threatened.
We face an odder sort of struggle towards odder
sorts of goals. We get the occasional existential bump
from death but the intervening years are eerily quiet.
We look for guidance but there is none. Where there
is no right to sorrow, what right is there to happiness?
Anxiety has filled the gap left by religion — material
anxiety in those whose souls have entirely shut down,
and in the rest, in those who cling to a vision of beauty,
a churning, ceaseless anxiety of the spirit.

James frowns, and is about to delete this unplanned outburst. Those who cling to a vision of beauty! He should have taken that job writing the copy for car adverts. But he doesn't delete it. Instead, he gives a bored sigh before nailing a final, unanswerable paragraph onto their doomed correspondence: a reconciliation of sorts.

> Art has explored all this too, with mixed success.
> But I'm not going to tell you how to spend your dirty
> money. We've each made our beds, and must lie in
> them. Do whatever you have to do to avoid falling into
> the boiling resentful rage of a failed life.
> Sincerely,
> James

'Dan. I was wondering.'

'Go on.'

'A lot of people who get diagnosed with something like this seem to keep a record. You know — a blog.' Dan looks at Natalie thoughtfully but says nothing. 'They can share their thoughts, not feel so alone. Help other people to understand what they're going through. Maybe help other sufferers, too. It's something they can do even if they get really sick. It's not like writing a book or something — there's no pressure. They can write a lot or just a few lines. And it means —' she hesitates.

'— they leave something behind,' supplies Dan. 'On the record. After they've gone.'

She nods. 'What do you think? You'd be so good at explaining things.'

'I think it's a fine idea. For some people. But not for me. I introspect as much as the next person. But I feel no desire to gift those thoughts to the world. When I write, I write methods, results, conclusions.' He gestures towards a physics journal lying on the coffee table. 'Not personal ruminations. I leave that for the artists.'

Natalie swallows her frustration. 'But hasn't this — this diagnosis —' that fucking word again '— hasn't this changed things? Don't you think it might change your priorities?'

'It has changed some things, but not others. I'm not really sure yet — I'm still thinking it through. We're all going to die. The difference for me, I suppose, is that I know roughly how it's going to happen. But I don't see why I would turn into someone I wasn't before. Blogger. Thrill-seeker. Fundraiser. I don't need to give myself a new purpose.'

'You're not going to be able to achieve everything you wanted with your electrons — you won't have time.'

He stares at the assortment of unlit candles standing in the fireplace, a twist of sadness in his face. 'I know. But who does? We all run out of time. I was thinking yesterday about how much I've been looking forward to seeing the Higgs confirmation. Pentaquarks. Neutrino mass. Gravitational waves. Dark matter. Viable fusion power. I'll probably miss most of those.' He looks at her and adds, with a laugh that cracks, 'Promise me you'll look out for them on the news.' Natalie feels tears darting into her eyes again. 'Whenever you live and whenever you die,' says Dan, composure recovered, 'you're sure to miss something unmissable.'

'You're not going anywhere just yet,' she says. In the silence that follows, her mind is made up. 'I'll tell you one thing that has changed.'

'What?'

'I want us to have a baby.'

Dan's start dissolves into a thin smile. 'I thought I'd find a way to talk you round, but this terminal illness ruse seems a little drastic.' Then the smile is gone and he shakes his head. 'But it's not a good idea anymore. I'm sorry. If you want reasons, I have three.'

Don't do this. Please.

'Dan, I want us to have a baby. I want —'

'No.'

Mike Vickers is fresh from his barber one crisp Saturday morning, the smell of talc following him like the material effusion of his privilege, when he encounters George, the Gas Man, on Jermyn Street.

'Just the laddie!' booms George. 'Remember what I said about life's rich tapestry? Well, how would you like to witness the purchase of —' his voice falls to a whisper '— *an actual tapestry*! Flemish. Exquisite little eight-by-six. Follow me.'

Mike is in two minds — decline jauntily to make clear that he won't be patronised, or accept and show this bumbling big-spender that the 'laddie' knows a thing or two about art. He checks his watch, a pre-bonus purchase, angling his wrist so George won't see the middling brand.

'Sure. Why not?'

George leads him down a side street and past half a dozen small galleries, glancing at windows and occasionally making derisive snorts at their wares. A narrow opening leads to a courtyard, and they stop at a black door with no shop window. A discreet plaque announces *Ira McFooley: Antiquities*. George glances left and right, apparently mistaking his tubby self for a person of interest to the world, and nods towards the doorbell with small, hungry eyes.

On the same day, James F. Saunders is in Scarborough, picking his way through a battleground of abandoned road works, hunching and flinching in a crossfire of rain and traffic spray. Little sodden sandbags lie slumped here and there like child corpses. He wipes a streaming nose, looks around and smiles. This town guards a scoop in the hostile coastline just as half-hearted as his native Bay, but an accident of geology provided a harbour here, and a sandy beach. These gave it a divergent identity that serves him well as a creative palate cleanser.

There is York, of course, but it's too far, and tainted by the risk of seeing one of the few uni peers still loitering there. Whether they recognise him or not, the pain is intolerable; on his last visit to the city he encountered an ex-classmate in the street — a fellow poet, now a successful journalist, whose career James once followed with interest — and she looked straight through him, would no more recognise him than a fly. Well, fuck them all. They'll soon have reason to remember him.

In the meantime, Scarborough it is. Seeking shelter, shoes wet through, James finds himself inside a bookshop for the first time in many months: a small Waterstones. Celebrity memoirs a speciality. It is an incontrovertible truth that while second-hand bookshops present comforting refuges to a writer the world has hitherto rejected, new bookshops are cursed. The shimmer, the scorn, the horror of failure. He drifts from table to stacked table, fingering the satiny covers with their sharp corners, bathing in a lake of bitterness. Invigorating, certainly: an antidote to creative exhaustion. His eye catches extravagant praise on the cover of a book that he once abandoned in disgust. Is it them or me? It's them, of course. He's learned to translate the absurd puff jargon: *thrilling* means shallow; *engrossing* is verbose; *mesmerising*, slow; *unflinching*, unsubtle; *stunning* means they couldn't think of anything to say at all. *Quite possibly the finest coming-of-age novel since Bambi. If you liked* Girl in a Bodybag, *you'll love* Girl in a Ditch. Murder me too and let's get it over with.

There are too many books in the world, of course. But there is too much of everything. James maintains a desperate belief in singularity: literature is not a bulk commodity. These thousands of worthless books do not pile up against its adamantine feet; rather, they are a stream babbling past harmlessly, endlessly, washing them clean.

He fixes his gaze on the place where his novel will stand, flanked by Sartre and Schlink; the infinitesimal crack between those unsuspecting literary comrades forms the sole egress from his life's impasse. He smiles. He's going to make it. He has sixty thousand words that glitter like the scales of a dangerous reptile: not one out of place. He's almost there.

And he knows exactly how it's going to end.

By March, Dan's right leg has given up the ghost and he walks with crutches. The change comes swiftly, over a few weeks. Because of the weakness in his hands, the occupational therapist has advised him to skip the hand-pushed chair and go straight for the electric model. It's already been ordered. 'You don't need it yet, of course, but let's be prepared.' Positive words that signify despair. 'I seem to be on the fast track,' he replies.

A defining characteristic of illness, in Dan's past experience, was that eventually you recover. It takes longer than you hope — sore throats evolve into colds that evolve into lingering coughs, blocking out swathes of the calendar; a poisoned digestive system keeps making one more frenzied ejection — but you do recover. The prospect of recovery is sewn into the illness with silver thread.

Now he's discovering the other kind, and the psychological flavour is unrecognisable. As different as *au revoir* and *adieu*.

He's bidding *adieu* capabilities he never even noticed possessing: kicking off his shoes; sidling between parked cars; opening childproof medicine bottles (the last a painful and symbolic affront). He feels a gathering sense of urgency even as his disobliging body slows down, and each passing moment carries the taint of impatience.

17. Glorious flood

'The most valiant are sometimes
the most unfortunate.'
Montaigne

Brenda's bus, having growled across the moors for half an hour, swings abruptly onto a side road. Suddenly you can't miss the sea, into which the land here — an unstable marriage of flatness and height, a toppling table with a broken edge — seems to want to tip you. A brown expanse tending to grey, specks of foam, the horizon blurred. Suggestion of a distant ship.

Now comes the irresistible hiccup of joy as she catches sight of James slouched playfully against the bus stop, hair curling from a flat cap worn not quite straight. So this is his territory, his stronghold: the village leaning over the tidal beach, shedding houses every few decades; the cobbled lanes; his small room a student's room, but a tidy one — bed, desk, bookshelf, coffee machine, flowers. From the window you can almost touch the sea. James tugs the curtain across it and they kiss, smiling so much their teeth collide. Blessed rightness of being together.

Now as a rule, Brenda doesn't do blow-jobs — one-sided wastes of a fuck (ditto the tickly converse) — but today calls for a gesture, and she's decided to make an exception. She unfastens his shirt buttons, slides lips to his chest, and resists, ignoring the slow burn of her own needs, when he tries to pull her towards the bed. Only when the insistent trickle of kisses reaches his stomach does the penny drop. He freezes, as if any movement might change her mind. A hyperventilating teenage boy getting it for the first time. He lasts about thirty seconds, and afterwards just stands there, looking dazed. She pulls his jeans up for him and they have a divine cuddle on the bed with their clothes on.

Later he takes her to a low, dark seafood restaurant about fifty yards from his room — there is only one, and it's perfect. He behaves with exaggerated gallantry. He's funny. Afterwards he leads her to a bench overlooking the village and wraps his coat round her, and they watch the lights benevolently trawling the horizon. She could get used to this. More drinks in his room. Then his narrow, creaky bed a nest of whispers and giggles.

The Mocks' street slumbers heedless beneath a blazing pink mackerel sky, as Dan eases himself awkwardly down the step onto the pavement. He can barely walk without the sticks, but he can still ride.

He positions himself astride his bike, helmet balanced on the engine, one glove off to operate his phone, scrolling with ever-so-slightly clumsy flicks of his thumb. Some of these he will never hear again — his final listen has already passed by, unnoticed. A Springsteen album. A Beethoven symphony. The same with everything, of course. More and more things as he gets sicker. Last this, last that. The same for everyone. But this list of discrete, named experiences dangles its complacent orderliness before his eyes and drives the point home.

And yet here he is now, alive. He doesn't normally listen while riding, but this isn't going to be a normal ride. It's a joyride. As the familiar names fly past, his eye catches Killing

Joke. Perfect. He checks the helmet's wireless internal speakers, activates the borrowed video camera perched on top, lifts the whole apparatus with some difficulty and slides it onto his head. Hits play on the phone, zips it into a sleeve pocket, pulls on his glove and throttles up hard. Wake these healthy slugabeds — ha! Strokes back the kickstand with his good leg. Joy already.

Out of town, asphalt flashing, surfing on a sea of inertial forces, Joke pounding into his brain like the grace of God. Somewhere in his mind, a dial has been adjusted. It's not so much that the goods at stake have shrunk in value, but rather his life's discount rate (Dan is up on his neuroeconomics) has rocketed. He accelerates hard out of a bend and feels the rear wheel twitch. His heart, somewhere under the leather and the storm of noise, is racing.

Brenda shifts, lets the inadequate duvet slip off her thigh and the cool morning air rouse her into wakefulness. James' short, regular exhalations weave in and out of time with the soughing of the North Sea. She could just lie here and bask in her happiness, but instead she lifts her head to survey the little room. Cold light spills under the curtains and across the desk: two emptied glasses, a bottle, the vase of cheery flowers, a plucked leaf that James folded around her fingertip — 'thy finger's taperness,' he called it, even though her calloused fingers with their bitten-down nails don't really taper.

And the laptop. His mysterious book is one of the private territories that must be opened up if they are to share each other's lives, to build an alliance. There are others, she acknowledges, but let's start with the book.

She dismisses his proposal to have breakfast in the tearoom, and instead carries pastries and takeaway coffee back to his room and lays them out carefully on the desk. 'You have the sea view, after all,' she explains brightly, 'and when you sit here tomorrow, writing your novel and feeling lonely, and the next day, and the next, I want you to think of our little breakfast.' James looks doubtful but doesn't argue. As he unplugs the laptop and transfers it to the bed, her eyes follow.

'Talking of your novel,' she says, 'isn't it time you told me about it? What's the subject?' James gives a reticent smile.

'It's difficult to explain.'

'Try me. Where's it set?'

'It could be set anywhere,' he answers, reluctantly, 'but it happens to be set just up the coast at South Shields, and in East London, and on a cargo ship out there. A coal ship. In about nineteen ten.'

'You must have to do a lot of research,' suggests Brenda, 'to get the details right.' She glances at his bookshelf. There are books, but not that many.

'To be honest,' says James, with an odd blend of self deprecation and arrogance, 'I don't really bother about historical details.'

'Then what do you bother about?'

Their eyes meet and Brenda thinks of the Harris hawk. Cornered. Suddenly the hawk eyes flash and he leans forward — he's going to spill the beans.

'Alright. Here goes. The ancient Greeks recognised at least four distinct bonds that we lazily throw together under the umbrella of love — you might call them desire, friendship, kinship and general benevolence. You might, but nowadays if you really mean it you're supposed to use the umbrella word: love. We also cram under there the attachments you feel towards a cat, a song, a view. Ice cream. McDonald's. You're even told to love yourself, which must be easier for some people than others. With me so far?'

'I think so.'

'Now why would our language, our most triumphant achievement, the whole purpose of which is to draw distinctions, why would it fail us so badly when it comes to this diverse jumble of affections, which range from the cheapest, most trivial of whims to what most of us consider to be the profoundest feelings any person can have? Is it really just laziness, or something more deliberate?'

Brenda feels a faint touch of foreboding, a sense that she might regret her insistence. She'd like to change to a lighter subject, but it's too late. 'You tell me,' she says, slowly dismembering a croissant.

Natalie Mock stands on the stinging bathroom tiles with bed hair and a man's T-shirt down to mid-thigh, holding a packet of pills. A red arrow directs her to the next pill in the sequence. Eat me and lose Dan forever.

Dan's three reasons for not having a baby were: for her sake, because she should be able to start again and live her life to the full with someone else; for his own sake, because it would — he thinks — make his predicament, his exit from the world, immeasurably more painful; and for the child's sake, because every child deserves a father.

Stated together they sound damning, but examine each in turn and it doesn't hold water. The opposing case, her case, is not a list. It is simply this: a child is hope and defiance against the terrible looming abyss of Dan's absence.

She looks up at her reflection. Some decisions she is perhaps entitled to make.

Dan rides hard, without a destination in mind, keeping the sun roughly behind him. Takes turnings he's always passed by and soon finds himself in unknown country. Everywhere the mocking vigour of early spring.

He accelerates down a long straight and thinks of all the misery lying ahead. The indignity, the frustration, above all the bloody wasted effort of all concerned. He can switch all that off with a flick of his hand. Later he'll be trapped, but right now, just a flick. His chance, right now.

But around each and every corner is more life, waiting for him. How could anyone willingly renounce it? His bike is a kinetic spark tracing these fertile wrinkles on the planet's skin, his mind a laser, projecting the perfect course on the road ahead, the rhythm guitar's staccato thump is heaven in his ears and crowds of adoring daffodils, ferociously abundant, are cheering him on.

He brakes too late for the next bend, much too late, and feels the bike let go of the road. He closes his eyes while the nest of forces unravels according to Newton's clear instructions, and the divine music plays on.

'It's deliberate,' says James, in answer to his own question. Brenda picks a crumb from the corner of her mouth. 'Our use of language draws distinctions but it also makes connections. We use the same love word for these things because they're all the *same* thing. "What thing?" you ask. What is this love thing? It's an emanation of the self. It's an involuntary manifestation of a part of ourselves that we cannot otherwise see — the deepest core of the self. Belief could be considered another emanation — if anyone believed anything anymore — but belief can be conditioned. Love can't.'

'If love is all about the self,' asks Brenda, her foreboding now tinged with panic, 'where does the thing — or the person — you love come into it?' James is oblivious.

'The object of our love creates the resonance,' he replies with a dismissive wave of his hand. 'But the thrill is in self-discovery. Love is a mirror. "Love thy neighbour!" we're told. But you *can't* choose to love, and you can't compel someone else to love. Love happens, or it doesn't. It always tells truth about what you have hidden inside you. Meeting you has helped me to understand all this.'

'Meeting me?'

'Absolutely. Before I met you, I was washed up — I was finished. I didn't know myself anymore. Believe it or not, I used to have this ridiculous plan to meet someone, to engage with someone emotionally, specifically to help me rediscover the person I used to be — I called it Project Q. Well guess what? Project Q came up trumps!' He points at her and laughs. She feels sick. 'You've been like — like an echo-sounder. Through the response I felt when I met you, and feel again each time I see you, I can see the very roots of myself, unreachable and ungovernable. It's a goldmine for my writing. I can see past loves, some just fossils, others still alive but twisted round on themselves. Some loves are extensions of these unyielding roots, while others are just sort of breathed out like smoke. But I've been able to harness it, this process of revelation, in the novel.' He points excitedly at the laptop. 'Whatever happens to us now, whether the resonance we're feeling lasts or fades, it doesn't matter, because this record, this testimony will remain.'

The cascade of words runs dry. James turns his exultant gaze from the laptop to Brenda's face. She's been hauled out of this once-happy room to a high and lonely vantage, looking down at her pathetic, mooning, love-struck self. His surprise at seeing something in her eyes he wasn't expecting, expressed in the sudden dropping of his saliva-flecked lower lip, shows him to be as deluded as her. He's about to speak, to question, when her anger detonates in a glorious flood of adrenaline. In one movement she leaps to her feet, snatches the laptop from the bed and turns towards the door.

'Brenda?'

By the time he thinks to leap after her, she has one foot on the landing. She waits for his approach, then flings the door into his face. She takes the narrow stairs in threes, silently rejoicing in his pain, swings into the hall and grapples with the latch of the front door. He crashes down the stairs just as she gets it open.

'Brenda! What are you doing? I didn't mean it like that! Stop, for God's sake! Give it back!'

He's getting it now too — the adrenaline rush. She meets his eyes for a moment, says nothing, leaps into the street and down to the ramp. Plants her feet firmly on the glossy, barnacled cobbles. Brenda Vickers doesn't throw like a girl. The Frisbee-spinning laptop flashes high. She turns her head and meets his eyes again just as the deep, dull thump of laptop meeting cold North Sea resounds behind her.

He's standing in the street, arms by his sides, nose bleeding, face like death. He has no words.

'Didn't you have a back-up?' asks Brenda, casually, as she strolls past him to the door of the cottage, climbs the stairs, stuffs a few belongings into her rucksack and returns to the street. His body hasn't moved — his eyes are still fixed on the point of impact. As for his soul, who knows? Who cares? Brenda walks up the street, away from the sea.

Her gaze wanders idly like that of a tourist, and falls on a shop selling fudge. She steps in, buys a handful of vanilla choc chip and savours it, piece by piece, as she climbs the steep hill towards the bus stop.

Brenda loves fudge. She can't help loving fudge. It's an emanation of the self.

18. Deadest thing

'There is ... not so much misery in us as emptiness ...'
Montaigne

James F. Saunders watches the heave and suck of the spastic sea. Stuff of madness. Destruction fantasy. He begins to shiver, then retches without warning. Stringy dribble of vomit and bloody snot on the cobbles. A gull swoops half-heartedly and veers away.

He turns, dimly registers Hugo's moonlike face watching from a window with his round, black, crater mouth. Climbs the stairs to his room: the room where his laptop, his novel, is not. His eyes search for it, disbelieving, and then, moderating their goal, seek out something to cleanse the puke. The whisky she brought. Laphroaggie. Laugh rage. Medicinal purposes, she said. He fumbles with the heavy foil, pulls the stopper and swills. Cleansing fire. Choking liar. Gasping choir.

Dan Mock can hear a bird singing. A greenfinch, if he's not mistaken. The other music — pounding drums, angry man shouting in his head — has stopped. He sees greenery squashed against his visor and smells its fierce distress, smells something else too, something delicate and lovely. He tries to move. Turns his head without pain. A limb which seems to be his arm rustles

173

some plants noisily, communicates a sensation of damp, and eventually presents a fully-functioning gloveless hand to the glossy problem of the helmet. He exerts his shoulders and another arm enters the fray. The helmet comes off and here is the wet, bright world.

He sits up. Daffodils. Everywhere. A flash of chrome above a nearby ditch. He crawls to a flint wall that his body apparently didn't slam into, gets an arm over it and hauls himself upright.

He looks down at his mud-streaked leathers. There's a small tear on one sleeve.

'And you?' he says to his leg. 'Are you going to fucking start working too, as part of this fucking miracle?' The leg twitches ineffectively. Dan looks to the sky and laughs.

James is on the beach. Tide down. Shoes wet through; on one a stubborn straggle of weed. The near-empty bottle leaves him only one coat-pocket to cram a hand into. The laptop corpse nowhere. Not content with destroying his novel, the sea has actually done away with the hardware. Acid bath murder.

Lines from the dead novel assail him. Flawless lines. *The sun a dripping sponge on my face, between rounds of brawling night.* Dismembered now, functionless, grotesque. It's all come to nothing, after all. Thirty-odd years of blur and blot. The deadest thing. Stupid phrase, he's always thought, but maybe Hardy was on to something. Wind oozing thin; yes, that too.

He turns unsteadily and sees the village now far away along the waste of mud and shingle. It seems easier to go on. Didn't you have a back-up, she said. His father used to plead, nag, badger: 'Write if you must, but finishing your degree will give you a back-up.' James has never believed in back-ups.

Mike Vickers is sandwiched between an English tearaway daddy's girl with indecent lips and an older Lithuanian lady of doubtful profession and penetrating intelligence; a Ghanaian model with a gift for deadpan one-liners sits beside Pete Walley, who is in his element; and Maurice, summoned by text, has just arrived wearing a vinyl zip-up shirt, to the general delight of the table. Mike's Amex card is behind the bar.

'I work in investments,' he admits to the ladies, 'but only until something better comes along.'

'Mike's idea of spontaneous,' explains Pete, 'is to buy monthly travelcards instead of an annual, in case he has to jam. He's that wild.' Verity, the tearaway, who has probably never purchased a travelcard, snorts.

'Michael,' purrs Maurice, slipping into his Anthony Blanche Brideshead act, 'you would have us b-believe that you have made a great sacrifice, that you have laboriously b-bricked up the windows of your imagination in the service of your career. But I rather think you are like the P-pantheon or La Madeleine — you were constructed with no windows. Only a single round hole in the t-top of your head.'

The table dissolves into hardly-warranted laughter and Mike meekly displays the ginger crown of his head to left and right. Maurice feels entitled to refer to Mike's flat as the far-famed masturbatorium. Pete keeps mockingly calling him the Jack of Hearts. The more drinks you buy them, the more freely they insult you. Interlopers come and go, contributing to the atmosphere of entitlement and little else. The abuse in James' emails tastes much, much better than this.

When he goes to pay, Mike is casually presented with a bill for eight hundred and three pounds. He glances at it just as casually and taps in his code. The manager slithers out from somewhere.

'I hope sir and guests had an enjoyable evening,' he fawns.

'It's salvageable,' shrugs Mike. 'I've had better.'

Just a drop in the shallow end of the swimming pool of digits he signed over to shrewd, twinkly Ira McFooley this afternoon, in exchange for an object rather smaller than a penny and of no special beauty. He feels sick both at the probability it's junk, and at the remote possibility it's not.

Life: you know it's a swindle, but you still buy.

James F. Saunders awakes in an unfamiliar metal bed. A police cell, maybe, or a hospital. His shoes are standing neatly in a plastic tray on the floor, stuffed with newspaper. Birds are chirruping. Without raising his head he tugs at the curtain and sees hard blue sky. Swaying tree branches — no leaves on them, just a few dozen of the sniggering feathered imps.

A motor starts up outside — a trimmer or a saw. The birds skedaddle and James thinks of Brenda. If I have not. Love. Her cold eyes, full of hatred. Out of control. What if she's done something stupid? The classic twofold melodrama; the double whammy. He lurches out of bed and tries the door.

It's not a police cell — it's the YHA at Stoupe Hole. Walkers, he's told, reported his wretched existence to the manageress, who ventured out onto the rocks at dusk and recognised him as Bay's unofficial writer-in-residence. She lets him use the phone for free — Brenda won't recognise the number — but there's no answer. No voicemail. He tries three times, then tries calling from his own phone, which he finds intact and functional in his pocket. Where Brenda should be, there's nothing.

Mike Vickers is awakened by his phone's *Ride of the Valkyries* ringtone and insistent buzzing on the bedside table. He turns apprehensively to the other pillow but it's untenanted. Ah, yes.

He and Lulu played a delicious, wordless game in the back of a cab after the club but then she left him hanging. Just a fragrant nuzzle on the cheek. Clever, classy girl. Mike's arrangement with Victoria is informal, of course, a pragmatic alliance. But there is a special sweetness in pleasure that leaves the conscience clean. In every bad night a bright spot.

Oh. Only now does he remember Ira McFooley. The confiding whisper. The uncatalogued item. The elaborate provenance, tantalisingly incomplete. George egging him on in that dimly-lit room where common sense has no jurisdiction. He slumps back, fingers planted in his eyes, but the phone is still chuntering. He submits. It's James, of all people.

'James, old man,' he croaks, with affected cheeriness. 'How nice of you to call. I was thinking of you last night. Among other topics dear to my heart.'

'Have you heard from Brenda?' James' voice is even more humourless than he remembers. A hint of urgency. James and Brenda: Mike has forgotten all about that curious match.

'Not for a while. Should I have?'

'I'm worried about her. We had a row. She — she's not answering her phone.'

'She rarely does.'

'We had a bad row,' James repeats. His whining tone resounds with guilt and defeat. Mike is surprised by a flash of suspicion.

'What did you do to her?' he asks, sharply.

'Nothing! We were — having a good time. She came to visit me. I was talking about my book, some things I said came out the wrong way, and she — she flipped.' This story sounds plausible, and Mike's suspicion recedes. He's seen Brenda flip, once or twice.

'I'm sure she's fine. I warned you not to mess with her.'

'Can you call her? She looked crazy. I'm worried.'

Brenda doesn't answer Mike's call. No surprise there. He texts her the single word *ok?*, which is an agreed signal. There is no reply. She's probably in the mountains. Fasting in the wilderness.

Mike dons a silk dressing gown, pads down to the kitchen and slices his grapefruit with a fiendish Japanese knife. A sensualist not only by inclination but by deliberate cultivation, his first refuge is always pleasure. The masturbatorium, indeed. He manspreads luxuriously in his Eames recliner and consults a mental library of fantasies into which Lulu might be inserted; the opening premises tend to be crude, but unexpected nuances often develop. They're a creative outlet of sorts: expressive therapy.

Afterwards, he sits looking up at his Damoclean chrome chandelier and feels utterly worthless.

Twisted headstock, broken engine mount, cracked wheel rim, bent disc: the bike, now at the garage, will fetch a few hundred quid for parts. Torn jacket sleeve. A scuffed boot. Dan's flawed biological machinery untouched. He reaches for his tablet and watches the wipeout video again: probably the last ride of his life. A wistful sense of what might have been.

Natalie has gone to the supermarket. They've always shopped together but he'll only slow her down. He, blitzkrieg shopper, round in seven minutes, expert judge of the fastest queue, will now slow her down.

The crash was an accident, he keeps assuring her, but she doesn't quite believe him. 'Promise me you wouldn't,' she said. 'Not without telling me. Not without —' She wept; he promised. I admit I was riding carelessly, he said again, but it was an accident.

Death is a bird of paradise: we all know what it is, but it can be many different things that aren't at all alike.

The vase on James' desk is nearly dry, and alstroemeria petals lie scattered among the abandoned plates and cups. One has fallen into the open pot of jam, another clings to its sticky edge. When you sit here, she said, feeling lonely, I want you to remember our little breakfast. Yes, he remembers it. The desk a crime scene. As his head and heart begin to clear, he feels not a trace of anger towards Brenda. You might as well be angry with a cornered leopardess for lashing out. Never love a wild thing.

As for the novel's destruction — that he might or should rewrite it does not even occur to him — since he woke up in the hostel this has lost its horror: a tragic twist is only really sad the first time. Now it's a simple fact in the sordid, inconsequential non-bibliography of James F. Saunders. Fitting, that even its tragedies disappoint.

The horror is rather in the drastically altered landscape of his conscience. His face twitches with disgust at the thought of Project Q. He wallows in the reproaches of Brenda's warmth, optimism and guileless generosity. Where is she, his accidental soulmate? Where is she now?

'Oi! James! Get down here!' It's Rob — Hugo's dad — below the window. James gets up slowly, mechanically descends the stairs and opens the door. Rob is wearing his cords and country check and has a sneer on his face.

'You really are a worthless shit.'

James stares at him blankly. Tell me something I don't —

'Do you know how old my son is? Well?' James casts his mind into the distant realm of last week and last month.

'Six, I think,' he murmurs.

'That's right. Six years old. When you talk to a six-year-old boy, you talk about pirates and dinosaurs and Kung Fu fucking Panda. You do not talk about loneliness and death and whatever fucked-up crap is in your miserable, retarded head.' James feels a bland relief; abuse from a hypocrite, that he can take. 'You won't be getting another penny out of me,' continues Rob, 'and I'll make sure everyone here knows just what a disturbed, pathetic creature you are. Christ — look at you. What was I even thinking, leaving him with you?'

Lacking the desire even to communicate his indifference, James moves to close the door but Rob stops it with a mud-splashed suede boot.

'One more thing. Hugo asked me to give you this.' He holds up a dirty black sack with something heavy in it. 'He found it on the beach. He says it's yours. You could think of it as a goodbye present. Enjoy!'

James takes the sack without a word, carries it upstairs, drops it in the corner of his room and tries to ignore it. There doesn't seem to be any point in opening it. So he's lost Hugo too. The solemn, big-headed boy was his largest source of income. Also, it so happens, his best friend. His counsellor. *Truth is none the wiser for being old.* Gone now. In for a penny.

After a while the sack's forlorn presence becomes overwhelming. He reaches into the wet plastic shroud, lifts out the laptop carcase and lays it on his desk. There is water behind the cracked screen, which flaps on its hinges without resistance; the keyboard and the various sockets are caked in wet grey sand; every surface is streaked and mottled by a sheen of salt. Even though it looks and smells precisely like Hardy's deadest thing, James cannot stop his hand travelling to the power button, which no longer yields to a push. Just above the screen, the inch of red embossing tape he stuck there ten years ago is somehow still clinging on, still announcing its one-word command in clear white capitals.

'*INCIPE.*' is what the tape says. Begin. But it doesn't matter that Steinbeck's dog ate one of his drafts, or that John Stuart Mill's stern father routinely tossed his son's first attempts into the flames. For James, *incipe* signifies nothing. He flicks off the tape with his fingernail and drops the stinking wreck into the rubbish bin.

19. Damage zone

'Poets have the feelings of common men.'
Montaigne

Natalie Mock always used to know right from wrong. The quandaries presented in novels and films; the behaviour of boyfriends; government policies; the responsibilities of multinational corporations; how to remedy injustice. She argued with friends, held her ground and usually won them over. Dan asked her for advice. 'I trust your instincts,' he would say.

In recent years, her instincts have wilted. She couldn't even decide how to vote at the last election, not, as some of her colleagues asserted, because all the parties were alike, but because she simply couldn't judge whose approach was the best. For every well-meant intervention, an unforeseen consequence. Is SmartAid, on balance, helping Africa? She hopes it is, but she's no longer sure. Should you bail out the borrowers or the savers? Protect the fishing communities or the dolphins? Is she a good person? Is she doing the right thing?

As she helps Dan up the stairs and they get ready for bed, she twice seems to feel a sort of pelvic twitch, an awakening, a latent treachery that she tries to ignore.

Brenda stands on the hulking summit of Carn Eige, one of the country's highest but least known peaks, and taps the tip of her ice axe against the trig's grotesque armour of hoar frost. Above, around and below her, the cloudscape shifts. Small, sharp details appear briefly between gulfs of nothing: silhouetted cairn on the neighbouring peak, shore of the angry black loch far below, feeble yellow hole-punch of the sinking sun, patch of scoured rocks that marks the way down. The wind shoves and snatches at her body and scalds her face.

This is the tenth and highest of the twelve tops. She's been walking for eighteen hours with barely a rest, by bright moon and impotent sun, and has four or five hours to go. She's seen nobody. The usual neat black rucksack is not on her back — she has no stove, no food, no map, no phone. Only her axe and the contents of her pocket: a pill bottle, a knife and a small forked stick.

Love — men — boys — what was she thinking? This empty world, this world of abundant silence, is her plenty, her pleasure and her satisfaction. There is relief — even elation — in the confident resolution that she will never again allow herself to fall in love.

She sets off down the narrow spur of snow in bold heel-biting strides. A cloud sweeps over and she loses sight of the ground ahead just as the wind, now behind her, bats her skittering down a sloping sheet of ice. Her arms fly up and she regains her poise, only for another gust to swat her off her feet. She feels acceleration in her gut, and rolls hard onto the singing axe. Its pick judders madly on the ice, breaks loose, sings again, skitters and finally sticks, wrenching her arms upward. She comes to rest with her hands numbly clinging, face crammed hard into snow like broken glass.

A tiny black speck, barely adhering to the white mountain's

breast, insignificant, redundant — now still, now shaking in silent sobs, now still.

The Box is heading for a flat first quarter. Stocks have been raging, but Mike only just got long — he missed the rally. January's profit would have been bigger if he hadn't forgotten to reset the virtual dials he fiddled in December. He remembered in February, cranked up his leverage and duly handed back all the year's gains. Banal. Like a dodgem car with no steering. If this was entertainment he'd ask for his money back. Instead, it's his career.

He hears nothing from Brenda for two days, and is feeling the deep, nascent prickles of fraternal worry when her answering signal arrives: *aye*. Nothing else, but that's enough. He means to text James, but finds himself calling instead.

'I've had a message from you-know-who. She's okay.' James doesn't speak for a few seconds, but breathes and whispers something to himself. He really was worried about her.

'Are you sure?' he says at last. 'Did she say anything about me?'

'I don't think she's in a talkative mood. But yes, I'm sure she's okay. She has her ways of dealing with things. How about you? Are you alright?'

'Me?'

'Yes — you. How's the book coming along?'

'I'm — I'm having a rethink.' His voice trails off weakly. Then he adds, 'Tell her I'm sorry, if you speak to her. Tell her to call me.'

Mike feels unexpected sympathy for this waster who stole his property, upset his sister and insulted his way of life — at least, he takes it for sympathy.

'Listen. James. I have a well-appointed spare room here. En

suite. Objets d'art. Heaving booze cabinet. Why don't you come down for a few days? I think we'd have fun.'

He takes it for sympathy, but it could be a cry for help.

Dan is travelling to work by train and bus. Nat gives him a lift to the station, and picks him up. People surrender their seats when they see the crutches; the ingenious bus lowers itself to help him disembark. The arrangement works. For now.

He's helping the tuberculosis team again. It took them months of painstaking effort to create their single tiny crystal of the crucial protein — the infuriating enzyme that helps TB to defend itself against antibiotics — and already it's been damaged by the harsh glare of the X-rays. There is disagreement about how to proceed. Dan is proposing a trial of the new microfocus beamline, but he admits they may only get one shot. If they illuminate an even tinier volume of the crystal, he argues, they'll be right inside the damage zone, right in the eye of the ionisation storm. The crystal will be toast, but they might just get a clean image.

His colleagues all know about the diagnosis now, of course: the sprained ankle story was never going to wash for long. There's pity on both sides as each unconsenting initiate receives his or her share of the knowledge burden and struggles for the right words. Some Dan tells himself, matter-of-factly — these have to react on the spot, and do so in unpredictable but telling ways — while others hear second-hand and have time to think of an appropriate response. The latter suffer the most: many, especially men, find their courage fails them and say nothing at all, but just conduct their interaction wearing an expression of exaggerated sympathy and avoiding any trace of humour. It makes for long days.

Among his wider circle of family and acquaintance, the

scientifically illiterate often suggest alternative treatments. 'Don't believe the doctors,' they urge, brushing aside the self-evident wonders of biomedical research. 'All you need is a deep detox. Let me send you some links.' A few tempers have flared — Dan's well-meaning aunt is no longer speaking to his father because of the latter's curt dismissals and warnings off. Even Natalie, usually a bullshit bloodhound, wavered after too much internet exposure and had to be steered gently away from the soft verges of quackery and back to reality.

Reality is palliative physio and unpronounceable drug that might give him an extra couple of months — a well-meant biomedical gesture that he chooses to accept with good grace.

James F. Saunders has shaved his head. An odd sensation, this cold, naked bonce — he keeps wanting to rub it with a towel. Fitting, though. Everything is fit and proper. For servicing the internal works he can't stretch to more Laphroaig, but the Spar offers a range of affordable substitutes. Cleansers.

He presses rewind, play, fast forward, play, intent on his mission to find the start of a particular piece of music. Years have passed since he sold his once-prized CD player to pay the rent, but at Christmas he found this dusty thing under the bed at his parents' house, together with a stack of hand-labelled tapes. Click, clack, whir. Rewind an obsolete term now, a lost metaphor.

Yes — literature being a roofless mockery of a refuge, James has turned to music, his oldest love-hate. His attachment spans several genres, but he has been clinging most tightly to certain albums of the Australian singer-songwriter he calls the Boatman. Any therapeutic benefits have, as usual, been impaired by his envious horror of finely executed art of any kind.

Despite sharing genes with his fiddler uncle Joe and a grandmother renowned for belting out fado, James was born with no trace of musical ability. He recalls feeling, even when Becks sang in the shower — adding her own jazzy spin to an apparently vacuous pop ditty — the same hunted, despairing shiver of inadequacy induced by a page of Nabokov at his best.

Ah, here: the pregnant hiss. Just time for a precursory breath, and it begins. Not the Boatman now — James has worn those songs out — but the last resort: his private anthem — the work he reveres above all others, above even the Exile's greatest novel. Reverence was, indeed, born in him the moment he first heard it, twenty years ago.

This close-guarded treasure is quite flawless, like no book or poem James has ever read: flawless like the freak apple he once addressed in fifty consecutive prose variations. Yet, unlike the apple, it remains flawless for eternity. He knows the composer's name, the gist of the text, the distant century in which it was first performed — but nothing else. He's never discussed it, never read a review of it, never listened to a jaded lecturer picking it apart, never heard it chosen on *Desert Island Discs*. Knowledge can be destructive; a second-favourite, Mozart's *Requiem*, once prized by James for its power to evoke a visual panorama of spreading wings, beams of light, precipices, has never sounded the same since his father, a man of little culture but much trivia, gleefully informed him that it wasn't all the master's work. It was, in fact, finished off by some random punter. Horrible.

But *this* piece, the private, secret anthem (or motet — let's not quibble), the one now serenely unfolding, unrolling its Latin syllables, stands in unsullied splendour. Why this obscure, uncelebrated piece, above all others? Which root of his being does it reveal?

He might as well ask, why Becks? Why Brenda? Why Brenda? Why Brenda? He might as well write a fucking autobiography. When the music stops, he snatches a sealed envelope from his desk and blunders down the stairs.

One delicately lingering Monday evening after a productive day at the lab, Dan waits at Didcot station for his train home. A repurposed wall holds an original timber-framed window newly painted in white gloss but lacking its panes: in their place a shock of unimpeded air that draws and fascinates the eye. Perfect transparency.

Dan smiles. Transparency is what he has too. He rejected the childish notion of fate at the age of nine, and so it has been humbling to have his own revealed in terrifying detail. Terrifying is the word for the sheer extent of incapacity that motor neurone disease has in store for him. But Dan will not yet submit to being terrified. The train arrives, its carriage windows open to admit the novel warmth of spring, and as he finally settles into his seat — another small battle behind him — he compares his own looming, creeping incapacity to other varieties.

There is incapacity that strikes without warning: car, horse, assembly line, climbing frame — a momentary freak that transforms a life. Paralysis, blinding, loss of a limb. How those few seconds — so easily avoidable but irrevocable now — would needle and torment! He has been spared that, at least: there's nothing he could have done. Then a different, bitterer flavour of trauma awaits victims of violence or recklessness — of drunk drivers, jealous partners, bungling thieves. Hatred an additional burden for them — seeing justice done. To be free of hatred, as he is, to be a victim only of the universe's general injustice: a profound mercy. And the universe can do worse, of course, can condemn the very young who haven't even had a chance to live. He's had half a chance.

So much for the circumstances of his misfortune. How should he evaluate the pathological details? How does that so-much-commoner fate than his, cancer, compare? More pain, probably (he reserves judgement). More tangible destruction. For many, a cruel and tantalising brush with remission; no such uncertainty for him. On the contrary, his diagnosis has brought more clarity, more certainty: his fate. And let's spare a thought for the wider, subtler net of misery cast by behavioural disorders — addiction, uncontrolled anger, dysfunctional families, unspecified or undiagnosed sicknesses of the soul. Digging a lonely hole — hurting those you need most. For Dan, instead — so far, at least — a cradle of generosity, good intentions and love.

There's one more misfortune to add to this by-no-means exhaustive parade of woe: just getting old, with its slowly gathering conspiracy of health gremlins. The big one. The inescapable elephant in the room of life. Arthritis, incontinence, memory loss, deafness, a dicky ticker, all weighing heavy against the supposed consolations of wisdom. With each passing year the odds leaning further in the wrong direction; the youngsters' world a foreign country; friends and siblings going or gone. Marriages skewed, like Dan's will be, into carer and cared-for, or the roles of child and parent humiliatingly reversed, or the lingerer a mere burden on the buckling state, a life reduced to an unsustainable statistic. The long, crabby descent. Decades, perhaps, to taste its unfathomable sadness.

Life without motor neurone disease, Dan concludes, is no picnic either. The more he ponders his predicament, the more he regards its fundamental substance as universal. The diagnosis has merely rearranged his woes, given them a vigorous shake like dice in a bag. The arrangement is unique to each of us, yes, but everyone has the same dice, and the same sumptuous, moth-eaten, ridiculous bag of life.

Mike Vickers appraises himself in the lift's mirror: a daily indulgence. The eyebrow cocks itself without his prompting. Would you trust this man? Another daily ritual — now lapsed — was to peer over the polished railings of the stairwell on his way to the trading floor. This was to commemorate his once overbalancing while hitching an intransigent sock en route to a meeting, and coming absurdly close to pitching over the rail; the meeting was a great success. I see you, old boy, he would murmur each morning to Death, smiling up at him from a depth of eighty feet. I know all about you. Turning away would feel like a gift, a lucky break — but somehow he lost the habit.

   He's meeting Dan tonight for one of their periodic chit-chats. If his old friend asks him what he's done with his fabulous riches, he'll say he's biding his time — gathering his thoughts before stepping boldly into a new life. Measure twice, cut once, as his dad would say. His experimental purchases of Life, by the yard or by the glass, so seemingly insipid or absurd, have, after all, a potent narcotic aftertaste. He forgets himself. Political hoo-ha about a double-dip recession appears charmingly abstract; old doubts have lost their sting. But the swimming pool of digits isn't a legitimate topic of conversation, even with Dan.

   Strolling beside the canal after work, Mike tries to conjure the spirit of their friendship. For the first five or six years, the two of them were merely rivals, eyeing each other coldly in the run-up to Exam Week and passing the hallowed Form Prize back and forth each summer. By the age of thirteen, each had studied the other's weaknesses so intimately, and found them to be so perfectly non-overlapping with his own, that an alliance seemed not just desirable but inevitable. The next two decades have laboured the point.

As he approaches the usual pub, a black cab pulls up outside. A pair of crutches emerge from the open door and a hand gropes at the roof, hauling its owner upright.

'Do you need some help?' asks Mike, stepping forward and opening the door more fully with a benevolent flourish. For once, he's going to be a good egg. The struggling invalid looks up and smiles wearily.

'Dan! Jesus! What have you done to yourself?' Mike helps him arrange the crutches and closes the door. 'You went and crashed the bike. Am I right? I knew you would. Closet adrenaline junkie.'

'You are right,' says Dan, 'but you're also wrong.' There's no sign of a cast on his leg. He's wearing a normal shoe. Mike has a sudden feeling of disorientation.

'Dan, what is it?'

'Buy me a bloody drink and I'll tell you.'

20. Tracing paper

'We are each of us richer than we think.'
Montaigne

There is, of course, no answer to James' letter. The involuntary yearning that may still be, for all he knows, an emanation of his buried self constantly draws his thoughts after it, northward. But his love (the conventional terminology) is wary now: to chase after Brenda — actually to invade her mountain retreat, to knock on her door and rap on her windows — seems unthinkable. This is why his limp, weary body is heading south, towards Mike.

The smarmy spiv isn't looking so smarmy when he opens the door. His face is flushed and puffy, his shirt creased, he didn't shave this morning.

'Speculation go bad?' says James. 'Pesky third world farmers get one over on you?'

'Shut up and come in,' says Mike. 'It's good to see you.' James walks into the well-remembered party space, now empty and mildly dishevelled. A bog-standard bachelor pad with added trinkets and stretched dimensions. Brenda stood there, and there.

'As it happens,' says Mike, already pouring from an open bottle, 'I did donate four million dollars to global markets on behalf of my investors today — but that's par for the course.' He hands James a predictably oversized glass, sweeps some obstructions off the sofa — a jacket, a blinking phone, *The Economist*, an auction catalogue — and slumps down. 'I also met an old friend yesterday — or rather, a young friend — and found out —' He hesitates, and the last remnants of his chirpy, salesman's inflection drain away. 'I found out he's dying. Has been for while, and I didn't know.'

James studies the frown drawing Mike's translucently blond eyebrows together. Privilege, he thinks, confronted by something that can't be bought off. The indignation! But James knows what it's like to lose friends.

'At least you know now,' he offers.

'I was his best man,' confesses Mike. 'I sort of compare myself to him, if you know what I mean. I've always felt like the two of us are just setting out, like nothing is ruled out yet. Suddenly he's out of the race, just like that.' Mike looks up at his ridiculous chandelier as though at a religious icon. 'Still, he's achieved more than I have. He's a world expert on — what was it? — *insertion devices* in particle accelerators. A finger in the pie of progress. Whereas I —'

'Your only achievement has been to perfect the art of *being* a total insertion device.' Mike nods without smiling.

'This job — ' he waves dismissively at the phone '— was supposed to be a temporary diversion. Work experience. In the last few years, since I turned thirty, I've started hearing a whispering, a warning that I need to get a move on and do something meaningful, but I haven't listened to it.'

'*Meaningful*?' scoffs James. 'It doesn't have to be meaningful. It only has to be useful — or scratch an itch.' He yawns, recognising no obligation to display pity he doesn't feel. It's nice to have a partner in failure, though. 'It's pathetic, isn't it, how we all fall for the same stupid delusions, just like our parents, and their parents, and everyone else on this deluded planet.' He rummages in his bag, extracts the leather-bound Montaigne and holds it out. 'Here.'

Mike looks at it blankly for a moment. 'Oh, that — are you sure you've finished with it?'

'Yes,' replies James, quickly. 'I'm sure.'

'I've never actually read it, you know.'

'That I can believe.'

Mike turns the book in his hands, frowns at the obvious new bruises, then opens it just a crack, as though committing a forbidden act, and peers inside. 'Crispin, my old boss, gave me the set for my thirtieth birthday. I was holding out for a bottle of '82, and didn't know what to say. He was very solemn about it. Should I read it, do you think? Would I get much out of it?'

'I don't know,' says James, reaching for the wine bottle. 'I can't remember what it's about.' He smirks at the label: what Mike *has* achieved is for the '82 to become his daily plonk.

Dan asks Natalie to help him up the ladder into their tiny loft. There isn't enough headroom to convert it — academic now — but last autumn Dan insulated and part-boarded the space. Slid the boxes of their least often-needed possessions into two neat rows. Cold storage in winter, in summer a kiln. Now, in spring, there is merely an ecclesiastical coolness as the Mocks kneel beside the open hatch, surveying their sentimental hoard.

In her row: a few large zipped portfolio cases; long carrier bags stuffed with storage tubes, rolls of tracing paper, balsa offcuts; CDs; a large backpacker's rucksack stuffed with old clothes — Dan's mind makes a glancing, involuntary connection to the stack of letters, the ex-boyfriend that he'd forgotten all about — a high stool; an easel he gave her that never saw much, if any, use. Before he knew her, she painted.

In his row: a heavy box of miniature soldiers from his childhood — his mind's eye sees the stacked rank and file, cavalry with paper pennons laboriously painted and curled, siege engines, winged beasts in lurid hues — once so prized, now a perplexing irrelevance. Irrelevant too the school essays, exercise books, embarrassingly bad artworks, his house tie — a decade in one box. Ah, but this is more like it: his homemade wind-up radio, his collection of fossils and rock samples in stacked ice cream tubs, his chemistry set, his Commodore 64, and finally, right at the back, just visible, bubble-wrapped barrel lying across the unboarded rafters, his telescope.

'Will you help me bring it down?' he says. Natalie knows what he's referring to, and sexily straddles the boxes to reach it. On his way down, with Nat guiding his useless foot onto each rung, he takes one last look before switching off the light.

James picks his way judiciously around Mike's flat. Sliding glass doors recede into walls; ink drawings are printed on huge sheets of metal; windows have both blinds and curtains for good measure; toilet seats hover and then come to rest gracefully like UFOs. Even the air, once exhaled or abluted in, is silently, protectively drawn away to accommodate a filtered inflow.

He feels the old twinge of possibility — that there's material here. This is life, after all, for better or worse. This is the age he's been born into, and every age has a story to tell posterity.

Over breakfast Mike tried to explain, to justify his profession. Even if we are just monkeys throwing darts, he said, we're necessary. We're oil in the works. We operate in

public markets using public information. Outcomes are
dominated by randomness in many enterprises. Whale-
watching tours. Test cricket in rainy nations. He claimed there
were industries with less honourable methods and worse
consequences. Not just satisfying a need, but creating one.
Bottled water, he suggested, piously. Every *second*, *thousands*
of plastic bottles are made, shipped, bought, landfilled. The
Minoans, he said, were piping water four millennia ago.
Whatever makes you feel better, replied James. Self-justification
is, of course, a battle he understands.

He surveys the booze cabinet and wine fridge, idly sends
heavy kitchen drawers rolling out and back on silent bearings.
This material disparity between two losers apparently a
meaningless accident. But no, not meaningless. The penniless
humiliation of the artistic life is essential and just, a test of
intention as well as resolve, and the mercenary's riches are no
different.

A cascade of electronic chimes breaks into his thoughts: the
doorbell. He might well have ignored it, but happens to be
standing at that moment in the hall. The heavy front door,
three inches thick, swings back from its lisping seal and there,
gracing with faded denim and khaki the grotesque, indigo
marblings of the corridor carpet, stands Brenda the beloved.

'Surpri—' she starts to say. Surprise does indeed reverberate,
ricochet between them, measuring out its own silent space.
James is doubly confused, ambushed by vivid imaginings,
decade-buried but scored deep, of the reunion, the reckoning
that he never had with Becks. He's practised this scene over
and over, but with the wrong script.

'Brenda,' he murmurs at last, drawn out across the threshold.
Thus I; faltering forward. 'You got my letter.'

Brenda steps back, her eyes child-wide. She steps back again, retreats. Then her face crumples into a mask of very grown-up disgust.

'Brenda. Wait. Just wait a moment. You don't have to say anything. Just listen.' She shakes her head, turns and hurries away down the corridor, duffle bag swinging. 'Wait! I'll leave, you stay.' He follows to the stairwell, hears her echoing steps below.

'I'm nobody — you stay!' he calls. 'I'll leave!' Then in desperation he adds, 'I'm sorry for what I said! I was confused!' *Confused?* These are the wrong words, he knows. The footsteps recede and a door bangs shut.

'Can't we just start again?' he pleads of the silence.

Back in the cavernous fraternal crime scene of a flat, he calls Mike, leaves a message telling him to call Brenda tout de suite and packs his miserable bag.

Brenda Vickers stands beside the canal, her body soaked in cold sweat and her mind a hot infusion of anger and self-loathing (a hint of dissolved sweetness is ignored). Why did Mike have to put her through that? What was he thinking? Why is the world so stupid?

Her phone buzzes in her pocket. She yanks it out: Mike. Her phone, she suddenly understands, is the surgical implant by which these hateful people control her. Invading her mental space with their pathetic, desperate sexts and their concerned family signals (commands, rather) and their rescheduled appointments, pressing their obligations upon her. She lets it swing for a moment between her finger and thumb, cracked screen abrading cracked skin, then flicks it spinning into the canal. Plop. The water is clear, and she sees it plumb the four or five feet to the bottom, raise a little puff of silt, and lie there, face up in the sun, drowning mutely. Out of your misery. An electronics serial killer now.

And she laughs.

Dan Mock relishes a practical challenge, and the crutches present many. The tool holster he wears round the house and lab accommodates his tablet, phone, tea flask, snacks, and anything else he needs to carry from one room to another. He's cushioned the crutch handles with gel-filled sleeves and armed the tips with all-weather rubber feet. He's had five cheap bar stools delivered, one for each room of the house (including one in the shower) for easy sitting and rising. His father, arriving with a toolbox in each hand and a sort of fierce, desperate joy at being able to help, has helped him to install grab handles in tricky places.

Yes, humans are adaptable in the face of incapacity. Practical victories encourage profounder internal ones. But Dan's disease harbours a unique scorn for such resilience. Just as he gains purchase, traction on his difficulties (and as he and Natalie even feel able to laugh at them), it changes the rules: deepens his incapacity and renders all his adaptations useless. Presents a snake to cancel all his laboriously-climbed ladders.

At the start of April, a quick hand up — from Natalie, a colleague or a fellow commuter — was sufficient to get Dan out of a chair. By the end of the month, it's not. Simply standing his body upright is a precarious operation, as it might be for a badly-made action figure. After his fourth fall, from which he is unable to get himself up, Natalie persuades him to try the wheelchair. Within a week, months earlier than he expected, it's his new reality. Ramps now his domain, stairs of mere sculptural interest with no practical function. Working from home less a leisurely treat, more a prison sentence.

And it's not just Dan's legs. His hands still work but he can't lift his arms above his head: shirts, yes; T-shirts, no. Shirt buttons: annoying. His voice has started to change, which is a bad sign. Its pitch has crept up a couple of notes, and it slurs when he's tired.

His parents think he and Nat should move house. They look at property websites, tick the 'accessible' box and send suggestions. But the two-up-two-down has its advantages: downstairs bathroom; central location; sunny front room where Dan sets up his workstation; gloomy back room a natural bedroom; plenty of space for guests upstairs. Best of all, the wheelchair neatly clears the kink in the hall by one centimetre, which gives Dan, tongue clamped in teeth as he manoeuvres, the thrill of unlikely success every time.

The car becomes a dreaded battleground of heaving and grappling, suddenly swept aside by the arrival of the Motability car in mid-May. You just drive straight into the back, like a drone docking in the mothership. As gadgets go, it's good.

These arrangements, foresighted concessions to practical needs, are similar, Dan imagines, to the preparations of expectant parents (Nat hasn't mentioned that idea for a while, thankfully). He too is expectant. Just like the nervous, excited dad-to-be that wasn't-to-be, he sometimes forgets what is going to happen despite the glaring parade of reminders. Each time reality bites, he feels an incursion of raw panic, incoherent antithesis of all his careful philosophy. The panic is that he doesn't even know what is unfinished, what unexplored in his dwindling life. He tells himself to get a grip.

Life is preparation.

Six weeks after his thoughtless betrayal (like all thoughtless errors, James' visit acquired this identity only after the fact), Mike Vickers has failed to re-establish meaningful contact with his sister. He has, apparently, driven Brenda to the other side of the world — to cheery, self-satisfied brother Austin and his New South Wales sheep station.

Faithless brother is a heavy charge to add to Mike's lengthening roster of worthlessness and wasted privilege, which swells and flexes under the awful magnifying glass of Dan's illness. However, like all early-stage addicts, Mike is blind to the connections between his various woes — in particular, he's not prepared to give up James. He likes James. His moment of madness in Ira McFooley's gallery was both in spite of, and inspired by James. And he doesn't want James on his conscience as well.

Mike is still spending, cycling grimly between restraint and profligacy. His friends have quickly come to expect and rely on his largesse, and when news of his latest extravagance fails to elicit the enthusiastic affirmation he craves, Mike finds himself calling James.

'I've just signed a rental agreement,' he announces.

'For what?'

'For a summerhouse. On an island in the river — Shepperton. River frontage. Punt. Hot tub. Cocktail bar. Baby grand. For the whole month of June.'

'I didn't know you played the piano.'

'I don't. But I can punt like a pro.'

'Sounds idyllic,' says James, dully. Mike falters for a moment, then presses on.

'I hope so, because during the week, it's yours. Your retreat. Sun-dappled, river-rounded change of scene. What can you write in four weeks? Two or three short stories? An avant-garde novella? Gatsby-on-Thames?'

'Very generous of you, but no thanks.'

'At the very least come to my garden party there on the

ninth.' James emits a savage snort of laughter that makes Mike wince. It hurts, and it feels good.

'What on earth are we celebrating?' asks James.

Natalie Mock's outward life is locked in a downward dance with Dan's. When he can no longer safely drive, Natalie can no longer *not* drive. When he can no longer stand at the kitchen counter, Natalie is committed to all the cooking and all the washing up. When he needs a shower enclosure, she loses a bath. One of the heaviest visible burdens stems from her resolve to spare him the banalities of terminal illness — navigating the bewildering web of well-meaning professionals and volunteers with their leaflets and ring binders, addressing perverse financial complications and, above all, filling in forms. Even three-score and ten is far too short a span to be filling in forms, Natalie reasons, so Dan's precious few months or years will be form-free if she can help it. In consequence, her downward-dancing outward life has a triple helping of infuriating, bureaucratic crap.

Her internal life is following a stranger, richer course. Each practical necessity has its attendant love-angel — patient, indomitable, ennobling, recalling helpless ministerings to her father but fledged now, matured, drawing out the very best of her once-doubtful respecting and cherishing of Dan. On the other hand, angel or no, each must be accomplished amid the pitch and roll of wretchedness.

Last night, she and Dan argued. 'I get it!' she snapped. 'I get that our future was a blank fucking page that means nothing to you. But this is not only about what might or might not have been, it's about what's happening right now — this long, dismal, slow motion goodbye.'

Dan nodded, as he might at a seminar, and replied, in that

calm, matter-of-fact voice that makes her want to shake him, 'A sudden death piles all its sorrow onto those left behind. At least a slow-motion goodbye is shared.'

'That's just it!' she returned. 'You're not letting me share it! Sharing it does not mean me turning into your fucking nurse.' She cried and said sorry, and he said sorry, and it ended.

The little plastic wand lies thoughtfully on the rim of the sink, considering its answer. Natalie's periods never exhibited much of a sense of rhythm in the bygone era before she went on the pill, so a missed beat need not be significant. But if. She recalls Dan's three reasons — the three tragedies he wants to avoid: his, hers, and its. He said, 'There is no divine decree tying you to me.' It was well-meant, presumably — it might even be true — but could anything be more hurtful?

She tries to stop herself looking down too early. Looks over at the new enclosure. Pictures the old bath, and herself, last year, lying in a marinade of diluted blood. Reaches back, elbow crooked, to feel the dint of the scar.

Her eyes snap down to the edge of the sink. One bar, clear and solitary as her own deluded plot. She feels a crashing wave of relief — only relief. If. If nothing. Not built for babies.

James F. Saunders remembers the Upstart suggesting that the first impulse after a humiliation is to look into a mirror. As for the Exile, his private prescription was simple: *Write it! What else are you good for?* The foundations of a novel cannot, he feels sure, be laid from unsorted rubble, nor from the still-hot, gelatinous matter of raw feeling. But poetry, perhaps. Yes, it is as poems, or fragments of poems, or poems of fragments, that James' benighted thoughts stagger back into the light.

The conjunction of several minor observations, each insignificant in itself, convinces him that the Bay locals have become less friendly. Rob's been dishing the dirt on him. Nobody in Bay much likes Rob, but the dirt sticks anyway. It's bank holiday weekend, but the Bay Hotel doesn't have any bar work for him. All very fitting. Sackcloth and ashes, tar and feathers, grime and banishment. Write it.

He writes four or five poems a day, takes pleasure in squashing them into perfectly round, compacted balls, and then, at high tide, sitting with his back to the usual bollard, flicks them one by one into the appreciative sea.

Natalie Mock is hauled out of a frantic dream by a gentle but persistent tinkling bell, apparently right inside her head. She had a beautiful baby in the dream, about the size of a baby gerbil, but then lost it somewhere in the house and searched with growing desperation, cursing her negligence. The tinkling bell is Dan, fully dressed, stirring a cup of coffee he's delivered to her bedside table. He grins. The clock says before five.

'Can you help me get the blunderbuss out front? We have to be quick.'

They stand on the pavement in the bright, birdsung dawn. Dan fits a sort of lid of dark glass over the front of his telescope, slots an eyepiece into place and points the barrel straight along the street towards the sun. He applies his eye and grins again.

'Tell me what you see.'

What Natalie sees, stooping over the telescope and applying an unpractised eye, is a luminous orange. There's a little round black spot on the orange, and some even tinier specks and marks.

'I think there's some dirt on your lid-thing,' she says. 'And maybe a price sticker — a round one.' Dan grins again.

'Look again at that round sticker.'

Suddenly her mind begins to grasp what she's looking at.

The orange — it's the sun — is bright at the centre, dimmer at the edge, as a thing would be if you were peering through a dimmer skin into a potent, glowing core; the marks are not on the glass but, shockingly, etched on the sun's fiery surface; and the black spot is something else again — not a sticker, not on the glass or on the sun but drifting somewhere in between: a celestial photobomber. A planet. She feels a lift in her stomach as the solar system suddenly seems not an abstraction on children's posters but a reality upon which she is lightly perched.

She looks up at the empty street, at the empty dawn sky, and at Dan's face glowing with excitement, and feels a violent heave of loneliness. When Dan is gone, this is what remains: a black stone circling a ball of fire.

'Venus,' whispers Dan, squinting, adjusting the telescope's aim to keep up with the rising sun. 'Not stopping. Just in transit. The next time this happens —'

'You don't have to say it.'

'The next time this happens,' he repeats patiently, 'we'll both be dead and gone.' He squeezes her hand, gently but probably as hard as he can. Our fragile existence may seem to divide us, he's saying, but really it unites us. Yes, but.

When she stoops and looks again, the black circle has drifted, silent and sure and without any of the fuss the rarity of this event seems to demand, closer to the edge.

21. Slap bang

*'How many improbable things there are, vouched
for by trustworthy people, about which we should at least
preserve an open mind, even if they do not convince us!'*
Montaigne

Mike tells Dan and Natalie to present themselves at Shepperton
Lock at four. There's disabled parking, he says; everything else
is arranged, he says. It's a blazing, pulsating June afternoon
with all that entails for the west London traffic, but they arrive
at the riverside only mildly late and mildly frazzled to find the
miraculous parking space just as Mike promised. A bronzed
boy in shorts and flip-flops waves them over to a launch
moored with its stern to the bank and a ramp already unfolded.
His lithe, undiseased body seems, to Dan, only vaguely subject
to the law of gravity.

'Mr and Mrs Mock?' he enquires. 'Guests of Mr Vickers?
Step aboard, please!'

Dan pushes aside a ripple of envy. He smiles at Nat, and
manoeuvres his chair with an appreciable remnant of that
satisfaction peculiar to self-taught expertise. The mooring rope
is loosed. Terra firma, traffic and the humdrum world drop
quietly away behind them. The launch glides in a breezy arc
around the nearest island, past a churning weir, a small marina,

a rowing club littered with more tanned bodies and boats, and a parade of houses with immaculate, dreamy gardens. One of the larger gardens is thronged with chattering people, and it is here the launch slows and backs up to a narrow landing stage. Dan steers down the ramp backwards and executes a graceful one-eighty on the striped lawn.

Mike is already strolling down to greet them, tongs in hand, wearing a novelty Statue of David apron over a pink shirt and dazzling white trousers.

'Old man,' he says, stooping to embrace Dan. 'Natalie. Quite an entrance! Welcome.'

It's hard to mingle by joystick, and though Natalie does her best to intermediate, Dan's sense of empowerment is soon punctured by the usual awkward smiles and greetings that assail them from both standoffish and overenthusiastic strangers. In fact, it's worse than usual. To some of Mike's friends he is invisible — even to some he's met before — to others a child, and to yet others he's apparently stark bollock naked. Natalie, fiercely protective and no expert at this game, sometimes makes things worse. Even the most innocuous small talk presents pitfalls to the awkward squad, and Dan finds himself wanting to let them get back to their party.

He has a feeling that not all wheelchairs would have the same effect. A sporty big-wheeler evokes the Paralympics, burly shoulders, basketball; it's the headrest, he suspects, that really scares people off. A proclamation of mental impairment, of drooling dependency. Dan doesn't even need the damned headrest — yet — but he's been advised to keep it in place, in case he gets tired.

'I wanted to throw a surprise party especially for you,' confides Mike over the barbecue, after their first circuit. 'Invite all your friends and family. I had the whole thing worked out.

But Nat thought you'd hate me forever for making you the centre of attention. So you'll have to make do with my friends instead.'

'Oh, but we *love* your friends,' jokes Natalie. 'Your friends are our friends.'

Mike poles out into the channel and swings gracefully upstream. The punt handles like a dream, providing a welcome fillip to his morale. Dan's arrival was a shock of the least flattering kind: the shock of new knowledge is honourable enough, but the shock you feel on seeing something you already knew to exist — the child victim of a civil war, what goes on in an abattoir, or your best friend's wheelchair — is an indictment of your internal dishonesty, and guilt follows close behind.

He takes a deep breath and adjusts his stance. Here, at least, is something that he can do well. When he should have been learning maths twelve years ago, or repaying his privilege in some other service to mankind, he was perfecting the art of prodding an elongated, upholstered crate along a river with studied nonchalance. It's gratifying to finally see a return on the investment.

Seated side by side on the velvet are Victoria, in a shoulderless red-and-gold number that's trying just a little too hard, and Lulu in floral perfection. Not a seating arrangement they would have chosen, but neither wanted to be the one left behind and they're both coping with characteristic grace. On the nearer seat, at Mike's feet, facing forward and with her simple straw hat obscuring his view of her face, sits Natalie. She didn't want to leave Dan, but he insisted. It's just possible that he wanted to escape her constant, ministering presence. Let his hair down.

Confronted by two of the most beautiful women he has ever met, silently competing to arrange their flawless legs to the most devastating effect, Mike nevertheless finds his gaze drawn downward towards Natalie. Her predicament troubles him in ways he hasn't explored — ways related to, but distinct from his pain and pity for Dan. When she turns her head to the left or right he gets an eyeful of pallid breast and looks up guiltily.

Dan's chair is positioned beside a sundial, which supports his beer at the critical straw-sipping height. After another gauntlet of uncomfortable niceties, he is relieved to find himself alone. It's not just the patronising and the awkwardness. Talking, laughing, nodding and even smiling are now for him the equivalent of running up steps or standing on one leg: manageable, but hard physical work for which he has a limited capacity.

The sundial's shadow rests on five, but it's gone six — the error resulting from some combination of incorrect accommodation of latitude and longitude, the ellipticity of the earth's orbit and British Summer Time. The inclined edge of the blade should lie parallel to the earth's axis, of course. Dan closes his eyes and feels the planet rolling through space, northern hemisphere generously tipped, for now, towards the sun and basking in its summer bath of photons, whatever charged particles happen to penetrate its magnetic field, and a comically large number of neutrinos (a few trillion of the unassuming little buggers are landing in his beer every second). Why is the planet tipped over just the right amount to create the moderate seasonal variations so conducive to life? Ah. Good question. It got tipped sometime in the earth's early history, of course, when the solar system was a jumble of rubble, possibly by the same humongous collision that created the moon.

But why just the right amount? And why are the sun's temperature and distance perfectly tuned to ensure those photons are conveniently energetic (for photosynthesis) but arrive with moderate, non-roasting flux? And why, after all, have the dials on the fundamental forces been so precisely and perfectly adjusted to permit star formation, heavy elements, complex structures and the habitable universe? And why has space-time itself been configured slap bang in the sweet spot (two or four spatial dimensions would be non-starters for life)? Why, indeed. Ah. Dan smiles.

The anthropic principle and its more personal corollaries constitute, in his view, a refuge of almost limitless therapeutic power. The answer to so many questions. Why are life's necessary ducks lined up in such a convenient row? Why did Daniel Mock come to be born, given the infinitesimal probability of his parents' union, and those of his grandparents, and his great-grandparents, and every scattered ancestor forever before? Why did he contract motor neurone disease? Of all the weirdly fucked-up ways to die. Why not the more likely heart disease, or cancer, or, for that matter, nuclear war? Why didn't that roadside wall of flint swat his incoming frame like a cricket bat? Why? Because. Because he's asking the question.

Of course, many people reject this line of reasoning — not only the superstitious, the faters, but many of his scientific acquaintance, both theoreticians and experimentalists. There is a kind of hunger for something more, a kind of —

'Sausage for your thoughts?' says a voice. Dan opens his eyes. A skinny, shaven-headed man has taken hold of his precious straw and is using it to shepherd a wasp out of the glass. In his other hand he holds out two sauce-slathered hot dogs precariously; perhaps a little unsteadily.

'Thanks,' says Dan, maintaining his serene, happy countenance. 'But I've already eaten. Thanks, though.' The man is wearing faded black jeans and a faded Nick Cave T-shirt. Not very summery.

'I'm James,' he says. Not someone Mike has ever mentioned. Dan took him for the gardener.

Natalie Mock can't quite hit it off with Mike's groupies. They seem nice enough, but that's just it — their politeness has the familiar flavour of crutches and wheelchairs. She feels the empty place next to her like a wound.

To an onlooker on the bank she's already what she'll one day become again: one of the girls. She hesitantly trails her fingers in the water, copying Victoria — it's pleasant for a few seconds but then something brushes against them. She wipes them on the seat and smiles weakly.

James F. Saunders has judged his preparatory inebriation well. A few drinks give his present consciousness a literary distinction — a grandeur, even — usually reserved for the regretted past or the dreaded future. His world's a stage, and hot sun pours down on him like a spotlight. The disabled man — presumably Mike's tragic school chum — is called Dan. He asks James rather doubtfully if he's a friend of Mike's. Doesn't like the cut of his jib.

'I suppose so,' shrugs James with a smile. It's strange, but true. 'Where is that slimy fucker, anyway?'

The man suppresses a smile. 'Showing off in the punt. My wife's with him.'

After a silence marking the moment when he might have made his excuses but chooses not to, James says, 'So what *were* you thinking about?'

'Luck.'

James is uncharacteristically ravenous and has just taken a bite of hot dog. The man seems disinclined to elaborate, so he valiantly shepherds the food to one side of his mouth.

'Last week,' he announces, 'my landlady found four double-yolkers in a box of eggs. One in a million. Doesn't win a penny.'

The man — was it Dan or Dave? — says something like, 'Clustering,' his voice slurring. He tries again. 'Classic example of a rare event that occurs in clusters. Young chickens, big eggs. Not really one in a million.' Ah yes, he was — is — some sort of science nerd. Doctor Who. Doctor Strangelove, maybe. James decides to advance the conversation, the dialogue, onto matters of substance.

'What kind of bad luck put you in the chair?' he inquires, simply. Mike never actually specified the disease.

The man calmly names it, the six Delphic syllables tripping off his tongue with no slurring. It *is* a nasty one. A clock ticker. *I'm not the only one who's cursed*, thinks James. *Worth remembering.*

What he says out loud is, 'I imagine one of the worst things must be the loss of — of *autonomy*. To be autonomous, your own person, in control of your life, able to be alone and act alone, you need your body to cooperate.'

The man frowns at this abrupt, Montaignian perspective on incapacity. 'Technology helps,' he says. 'The chair, the computer, above all the internet.' After a pause, he adds, 'The other side of that dependency coin is that I appreciate the people I love — my wife and my family — and they me, I suppose — more than ever before. More than would have been possible before.' This observation stings. 'Are you married?' pursues the man, relentlessly.

'No. But I take your meaning. I've experienced something like it. Only a trauma makes love real. Without a trauma, love dissipates. Takes itself for granted. Wouldn't you say?'

The man nods. 'Yes, I would say that. Love — I'm not speaking grandly here, just about what everyone feels for the people closest to them — finds a purpose.'

Natalie fidgets. She can feel her legs and feet burning even under the sunblock. At last, Mike turns the punt and the river's lazy flow helps them back over the same Ratty and Mole territory. As they round the tip of the island, a window between two willows slowly opens to reveal the pastel collage of the throng on the lawn. Burbling voices. She's relieved to see Dan still where she left him, looking cheerful — in animated conversation with the oddly-dark figure of a man. A curtain of willow fronds drifts again across the scene, and she leans to one side, trying to identify Dan's new friend.

'Whoa there!' says Mike, flailing for his balance as the punt tips. 'That's neither big nor clever.' Victoria giggles and leans too, and some banter commences — but Natalie isn't listening. Her eyes are still fixed on the duo beside the sundial. The landing stage approaches.

Without a sound, the gin and tonic in Natalie's hand slumps over, depositing a many-petalled effervescent bloom onto the cushion where Dan would have sat.

Mike Vickers carefully applies weight to the pole — an expert puntist's clothes are never wetted by so much as a drop — feels it slide a good foot down into the primeval mud, and leaves it standing there to trap the punt against the landing stage. He disembarks nimbly, dries his hand on a handkerchief and offers it to the ladies. Victoria. Lulu. Natalie.

'Nat?' Natalie clambers out distractedly, knee first, ignoring his assistance. She's spilled her drink across the seat. 'Are you alright?'

'Fine,' she replies, distantly, looking past him. 'Fine.' She straightens but makes no move away from the bank. Mike follows her gaze to Dan, who's talking to, or rather being talked to by, of all people, James Fuck Fakes Saunders. Jesus, thinks Mike, seeing James' inelegant get-up. If you're going to come, at least make some sort of effort. At the same time he feels a surge of relief that his fairy godbrother is here.

'Come on,' he says, touching her arm. 'Let's go and rescue your dearly beloved. And I'll introduce you to someone.'

Natalie drifts forward, murmuring. 'Is this some kind of —'

James F. Saunders didn't expect to meet Death on this gin-soaked lawn, let alone Love. But here They both are, sitting in the same electric wheelchair. More self-satisfaction than self-pity. Love conquers all.

The man smiles suddenly, and half-raises a hand to wave. James turns to see Mike prancing up from the riverbank with his bevy of ladies. Two of them — one imperiously tall and dark, the other imperiously blonde and tanned — diverge towards rival party factions, leaving Mike with the third. The third is a freckly redhead, all of about five foot two.

The cheerful backdrop, the staging, falls away. *Every hour, on the hour.* Even to the original air-blue gown. No. Yes.

Dan can't easily shade his eyes. Venus is still up there, tracing out her less fortunate ellipse, thirty million miles closer to the blazing sun, out of line now but still lost in its dazzle: the slenderest eyelash of a backlit crescent, if you knew where to look.

'Nat tried to drown us all,' says Mike. 'We had to tie her up and lock 'er in the foc'sle. Afternoon, James, old chap. So good of you to make it after all. Now, who needs a drink?'

As Dan looks up at Mike, he notices Mike's gaze wander with a frown across to his scruffy, plain-speaking friend, James. Dan's own gaze wanders from Mike across to Natalie. Suddenly, the earth that he again feels rolling on its axis is a planet whose laws he doesn't understand quite as well as he thought.

His wife is standing as still as the sundial, her blue dress slightly rucked on her hip from sitting in the low seat of the punt. Her face is expressionless, but has the barely perceptible colouring and the extra-glossiness of eyes that always betray her discomposure. The fingers of her empty hands, at her sides, are held just a little too straight. She looks like she might break into a run. She looks magnificent.

'Is someone going to say something?' Mike's voice, far away.

Dan drags his eyes from Natalie and directs them up, up, towards the focus of her attention, James, who is standing at his side. James glances down at him. Their connection, their understanding has been displaced by something else. James looks back at Natalie. He seems at last to breathe.

'Hello, Becks.'

22. Living thing

'My mode of living is the same in sickness and in health.'
Montaigne

Natalie Mock, née Beckett, feels herself to be in two places at once, and in each place she is a different person. One of the two is laughing, sliding down a snowy slope on her backside, with her boyfriend clutching her from behind, his weight pressing her to accelerate. They're out of control, going much too fast, but the hill miraculously steers them past each threatening rock or tree, and they come to rest in a painless tangle with cold hands and ears and arses, and hot hearts. It's her twenty-first birthday.

The other is here, in this sultry corrupted Eden — wife, carer, homeowner and unfulfilled office pen-pusher. James is in both places, and he hasn't changed a bit.

James F. Saunders, seeing the changes wrought by ten years in a remembered face, feels a sickening, thrilling jolt — the wake left by time's thundering passage. It's not that Becks has aged in any trite, pejorative sense. She looks wonderful, in her Becksish way. But in that instant he sees for what it is his long-preserved, long-treasured sense of their star-crossed union — it recoils from her undeniably, unanswerably altered reality, back into the distant past where it belongs.

'Why does he call you that, anyway? "Becks."'

'He always did. It's the name he first heard — it was a school nickname, and I was backpacking with a school friend who used it. He sort of adopted it.' Natalie doesn't add the recollection that James said he preferred Becks to Nat — the sound, the strength of it — and that at the time she felt the same.

'Huh,' says Dan, nodding as though assimilating a significant fact. 'You never told me that. The funny thing is, I always imagined him as a Chris.' Natalie knows she shouldn't find the subject uncomfortable, which only compounds her discomfort. 'Have a few moments with him,' adds Dan. 'I don't mind. In fact, I'd rather you did.' Then he smiles. 'Mocks.'

'I don't think I've got anything to say to him.' But Dan quietly, sincerely insists. This, apparently, is an ordeal that must be gone through.

'Hello, Becks. It's great to see you.'

'It's good to see you too.'

James takes note of the moderated adjective. 'You look great. Grown up. Sort of, er, womanly. I'm really sorry about your husband. It must be hard. Seems like a great guy.' This is where James' decade of wordsmithery has got him: great to see you, you look great, seems like a great guy. But he finds he's not afraid of using the wrong words.

'We do okay. And you — you're here on your own?'

James smiles and nods. 'Yep.'

'Where do you live?'

'Yorkshire. On the coast. After uni I didn't get far. You?'

'Reading,' she says, with defensive force, and then adds, perhaps in mitigation (though James hears too a note of reproach), 'I work there.'

He savours the next pause. It could last almost forever because of what he's going to say at the end of it. She's looking through the willow fronds towards the sparkling play of evening sun on the river. It's beautiful. Mike was right — he could write here. Or just exist here, for a while. He breathes in. And out.

'Have you ever thought about me?'

Becks — Natalie — glances up with an eyebrow raised derisively, but then says, 'Once or twice.' James is surprised when she adds, after a pause, eyes fixed back on those miraculous, ever-changing, never-repeating reflections, 'You?'

He smiles again. 'Once or twice. Sorry for being — back then — the way I was —'

Natalie shakes her head, raises a hand to cut him off — lightly veined now, ring on the finger. 'It's not even a thing.'

James has finally, in the last hour, comprehended that their unresolved quarrelling is not a thing — not a living thing — but she says that as though it is.

Mike waits on the landing stage. His best old friend and his best new friend are, it turns out, connected. That this connection runs through the body and soul of Natalie is, today, oddly unsurprising. The launch glides into sight and backs up. Mike nods at the boy, presses a twenty in his hand. At length, Dan and Natalie emerge from the house — their toilet mission accomplished — and negotiate the ramp he's had fitted to the patio steps.

James is talking to Pete, his original discoverer and champion, and waves a casual, friendly farewell to the Mocks as a single entity.

From now on, Mike's going to be there for them. This resolve, like James' farewell, finds it convenient to address the two as one. But as the launch swings out into the channel and the Mocks themselves turn to wave, and as love and sadness well up in Mike's stunted heart, the eye he catches is Natalie's.

Winter is a surprisingly chilly affair in Kentucky, New South Wales. Brenda likes the cold, of course, but isn't dressed for it, and blows on her hands as the cabin warms up. She imagined a rustic log cabin, but it's more of a portakabin. On the wall there really are pictures of prize sheep wearing rosettes.

'Can you tell me again,' says Austin, thoughtfully scratching his stubbly jaw so that muscles bulge in the crook of his arm, 'exactly what this bloke of yours did wrong?'

Brenda feels her chest tighten. 'He admitted that he was just using our relationship as material for his book.'

Austin chuckles and shakes his head. 'Christ, Bren — sorry, I don't mean to laugh. But you do pick 'em. And this would be the book that you, er, relieved him of.' Brenda nods. 'And Mikey knew this, and took his side?'

'I don't actually know what Mike knows. But James was in his flat. Opened the door to me, like they were best mates.'

Austin grunts and nods, as though his point had been made. 'And I guess this author bloke went spare when you — took your revenge. Since his precious book was all he cared about, I mean.'

'Not really,' answers Brenda. 'He wanted me back.' Austin grunts and nods again, letting the implications of this fact, whatever he considers them to be, speak for themselves.

'Still,' he sighs, cracking a can of imported English cider, 'plenty more tups in the rut, as they say.'

Austin thinks the best of everyone. Always has. One result is that he lives in a portakabin. Another is that he always seems to be happy. That's why Brenda came here, buying her ticket with Mike's unused fifties — that, and the certainty that Austin wouldn't try to make her see a doctor. They both know she's unwell, but they believe in other kinds of treatments.

Mike Vickers sits forward on the perverse reception-area chair, elbows on knees, fingers bridged, waiting his turn. The sales rep thumbs her phone intently. This is the culmination of three months' schmoozing — a finals pitch, a direct contest against one or more unknown rivals. Thirty minutes each in front of the investment committee, and Mike's up next.

The MRI's lacklustre, dodgem-car year has continued, but last year's bonanza keeps prospective investors interested. Past performance is no guide to … but nobody listens to that, least of all the professionals. Mike has learned to push the miraculous doublethink that while the MRI program itself is a ruthless algorithm immune to all human foibles, its investors also gain some sort of unspecified access to his firm's world-renowned human traders and economists, its superstar sparkle. CIOs don't want to hear that the strategy is just fresh-faced Mike, a standard issue desktop PC and ten thousand lines of inherited code.

The marketing team have helped him out with a new logo inspired by *CSI*, or maybe *ER*, and a glossy brochure. They can't improve on Mike's immaculate charts, of course — he has an A* in geography and he's not afraid to use it — and the magic show doesn't work in hard-copy. But the new introduction, emphasising his firm's peerless reputation and limitless resources, doesn't do any harm.

A door clicks somewhere, releasing a waft of voices and footsteps. Mike's rep looks up from her phone, smiles nervously and mouths, 'Here we go.' The outgoing rivals stride into view, and the smug, confident little smile that Mike has prepared for them dies on his face. His adversary — hawk nose, crooked tie, greying hair slightly wild — grins broadly.

'Michael. Fancy that. May the best man win.' It's Crispin. Crispin, ferocious boffin-in-chief, who should be in Hong Kong, and he *knew* he was up against Mike. Which means this battle is lost.

The muffled, resigned yelps of his neighbours' midlife therapy transport James F. Saunders back to the night before he started his late novel. The ghosts of Byron and Van Gogh, wasn't it? The spectre of death. All just repetition from here on. It's easy to wallow in dark thoughts when you're holding a luminous lifeline of hope, as he was then.

He frowns at the ceiling. He could have emailed the novel to himself — he even thought of doing it, about forty thousand words in — but he didn't act. Why not? He doesn't know. Its absence is still palpable — it *is* like a death, but a death, perhaps, of someone he misses less than he expected.

Is it time to begin the next doomed cycle of repetition? The altered landscape of his life would demand a very different book now, of course. A more — dare he even form the words in his head? — a more *grown-up* sort of book. Or — this new thought, impossible before his impromptu reunion with Becks, hits him like a tomahawk, and he gasps audibly — is it finally time to call it quits? Is this the end? And if it is the end, so what?

A breeze from the open window wafts, caresses, consoles James' face in the darkness. The neighbours are all fucked out now, and wavelets are crisply slapping the shingle. *Kesh; kesh; kesh.* If this is the end of his endeavour, his writing dream, then there will be, after all, no special legacy for James F. Saunders, no lasting work to touch the hearts of readers yet unborn, just as there will be no solemn slab laid down to mark his eventual passing, trod by reverent feet, but instead, crammed out of sight, unloved and tended by contract, a grubby little pellet of reconstituted stone.

Dan Mock, stuck indoors on a day of roiling clouds and hot, glistening pavements, has driven his chair to the front window to watch, hear and smell the latest downpour. He slides a weak hand through the opening. If he could, he'd lift the sash high and stick his head out.

He has mixed feelings about the peculiar re-entry of Natalie's ex into their lives. For himself, he is glad: he feels like a missing puzzle piece has been pressed into place, or a stubborn Sudoku grid has resolved itself. But meeting James seems to have upset Natalie. Dan is sympathetic rather than suspicious — he's not sure whether this is because James did, after all, turn out to be a bit of a loser, comfortingly unimaginable as his successor, or whether the jealous impulse has receded with his illness, just as the sex demon itself has relaxed its grip (the apparatus still functions, surprisingly, but the balance between his higher and lower selves has shifted).

But no — jealousy hasn't receded: it has merely changed colour. The thought of Natalie having children with and growing old with another man — not with him, after all, despite everything they've been through together, but with someone else, someone who thinks different thoughts, feels different, smells different, stands an alien razor in the bathroom cabinet — this thought conjures no indignation now, but only a grey, fathomless sadness. The more firmly he resolves that she *must* one day find someone else, that she *must* be happy without him, the further he slides down into his private, jealous sorrow. But still, she must.

Last Friday they went to watch the Olympic swimming. Once in a lifetime, people say. A nine-hour round trip for eighty minutes of frenzied splashing and churning. Not much of a spectator sport, swimming, you'd think, but it was fun. Mike offered them tickets for Saturday's athletics, but Dan declined — he wanted Nat to see her swimming, and consecutive days would have been too much. Instead, they watched what the papers are now calling Super Saturday on TV with Mark and Rachel. Dan felt an echo of his childhood fascination with records and results, a whisper of envy for all that flowing motion, and a resigned sense that in staging such spectacles, in relentlessly overdoing it, humanity is trying just a little too hard.

On the long drive round the M25 to Stratford, the topic of James cropped up a few times. Gritted teeth from Natalie, reluctance, even now. Memories that shine a light on life choices and life outcomes, perhaps. A loser James may be, but he can still take the bins out. Dan is slowly coming to accept that there will be no great opening of hearts. Their relationship is strong but also bounded.

They drove home in silence, weary and hoarse from cheering on the titans.

Natalie ducks under the shop's porch and shakes herself down. As she stalks past the fruit and veg, her foot slips on the wet floor and she flails wildly to stay upright. 'Oh, no you don't,' she whispers. No room for her to get injured these days — no slack in the system.

The item she needs is shelved meaningly between the condoms and the tampons, in the aisle reserved for accessories to adult life — razors, deodorant, multi-vits. But as she nears the tills, first her eye and then the rest of her is drawn up a different aisle, one she always skips on the weekly round. First, a preparatory run of dog and cat food, and then — babies. Faces like grinning, gap-toothed pumpkins, everywhere you look. Giant shrink-wrapped slabs, seventy-two nappies in each, are on offer: three for two. How much do babies crap? Baby-dry, baby-snug, baby-soft, huggie-snuggie-snot-nosed-cherub. Stacked crates of baby formula look like something you'd see at a builder's merchant. Nappy bags. Breast pumps.

She couldn't do all this, and look after Dan as well. Could she? Should she? No slack in the system. She retreats to the tills, tosses the test on the nearest conveyor belt and avoids eye contact.

The rain stops abruptly but Dan stays on for a moment, listening to the daytime traffic as it calmly, sedately shears the flooded streets. He should be working, but instead he's been reading about the law. He already knows that euthanasia and assisted suicide are illegal in England, but it's worth making sure. A patient can refuse treatment, and indeed can issue legally-binding instructions in advance. Yes — his leaflets told him that. In other words, the illness is allowed to kill you, to play God, but no one else is. What if the illness doesn't play a decent god? What if it takes you far enough to make life utterly miserable, whimpering at the roadside of existence, and won't finish you off with a spade? It'll be alright, the illness whispers, with a malevolent wink — trust me.

The law is an ass, but Dan is not the person to fight it. He's not prepared to spend his last days on earth making adversaries of principled, well-intentioned fellow men and women. Nor is he the person to 'raise awareness' by getting his face in the papers, or, for that matter, the person to raise hard cash for research. He leaves these worthy tasks to others.

Is he selfish? He hopes not. In the cause of science, not his own, he has signed up to all the trials he ticks the boxes for, although most have disappointingly modest ambitions — counselling therapies, a better way of tracking symptoms, an adjustable collar. Magic healing potions are conspicuously absent. Apart from the trials, rather than reinvent himself, Dan has decided to live his life according to the same principles he hazily espoused before his diagnosis, but to follow them more strictly: do what you're good at; do what you love; do what you think is right.

If, thanks to Dan's elaborate ranks of magnets, the synchrotron can deliver to its customer experiments shades and flavours of blinding light that it couldn't when he began, and if those shades and flavours help to answer questions that couldn't be answered before (the tuberculosis team did get their image; a grainy print-out is taped to the wall by his makeshift desk), and if just one of his sixteen published papers — or his work still in progress — ends up nudging human understanding in the right direction, he'll have achieved something.

If he manages to find pleasure and wonder in the world, even as his means of engaging with it disappear one by one — yesterday he took a nostalgic mathematical tour through Maxwell's equations and their many elegant implications — he'll have achieved something else.

And if he somehow succeeds in bequeathing Natalie, and his family and friends, a legacy of good feelings, feelings that engender strength and self-belief rather than despair, he'll have achieved something yet more. Success and failure are both assured; achievement comes in the shades and flavours.

Dan concentrates for a moment to execute a swallow, and again to effect a satisfyingly deep sigh. It is somehow reassuring to be reminded how lightly he has touched the world. This room, the moulding on this window frame, the tiny heart-shaped pock of rust on the fastening — they were here before him, and will be here long after he's gone: quietly, effortlessly existing.

At first, Brenda Vickers finds herself to be quite an attraction at the sheep station. The shepherds and shearers see few enough women, it seems, fewer even than the dour Highland foresters, and fewer still who'll fearlessly try their hand at manhandling a ram or herding a deafening woolly torrent through the chute. Any uncouth behaviour from the men is returned in kind.

She spends a few evenings at the bar with a gentle veterinary student from Argentina who's finding the job less pleasant than he bargained for. He's a mountaineer of sorts back home — Brenda forgives him some mild exaggeration — he has a good heart and his accent is gorgeous. They like each other — they have no particular reason not to. But it's not the same. There's a missing ingredient whose taste she can still remember. If this is an experiment, the results are clear.

Meanwhile, a few of the shearers realise that she's not quite right, not quite normal. They remember her put-downs and turn mean. 'Keep calm, boys,' they murmur when she passes, hands shaking in mock fear, exchanging grins at the running joke. Austin, so contented when she arrived, finds out and reacts with fury.

She also misses, more than she expected — there are mountains here, after all — the ancient, storm-rounded, midge-swept hills of home. She can't stay.

Meanwhile, James F. Saunders collides head-on with a job — one he would have found intolerable before his encounter on the Shepperton lawn. After determining that Whitby Library does not hold a copy of Nerval's *Sylvie*, which he has a sudden, scholarly yen to reread, James locates it in the town's bookshop. Unwilling to fork out ten pounds for the slim volume, he starts reading on the shop floor. Between chapters he moves about, pretending to browse, brushing his fingers over the neatly-stacked wares. The shelf bearing Salinger, Sarraute and Sayers registers no particular significance. He frowns, then smiles — the shimmer and the scorn have quite disappeared. He might as well be in a hardware shop.

After a hundred pages he's politely accosted by the manager, a sardonic, savvy woman in the late stages of pregnancy. They start talking about Nerval and the Romantic movement, and one thing leads to another.

'We're looking for someone prepared to work weekends,' she explains, hesitantly. 'For six months. After that — we'll see.'

'Weekends mean nothing to me, except fewer buses.'

'Are you mobile? You could move here, to Whitby, perhaps.' James thinks of his meagre possessions, and his pariah status in Bay.

'Yes, I could do that.'

So he finds a flat, still within earshot of the sea; gives notice to Mrs Peacock, promising to visit. Counts the days, and measures his internal adjustments. 'You haven't changed,' Becks said when they met, her tone measured, deliberately neutral. She couldn't see, in that moment, what he's become. Or maybe she could see precisely what he's become, or what he hasn't become, as the world has grown up around him. The friends, the admiring disciples all gone now. The nightclubs unwelcoming or closed down. The attitude unbecoming.

But now some stubborn lever has shifted. Seeing and speaking to Becks has effected a recalibration, has swept his expectations into line with his reality, and there is much more relief in this change than discomfort. Ambition is a stomach ulcer, healed now.

Again and again he settles himself into the warm, fragrant memory-bath of Becks' tragic splendour, her admission that she's thought of him, her reciprocal curiosity, that veined hand that used to hold his so tightly on rope bridges and rafts and reaching across from one sleeper-train bunk to the other as they rattled across a night-blotted world.

He takes from his shelf a copy of the York University magazine dated 2002, lets it fall open at a familiar page, and decides that his second-prize-winning poem needs an extra, final stanza. He wrestles with the ten lines for an hour, subdues them at last, writes out a fair copy, studies it judiciously, and then screws it into the usual tight ball for committal to the sea. Amen to an idiot prayer.

What puzzles him is that each time he remembers Becks, Brenda's absence gnaws at him. Brenda-guilt and Brenda-love. Perhaps a trace of Brenda-hope. Those, after all, are his reality. He writes *Dear Brenda* across the specious blankness of page after page, but nothing is sent. And still he thinks of Becks.

Becks, Natalie, stands in front of the bathroom mirror, calmly putting off the pleas of her bladder. She turns her head a little, lifts her chin, tries a different mouth. The puffy grey nubs under her eyes aren't a good look, but she feels worse — bad enough to threaten the breezy competence that she wears each day like a uniform. Bad enough to need an explanation.

She tears open the slim packet she bought last week and unzips her jeans. Dips into the singing cord of pee, extracts, watches. The tiny front of wetness advances rapidly, overrunning the window while she's still in full flow.

She waits the obligatory sixty seconds, tilting the wand this way and that, weighing its physical substance, watching the play of light. No, this isn't a dream, and she isn't seeing double. A flash of primordial triumph is overwhelmed by panic. Oh shit oh shit oh shit.

23. Two halves

'The soul's greatness consists not so much in climbing high and pressing forward as in knowing how to adapt and limit itself.'
Montaigne

Mike Vickers casts a jaded glance across his screens, locks his computer, grabs his sunglasses and slips out of the office. He never really believed in his success, so he doesn't take failure to heart. He lost the finals contest, of course, and the barbed feedback left little doubt that he lost to Crispin. He's heard a rumour that his old boss is charging half the fee for MRI 2.0.

Last week he was sent a link to an article announcing that the Americom pension fund, his biggest investor, has a new CIO, and that his old sparring partner, the ambitious young woman in green, has been tasked with overhauling the hedge fund portfolio. Transparency and cost-effectiveness are to be the new watch-words, says the article: neither is a strong suit for the MRI. Mike expects the notice of redemption any day now.

In July the system gained a healthy three per cent, and for a few precious days the year's performance turned from red to black (before fees, of course). But this bounty soon trickled between its careless algorithmic fingers. George's grand predictions at the urinal have been flushed away like so much coffee-charged piss.

Mike paces the streets slowly so as not to sweat, jacket slung over his shoulder, and finds himself in a small park littered with the rejoicing bodies of office workers showing off their holiday tans. Bodies above, bodies below: like most of the city's favourite lunching spots, this was once a burial ground. A many-layered lasagne of corpses, eighty thousand in all. The headstones have been respectfully cleared away and stacked along the boundaries, all except one large gated tomb — retained for aesthetic merit, the information board says, but crumbling now, pompous occupants long forgotten.

As Mike leans against the hot, white stone, shaded eyes wandering over the carnal cornucopia with its summer dresses, its kicked-off shoes and its gorgeous legs in a hundred inventive attitudes of repose, he tries to reconcile this vague awareness of bodies above and below, of Natalie, of Dan, of the living, the dying and the dead. Dan's illness is a window, facing downward.

His phone chirps: a message from Crispin, the first since the day of the übernerd's dismissal, sixteen months ago. That old 'good luck' message is helpfully displayed above the new missive, which reads: *Michael, hope all well. Want to meet for lunch?* C. Bookends to Mike's fleeting career as the Rocket Jesus.

'*What?* What is it?'

The Mocks' meals take longer than they used to. Meat has to be pre-chopped; spaghetti is off the menu. Dan spears and lifts his food with a clumsy, repeating motion and chews slowly, trying to avoid mess. They've developed an understanding that Natalie will do about three-quarters of the talking, but all this week she's been giving one-word answers. Now she holds

Dan's gaze, then exhales slowly and for a long time, so that when she speaks it must be with the last whit of breath in her swimmer's lungs.

'I'm —' (a needle-sharp ray of realisation dawns as her lips purse to form the 'pr') '— pregnant.'

The earth is rolling again, cornering, and Dan tries to find his balance. Out of all his incoherent reflexes of thought and feeling, the first to take expressible shape is a simple question of process.

'But how? Did you forget your —'

Natalie is already shaking her head. His jaw drops; the fork eludes his clumsy grasp and clatters on the plate. Natalie slides off her chair and kneels beside him, takes his greasy hand. The muscles of her face slowly draw back in a spasm of silent crying. She might be eight years old.

'I don't want this to be the end.' She mouths her confession, barely whispering. 'I can't just start again. You can't tell me to start again.'

The repercussions that Dan has already traced out during long, painful meditations, that he was determined to avoid and thought he had, catch up with him in a sickening rush. A child. A child whom, at the rate he's quite literally going, he will never hold or kiss; a mystery he will never unravel, a priceless treasure he will have to let go: hello, goodbye. And a chain fixing Natalie to the past, making impossible that renewal, that reinvention he's imagined for her in the nobler corners of his mind.

And yet at the same time he perceives the wonder of it, the miracle, like a faint, cold, dawn light falling across this tangled web of sorrows. And he recognises the tribute, the act of devotion: binding the future to the past.

But sharper and closer than either the sorrow or the wonder is the acute sting of misapprehension, of his blithe failure to comprehend the only person he can ever hope to comprehend. Would you call it a betrayal? (Stupidly, Dan's memory snatches at the only available comparator — the time Mike nabbed the '92 science prize after stealing Dan's idea for his project — then flings it away in despair.)

'I can't believe what you've done,' he murmurs, at last. 'I just can't believe you've done it.'

Natalie's face has recovered itself, become a grown woman's again — his wife's again — though still streaked with tears. She wipes them away with precise fingers.

'Well, I have, so let's make the best of it.'

James has almost finished packing, the Boatman drawling softly from the tape player, when Mrs Peacock's doorbell rattles his Anglo-Irish-Portuguese bones. She doesn't seem to be home, so he traipses down the stairs himself and finds Trudy standing in the road, looking pained, with her hands resting on Hugo's narrow shoulders. Could James look after Hugo for an hour or so, just this once? The wounded look on her face is not, in fact, embarrassment at having to go back on Rob's angry vow, but actual physical pain — she has a cracked tooth. Hugo, who has made his mouth as small as possible in an effort not to smile, looks like a solemn, pinched little wizard.

Upstairs, the boy's triumphant grin crumples into a frown.

'Why are all your things packed up?'

'I'm moving to Whitters. Whitby. I'll miss you.' Hugo's frown deepens to its full tectonic grandeur.

'Why?'

'Because I've found a job there.'

'You already have a job. You're a —'

'I know, but I thought I'd try something different.'

Hugo perches on the edge of the bed, still frowning, legs

kicking to further express his agitation.

'Can we go and sit on the fish and chips bench?'

'We can try. Last time I went up there, about twelve hikers were trying to squeeze on at once. I'll just skip to the loo.'

After James has left the room, Hugo's eyes wander dolefully over the empty shelves and gaping wardrobe. He recognises a small rectangular shadow on one door as the former site of James' faded cut-out picture of the staring man with glasses, moustache and brimmed hat, now gone. His gaze finds its way to the rubbish bin, which is crammed with papers. Yes, the picture is in there, and beneath it what looks like an unfinished letter. There's an addressed envelope, too.

Hugo lifts these items out — then, hearing James' tread on the stairs, stuffs them into the writer's notebook that he proudly keeps in the pocket of his shorts.

The latch on the Mocks' front door has been changed and lowered, after Dan found himself unable to admit his physiotherapist last week. Even his customised litter-picker failed him, and the consultation took place through the letter slot.

He hooks his weak fingers over the new latch and reverses the chair so the door can swing into the hall. There they are: his mother and father, laden with bags. There is still something unsettling about looking up at them rather than down, a familial ache so tangled in all the other sadness that he doesn't examine it too closely.

Age is making of them something slightly comical, but no less lovable. His mother was fine-looking, an auburn warmth in the dark hair that she has always — except a brief bob-stint in the eighties — worn long. She probably dyes it now, but he doesn't know for sure. He has a theory that the moment she stopped believing in her physical impact, it disappeared like a broken spell.

Physical impact is not a concept anyone would associate with Dan's father, who, though an ingenious, energetic and honourable man, has always had the bearing and features of a squirrel. His shoulders are stooped and narrow, and his face has a puckered look as though not quite finished, not fully inflated — a trait visible but mercifully diluted in the faces of Dan and his sister. Dan remembers painfully acknowledging to himself his father's shortcomings, sometime in his mid-teens while watching Mr Mock and Big Vince Vickers in conversation after a school function: mouse and man.

Of course, the physical ageing process seems laughably benign beside his own degeneration. It's the behavioural changes that Dan really notices — the bickering of new retirees with time on their hands, the fussing, the stories told or questions asked twice over, the missed cues, the odd habits, the pullovers worn on warm days.

He and his father discuss modifications that might be made to his wheelchair — an ongoing project that brings both pleasure — and everyone teams up to move him to the sofa while the old man sets to work. Each time Dan leaves the chair, marooned now wherever he's put, he recognises its transformative powers — powers not unlike those of the much-missed Yamaha, but with a different frame of reference. He calls the chair Shadowfax.

With Natalie, who has been promised and fully deserves a day to herself, he exchanges a nod of understanding, that she is to relax and not worry about him, and that their bombshell of a secret is safe, as agreed. She leaves the house briskly, carrying, for once, nothing but a small handbag. Mr Mock then steps out to buy some parts from the electrical shop, leaving Dan alone with his mother. She offers him more cushions; offers him tea; offers him a shoulder rub.

'Mum, you don't have to nurse me.'

'I'm not nursing you,' she retorts, straightening his pile of science magazines. 'I'm mothering you. Deal with it.'

The sliding doors snub Natalie for just long enough to break her step and slop a scalding dribble of coffee over her thumb, then grudgingly part. She enters the busy station and selects one of the intersecting queues for the various banks of ticket machines. It's a jolly, Saturday-morning crowd, bound for early-season football matches, open-air concerts and days out with the kids. In front of her: a silent young couple carrying huge rucksacks, holding hands, destined for adventure. Natalie feels a flash of envy, but she too is free today. A day off. Dan-free. Time, at last, to reflect on the damage she has caused.

Dan said he could never have done what she did. He's right — both because he is not a schemer (his intended meaning) and (more to the point) because he wouldn't have got away with it. In his place, she would have recognised that the matter of babies wasn't closed. His observation echoes the subtext of most of their quarrels: the moral gradient between thoughtlessness (Dan) and meanness (Nat) — which way does it tilt? Most people, in Natalie's experience, tend towards one fault or the other, probably because in the face of sporadic thoughtlessness — the box of chocolates finished off accidentally, the forgotten favour, the mood cues missed — the considerate must occasionally resort to calculated meanness to even the score.

This time it's different, of course, the scale unprecedented, the consequences profound. Dan hasn't mentioned the possibility of terminating the pregnancy: he knows his rightful jurisdiction, as a man, and as — she feels the hot prick of tears — as the one to whom it soon won't matter one way or the other.

A commotion in the queue behind turns her head: a pushchair has tipped backwards under the weight of a bag hung from its handles. The baby is safely strapped in but startled, and lets out a choking scream. The parents right the pushchair but don't think to comfort its occupant — or are weary of comforting. They argue instead. The baby can't see them and cranes its head wildly, then fixes wide, streaming eyes on Natalie. It freezes for a moment, out of puff, then hauls in another lungful and flings it out with ear-splitting abandon.

Her heart lurches: in all her long experience with images of suffering, she has never seen such a hysterical mask of misery.

'It's got some poke,' murmurs Mr Mock admiringly, as he accelerates the Motability car down the M4 slip road. Dan smiles: he hasn't been alone with his father for a long time. Mrs Mock is following in the other car; if she loses them, she has the satnav.

Dan turns to look at his father's familiar, mousy profile. The baby bombshell has changed everything, including his feelings for his parents. They will be overjoyed, of course — they never had the option of starting again after he's gone. Before, Dan's overriding urge when he saw them was simply to apologise for amounting to nothing, despite all their patient parenting efforts. Now there *is* something, but it's a gift given unwillingly. The guilt remains.

'I don't really know how to say this,' he begins, without clear intention. 'I know it's not my fault that I've got this disease — but — I still want to say sorry. I'm sorry that I'll never be able to repay what you and Mum invested in me. Or even put it to good use. Instead, I'm just taking more. More looking after, more worrying. And this time — it's all for nothing.'

The car is noisy and Dan's voice, a mewing monotone now, doesn't project. But his father gets the gist. Mr Mock shakes his head slowly, keeping his eyes on the road.

'Let me tell you something your mother and I have discovered — or remembered — this year about being parents.' The studied calm in his voice reminds Dan of stern, reasoned tellings-off in years gone by. 'You do hope and expect your kids will outlive you — of course you do. That hope, that miraculous continuity is one of the things that keeps you going through the — shall we say less glamorous parenting duties. But from the first moment you find out you're going to be a parent, you sense that you're involving yourself in forces that are out of your control. You can't even choose whether it's a girl or a boy, let alone whether he or she will be healthy, or happy, or clever or kind. Childbirth is no longer the roulette it was for millennia, but it's no game. Things go wrong. Some of those things — those outcomes — can't be righted, but just have to be lived with. If you get lucky — as we did for thirty years — you *feel* lucky. And if you don't, then you adapt.'

'Adapt in what way?'

'The hopes that you have for your child — that we have for you — they sort of evolve. They don't just disappear in a puff of miserable smoke. What we hope now — ' he flicks away a tear, but his voice remains steady '— is that you'll continue to meet this challenge with the great courage you've shown so far, that you'll feel loved, that we'll be able to help you to get the very most you can out of life, and that —' he falters, not quite able to say the last thing on his mind. Instead he bats the indicator stalk as the Windsor turning approaches.

'Thanks, Dad.'

'Don't thank me — thank your mother. She helped me to understand all of this. But she wouldn't be able to tell you, so I have. So there. Last week, we were having a bit of a trip down memory lane, and —'

Dan isn't listening. He's thinking that he will never take that complex parenting journey, and his own child won't remember him.

It's been windy: twigs and immature conkers litter the paths, making for a bumpy ride. Dan has requested this park visit; he has to do that now — request things. He can't just get up and go. James, Nat's ex, was right about autonomy being a treasure.

The Mock trio makes its way slowly towards the statue on the hill. Passers-by ignore Dan but flash sad smiles at his parents. A bout of good-natured bickering commences over Dan's head — something about his sister Laura and whether her latest business venture will succeed. A swooping crow catches Dan's eye — dips low, wheels round into the wind, stalls and lands neatly on a tree-root. O, joy of a skilful action! Suddenly he wants to be alone. This urge strikes often now; he values careful observation of his surroundings, flights of fancy, rumination. He remembers the same impulse before exams or important lectures — fear of the big event catching him with disordered thoughts.

Presumably he still has a right to solitude. When the time comes, will he want to be alone?

Brenda Vickers kills the van's sputtering engine, strides up the little path that badly wants weeding but won't get it, opens her front door. She's been driving in her work boots, which are still caked in peat and sawdust, and she nearly tramples an envelope lying on the mat.

James. Again. 'Seriously,' she murmurs. After all this time, he hasn't given up. She stoops, and the familiar bitter-sweet indignation gets a jolt when she feels something lumpy in the envelope. Christ, what now? His ear? She closes the door slowly, leans against it and inserts a grimy, nail-bitten finger.

Inside is a folded letter enclosing a second piece of paper as creased and bedraggled as though put through the wash, and a large, flat seashell. In Essex they used to call them otter shells. This one is a beauty, smooth and grey on the outside, striped with fine, concentric lines of orange, and inside a creamy white. Its two halves are still joined by a tenuous, wobbly hinge of tissue.

The letter begins in James' meticulous hand — *Dear Brenda, I am not asking you to come back to me, but* — then it stops, to be taken up, apparently, by a young child writing in pencil.

> *I found this in Jameses bin. Hes too scarred to send it, so I will. He writes poems and throws them in the sea. I saved one for you and dried it out. Hes going soon and Im going to miss him. You can have my best shell from the beach here to remember him.*
> *From Jameses friend, Hugo*

Brenda opens the stiff, wrinkled fragment. The writing, though smeared and faded, is still legible. It's a poem.

> *Every hour, on the hour: silence. Faceless*
> *Clock of memory waving your white hands,*

There are eight more agonised lines, and the poem is signed in the bottom corner with what can only be kisses.

24. Not enough

'No proposition astounds me.'
Montaigne

Beneath George III on a gargantuan copper horse, Dan Mock sits on his own copper horse, his electric wheelchair with its new off-road tyres, and looks down the Long Walk towards Windsor Castle. Tiny, harlequin figures in congenial groups crawl here and there. Beyond the castle — head and shoulders perched on the Walk's tapering skirt — a sumptuous grey-green horizon. You can see the curvature of the earth from the top of Everest, people say. Well, Dan can see it plainly from right here, at an altitude of two hundred and twenty feet. Nature abhors a straight line, after all, just as electrons aren't too fond of corners.

Nearly three miles to the castle: a fanfare sounded from its battlements would take, what, twelve seconds to reach him. A determined snail would cover the ground in four days. The flash of a mirror held by Rapunzel at her window, a seventy-thousandth of a second. Fast and slow, big and small. How much of human life is orientation?

We are, thinks Dan, consciously opening his frontal lobe's throttle valve, speckles of mould on the surface of a moist, gassy sphere of rock left accidentally whirling around a pathetic star. This devastating Copernican heresy is now a commonplace — the blue marble, the third stone. Yes, yes. But wait! Speckles of mould? Yes. Really? Yes: me, you, the baby. Three speckles. Our nondescript star buried in a big wheel of stuff. Big, big, yes. Stuff — heavy bits and bobs — gathers itself into these wheels. Big-bigger wheels devour big-littler wheels. Between: space, emptyish (quantum cameos like popping candy). Gravity a pull; angular momentum a dance. The stuff created out of energy. The energy happened — bang — because. Because we're asking. Who's asking? Mould. The universe a finite bubble of being with no edge, no outside worth worrying about, only an inside. Observable. Energy conservable. Quantum swervable. One of many? You choose — it doesn't matter. Creator? Word games and mind games, only. Harmless fancies, yes. But the thing itself no speculation, no hypothesis, no fable — arranged in plain sight above our heads, the arm of our galaxy hanging there like one stupendous fucker of an arch, others beyond it, others beyond them, and beyond, and beyond. It took us a long time to figure out what we were looking at; to forget again, not long at all.

And the mould itself, the curious infestations on that sun-bathed moisty marble — what of that? Soup accident, yes. Outlandish molecules stumble on the property of self-replication: a chemical freak that simmers discreetly for aeons and then suddenly, recently, gets out of hand. Mutate, select, repeat. In the blink of a geological eye, the planet is crawling with beasties. A single forest that stretches to the curved horizon is home to a trillion trees. Every tree a world, every leaf, the gut of every bug.

Replicating, fornicating beasties, each a thermodynamic house of cards, improbable, expendable, ready to dissolve: if a lucky few perform their party trick, their replication, that's enough. Mutate, select, repeat. Can't pause it, can't switch it off. Repeat, repeat, repeat, and then — a gasp, and a hush. Another, stranger accident. Self; angst; not Eve who ate the apple but that blind watchmaker gone berserk. Repenting now, perhaps.

One red kite keens loudly above and another replies; a buffet of wind lifts Dan's hair and lays it down in the fair approximation of a caress. With three strokes, the shadow of a long, low rag of cloud recolours in softer tones the western row of trees, the walk, the eastern row.

Mould with attitude. We are. But material orientation is not enough.

The heart of Mike Vickers is about as heavy as the mahogany box that he sets down on the table beside the drained glass and empty bottle of '82. He flips the clasp; the lid swings back until restrained by two gold chains. Mounted and framed inside it, as though on the screen of a ridiculous laptop, is a print of the famous, luminous portrait. In the box, two snug, artfully arranged compartments: a leather folder (letters, memoranda, copies of wills all in slip cases — the provenance) and a small, velvet-lined and Perspex-lidded display case.

Mike locks eyes with the portrait's subject. Receding hair, discreet lippy, a nose that swells as you look at it. Sly bastard. Wheeler-dealer. Winner. Mike, by contrast, has been well and truly rumbled: fraud, bluffer, loser. The other box — the MRI — is to be closed. 'Nothing personal,' said the Generalissimo, cheerfully, eyes already wandering back to his screens. 'Wrong market for us. Live and learn. Spot for you on the execution desk.'

Victoria is looking for something more serious; Lulu is in Milan and might not come back; Carmen has just announced her civil partnership on Facebook. Good luck to them. Nothing personal.

Time for that clean break? PhD? Hobby farm? Not-for-profit? Dry stone walling? He looks down at his slim, pinkish fingers. Never built so much as a Lego tower. All the maths forgotten. At that moment, realisation opens a scathing yellow eye: the fault doesn't lie in his profession. His half-hearted defences of the investment industry are all basically, depressingly sound. You don't have to lay actual bricks one upon the other to contribute something useful. The fault lies rather in himself. In his own incapacities and bad choices: the world's technicalities a mystery his brain is not equipped to penetrate, its moral endeavours unfathomable to a shallow heart. A swindled silver spoon up his arse. Good for nothing.

He opens the small display case, pinches the glinting object from its velvety cleft and holds it between his finger and thumb. Looks at the portrait, at the object, at the portrait, back to the object. Dan has his electrons (and more), Brenda her mountains, James his words — even Pete Walley, it turns out, plays mean improv piano. Mike Vickers has this only. His one claim on the universe, staked by means of a transaction.

He rises, walks to his colossal hall mirror. Holds the object up to its rightful place. Stares. Leans closer, closer, until his forehead is pressed on the glass. Stepped in so far. Stepped in what? How far?

Shakespeare's putative earring slips from his worthless fingers, glances off his shoe and rolls onto the doormat. He doesn't stoop to pick it up.

Natalie's friend Rachel raises a questioning eyebrow when she orders an Appletiser in the riverside gastropub, and Natalie has to laugh and shake her head. A curious thing, how pregnancy begins with a flurry of lies.

The little art festival was surprisingly good. She might even dig out her pen and ink when she gets home. One particular portrait triggered a shiver of sadness — an act of preservation, deeply personal, infused with knowing as no photograph can be. There is no portrait of Dan.

But this is a day to speak of other things. It is Dan's absence, after all, that restores Rachel to her intimate, confiding, insightful best. The two friends eat, talk, laugh and treat themselves to dessert. As they part — one to her car, the other towards the station — they solemnly agree to reconvene. Rachel has already driven away when Natalie frowns abruptly and turns back to the pub.

The monochrome faces of a hundred ladies with bouffant hair stare down from the papered walls and door of the toilet cubicle. Even the ceiling. Some of the faces are smugly smiling, some scornful, some apparently ready to pass out; a few offer pitying frowns. Black and white chequerboard floor, white porcelain, black seat.

Somewhere a cistern falls silent, so that the only sound is Natalie's breath ringing in the reverberant space. In the white bowl, glaring up between her white thighs, and blotted thickly across the white pants hammocked between her white knees: a precipitous shock of scarlet.

Dan exerts his fading muscles to shift in his chair. A spot of rain pricks his windward cheek; tickles pleasantly — unreachable, unwipeable there. He stares into the distance, northward along the Long Walk, still engaged in orientation.

Mould with attitude. Indeed — in one hot and fertile sweet spot, the intersection of improbable statistics, mutate-select-repeat happens upon a configuration with unprecedented élan.

A mechanism unknown in all the earth's astonishing biological engineering: reason. The power to exploit and subdue. Reason masters fire; annihilates with spears the stupider beasts; invents farming instead; axe, rope, wheel. Clear-fells whole countries, slashes, burns, replants, makes deserts bloom, dredges a harvest out of helpless oceans, slaughters and weeps at the slaughter and slaughters again.

With tenacity and courage it crosses oceans and deserts, adapts in the face of searing heat, cold, drought and disease, claims the whole planet as its domain (and in recent times, recrosses those oceans solo and unsupported, by canoe or balloon or pea-green pedalo, just for the hell of it). It's not goodbye to the universe for Dan — the universe recycles its waste — but goodbye to this inadvertent biological venture, this wide game frantically cross-hatched by triumph and despair: this society of humankind.

Goodbye to the untold microstructure of history — its countless individual struggles and sorrows, scoring their vivid colours one upon the other, overlapping, intersecting until the very soul of the species is saturated and numb, its characteristic anxiety born of the possibility it might forget all this vital substance and remember only the outlines, the peevish machinations of politics, dogma and war. Even now, at this very moment, as the day begins to turn above this million-footworn paddock west of Londinium and the season follows close behind, the flood tide of humanity rises. Trickling, prickling along the Eurasian Steppe, the Rift Valley and the Gangetic Plains, Yangtze and Orinoco, Appalachia, Patagonia, Arabia and the Norfolk Broads, fierce, private longings that never find expression, wells of loneliness, prisons of enmity and fleeting intermissions of joy. Acts of gross stupidity. Unreason. Madness. Rage. Acts of defiance, of quiet, untold fortitude, of generosity and love, inundating with blood and tears the ever-absorbent, ever-renewing earth.

Goodbye to the human form, strutting and bopping along the delicious fine line between existential grace and sexual sorcery; to harmonious voices or those merely kind or sincere; to transcendental smiles; to the stranger's face that takes your breath away.

Goodbye to labours of love, to marvels of engineering and imagination, to music of such omniscient loveliness it might have cascaded from the gods, but was in fact dashed off one Sunday afternoon over the billiard table. Goodbye to skulduggery and to earnest discourse, to stacked tomes of ethics, philosophy and law. Goodbye to the million hearts in mouths as the ball balloons over the bar; to the stunned theatre audience, sharing a moment unrecordable but lingering like a shape on the retina; to long-awaited headlights on a foggy night, throwing shadows like black windmills; to the old busker, lungs ruined, who jangles his strings tunelessly, stops them with a sad, remorseful hand (wife long-suffering, now long gone), and then dives into the twelve-bar blues.

Goodbye, too, to the arms race between means to destroy and motives to desist, galloping to its inevitable, poetic end: the bomb. Stuff of myth. Only one outcome. But the species holds fire, we hold fire — screw that, we want to live, too much, more than they do in the myths. We dance Gangnam Style instead. Savour a brief heyday of partial peace and unequal plenty. Indulge in glass phalluses half a mile high, engrave poems on grains of rice, stick flags in the moon. Build colossal experiments underground. Kick a ball around. Sip flat whites and chillax.

Yes, the involuntary wide game of humanity is something like this. Its players come and go. Meanwhile, nature maintains a ruthless blast of indifference, cleansing, laying waste without

vengeful motive, by storm or by disease; but not always —
sometimes sympathetic to our predicament or seeming so, in a
moment of dappled calm, or in swifts flying low at twilight,
crying out the very same tuneless song of sorrow.

Goodbye to all that.

Dan stirs and blinks, his bout of orienteering complete for
now: the foundations laid. He is not ready to address his
goodbyes closer to home. Larger spots of rain peck at his face
and eyes, and streak the great stones of the pedestal beside him.
There is an inscription: *PATRI OPTIMO*. Best of fathers. A
mocking eulogy that finds an accidental mark two centuries
on. Putative pater-to-be Dan bumps and wobbles down the
slope to the start of the walk.

There he pauses, a small, sedentary figure, parked on the
starting line of this monumental home straight. Suddenly the
brooding sky unveils a flood of late summer sunshine, and, at
the same instant, fills the air with hard, shining, autumn rain.

From our distant vantage on the Walk we can only just
make out Dan's hand pulling a plastic bag from the side of the
chair and covering his precious joystick. A few figures hurry
past without noticing him, in search of shelter. The chair rolls
forward along the rain-slick asphalt, wheel-deep in golden
spray. From here we cannot see the finger finding the new
switch or hear the wavering hum of the auxiliary electric motor,
and we do not expect what happens next.

With a soft, distinct *thwack*, a black umbrella opens above
the wheelchair, whose occupant continues resolutely towards
his rendezvous.

25. How deep

'If you do not know how to die, never mind.
Nature will give you full and adequate
instruction on the spot.'
Montaigne

The lane runs on and on before the headlight beams, straight and narrow as a chute, while the dashboard clock adds another minute to its damning score. There are no signs, but James F. Saunders can feel the sour, potent gravity of the sea. Here, at last, are some houses; a pub, The Gun; a small car park, and beyond it a suggestion of yachts' masts and a primeval darkness.

The car park is deserted apart from a few vehicles crouched and frosted in the shadows and two cars incongruously gleaming beneath a lamp: an Aston Martin and a Motability car.

'They've gone without us.'

'They wouldn't.' James swings the van alongside, stops the engine and opens his door to the cold, silent dawn. 'Not when we've come so far.'

'I told you they would.'

But they haven't. The outer silence is broken by the unmistakeable sound of a hand-dryer and a door banging, and a procession makes its way into the car park from what is evidently a public toilet.

Natalie Mock feels ridiculous in her wellies, waterproofs and woolly hat. Dan and Mike cooked up this escapade while Dan was in the hospice. Sea-fishing in November. Will it be safe for you, she asked; Dan can still do withering looks. Fine. Whatever. She slings the rucksack over her shoulder (medicines and other necessaries — each month it grows heavier) and follows the conspirators out into the car park; two newcomers are standing under the car park's single lamp.

'It *was* them,' says Mike, pushing his old friend's chair. 'Time and tide, people — time and tide!'

James has changed more in eighteen months than in the previous decade. He has a beard now — not like Dan's regrettable Crusoe tribute (they abandoned the daily shave last summer because of skin irritation), but a neat goatee that suits him. His characteristic forward hunch — to Natalie always a signifier of eagerness, of leaning in, rather than weakness or burden — has been ironed straight. He shakes Mike's proffered hand with ironic emphasis, then without hesitating stoops and warmly grasps both of Dan's gloved hands where they rest on the arms of his chair.

'Dan. Good to see you. Sausage for your thoughts — remember?' Now, finally, he turns to her. 'Natalie.' The name still sounds odd on his lips. He leans to kiss her and gets a faceful of hat and waterproof jacket.

'Hi.'

Beside James stands a woman — yes, it is Mike's sister, though she's changed too since Natalie met her, just once, at one of Mike's parties, perhaps six or seven years ago. She seemed very young then, an awkward, big-boned student dressed in black. She's still dressed in black, and has been sort of squaring up to Dan, not sure how to greet him, but now gratefully follows James' example.

'Have you got wellies and things?' asks Natalie, stupidly. It was Brenda who told them all what to bring. 'The fisherman guy — Reg, Ron — he's waiting for us on the boat.'

'We'll be ready in two shakes,' says James, throwing open the back doors of the van.

'Have you got the provisions?' asks Brenda.

'Vittles for both fishy- and humankind are all aboard,' replies Mike. 'Sandwiches still hot. We'll sort the ramps out and see you there. You can't miss her — name of *Andromeda*.'

Jupiter is the last survivor in the dawn sky as the squat, rusty *Andromeda* chugs along her buoyed channel, past the mud flats, the lighthouse, the old fort on its precarious sickle of land, and out into the mile-wide neck of the Solent. Though the morning is perfectly clear and still, the sea bears in a remnant of swell from the Atlantic. It glints like molten lead under the bow and then reappears astern, savagely sculpted into rearing, glassy waves that hang, slump and tumble into lanes of foam.

Dan Mock taps a question into his keypad with his left thumb, his last moveable digit: *How deep*. The electronic voice is drowned by the engine, but Nat reads the words and relays them to Mike, who ducks into the cab and asks Ron. 'Eighteen metres.' Is that all. Strange.

Dan allows his senses to feast. After the well-meant, comfortable blandness of the hospice, every authentic world-morsel is precious — the mewing retinue of gulls, the bright, tangerine glow seeping up behind the Isle of Wight, the mingled smells of diesel and marine sulphur. And bacon: Mike, Brenda and James are all attacking their butties. Dan hasn't bitten into a rasher of bacon for at least a year. But he isn't vexed by the others' enjoyment — or only a little. He's grateful to be reminded.

They round the ghostly chalk spires of the Needles just as the late autumn sun peeps over the island, narrowing the friends' five pairs of eyes and painting their faces with a wash of gold. The engine stops, the anchor chain rattles, and a deep quiet descends. The Channel plants gentle, slapping kisses along the *Andromeda*'s hull.

Mike Vickers feels triumphant. The weather is perfect, Dan's assurance that he's comfortable and enjoying himself quite believable: the controversial outing is already a success. The small matter of inadequate insurance was resolved with a couple of fifties. There were no bites from the first drop, but does it matter whether you catch anything?

General exultation can't help the twist of specific revulsion on his face as he pokes around in the bait bucket. Some of the squid are still half-frozen into blocks, while others — whole or in pieces — are floating loose in the grey water. Eurgh.

'You're getting off lightly here, old man,' he says to Dan, whose eyes swivel from the horizon they have been surveying. He taps a reply and hits play: *You always were a big girl's blouse.*

'You're supposed to be *attracting* the fish,' Brenda teases. 'The bait is supposed to look irresistible. Yours looks like a —'

'Like an instrument of torture,' supplies Natalie.

'You need to jam that hook right through the thing's body, and then stick the barb through the eyes like I showed you. So it's hidden.'

'I'll try my method, thanks,' replies Mike, wiping hands on his now-filthy handkerchief, taking up his rod and releasing the spool.

Again there are no bites, but as they reel in, the tip of Natalie's rod starts to flex. They all crowd over to her side to see what creature of the deep might find itself hauled up to the light. It looks like — a very small, leopard-print shark.

'Doggie,' says Brenda. 'We throw her back. Watch out — they have skin like sandpaper.' She helps Natalie extract the hook from the poor creature, which twists and curls around her hands, weird, sleepy eyes dazzled and blinking, mouth gaping.

'It's bleeding.'

'It'll be fine. Character-building. Story to tell the grandkids.'

When Mike gets his own bite, feels the unmistakeable heft of it and begins reeling in, his mind hums with childish speculation. Alpha male catches alpha cod. Saves the day. Three cheers for Mikey. When the quarry reveals itself to be another dogfish, and a small one at that, his disbelief quickly turns to quiet, unaccountable satisfaction that he and Natalie are the two pioneers. A team.

Later, after a coffee break, and with the new baits down for just a few minutes, Brenda sweeps her rod back and begins slowly, carefully reeling. A frown of concentration that Mike remembers from long ago.

'This is the one,' says James, scrambling across to watch. 'I can feel it. The White Whale.' The first thing they see is a huge mouth, then two round, black, staring eyes.

'May I present: dinner,' declares Brenda. But the cod, when netted and brought aboard, is no whopper. Ron holds up his wooden rule, shakes his head and jerks a thumb towards the sea. It's just a baby.

'Good eating on that,' says James wistfully, as they lean over and watch the dazed fish right itself and flop down out of sight.

'Don't worry,' says Mike. 'Plenty of time yet.' But the morning slips by and their cavernous catch-bucket presents a mocking emptiness. Soon the favourable, sluggish waters of high tide are gone and the current drags at the lines, lifting the bait off the seabed where the elusive cod feed. Natalie keeps asking Dan if he's had enough, and he begins to waver. *Yes, soon,* he taps, *back aching, feet cold, maybe one last go.* When the final baits are down, he taps again: *Straw poll. Is it skill or is it luck?*

Brenda Vickers tries her rod gently and lets out ten feet of line. As teenagers she and Austin used to dabble from Southend pier and a few other local hotspots, but she's never fished from a boat. Her presence is a favour for Mike, and for James.

She remembers Dan, of course. When Mike explained how sick he was — that he can't move or speak, but that mentally he's all there — she found herself making excuses for not coming: it sounded so awkward. James talked her round, said he wanted to meet the guy again — said it might be their last chance. That's his story. But let's not forget the minor detail that Natalie has been bizarrely outed as James' ex. Mike says she's met Natalie before, but she doesn't remember. Forgettable, perhaps. Or just one of the many mortifying nights blotted from Brenda's memory.

Check my kibe. Check my kibe. Check my kibe.

Check my what? Dan's eerie electronic request rings out in the silence. Brenda turns to see his rod twitching violently. Check my line. She hesitates a moment, but everyone else looks at her so she grasps the rod and lifts it from the bracket. It's nearly wrenched out of her hands.

'What is it, Bren?'

'Dinner!' says Mike. 'Dan, you actually are the man.'

'If you ask me,' says Ron the skipper, with a twinkling eye, 'I wouldn't say that there is a cod. You might want to let out some line. Tire it out.'

The creature is swimming fast and erratically, so that one moment Brenda has to pay out line, and the next it goes slack and she reels in frantically.

'What the hell is that thing?'

'It's a shark or something,' says Natalie. 'Can't you let it go?'

Dan's eyes are fixed impassively on the sea. He looks like he doesn't give a shit, but when he glances down and taps his keypad, the message is: *This is bloody brilliant.* He plays it again. They laugh and cheer, even po-faced Natalie.

Suddenly the angle of the line changes. This plucky old gal's coming up. The surface breaks fifty yards away: a flash of creamy white belly. Brenda reels hard, and her adversary thrashes air again, much closer.

'What the fuck is it?'

'It's a conger. A big one.'

'Can you eat it?' asks James. Ron pulls a sour face.

'Rather you lot than me.'

'It's all we have,' says Mike. 'We'll take it.' Ron's eyes twinkle again.

'Oh, "We'll take it," he says. If only it were that bloody simple. Can we move this gentleman back? And you, Miss — keep well back too.' The five- or six-foot eel, thick as a man's leg, thrashes madly in Ron's biggest net. 'Take that priest,' he snaps at Mike, pointing to a short wooden club, 'and give it two sharp goes on the noggin.'

Mike looks helplessly at James, who turns to Brenda with a pleading smile. For Christ's sake. She makes good contact and the beast goes limp, but as they try to tip it into the crate it rears up and breaks loose, thumping around the small deck and lunging left and right. Everyone retreats, cursing. Brenda circles cautiously and, when the eel slumps for a moment, exhausted, jaws silently working, she gives it a mighty whack. Ron steps in quickly, traps the beast's head between his boots and with a sharp, rusty, two-pronged stake severs its spinal cord.

'Do not go gentle,' murmurs James, in the stunned silence that follows. Dan taps his keypad.

There's a lesson here somewhere.

James F. Saunders finds himself alone in Dan and Natalie's living room-cum-office-cum-dining room as the mantelpiece clock — a brass thing with spinning balls — chimes seven. Dan is resting. Mike and Natalie are in charge of the cooking, but have recruited Brenda to assist in the formidable and frankly obscene task of skinning the eel.

The clock is a bourgeois anomaly in a room which, if James didn't know the family circumstances, he would ascribe to an over-imaginative twelve-year-old boy. Mounted on the ceiling is an enormous poster print of outer space — one of those Hubble photos peppered with galaxies like snowflakes in a torch-beam. A dozen more posters on the walls: a motorcyclist leaning into a bend, knee almost touching the blurry road; a pelican gliding low over water; the earth seen from the moon; a topographic map of the Chilterns; a suspension bridge rising out of fog; the periodic table; a photograph of a blackboard covered in equations; an enlarged, incomplete Sudoku grid.

So this is where Becks has ended up. There's not a single image that James would choose to place on his own walls (the eye candy now exhibited in place of his discarded Joyce icon: nothing), and he could never live with a chiming clock. Is this what happens to people who are dying? They revert to childhood? Dan doesn't seem childlike in person — or childish, for that matter. More like a prophet. Perhaps it's James' own incapacity — his burned-out soul — that sees something juvenile here.

He sniffs his fingers. Despite much scrubbing in the hotel shower, they still smell of fish. And he didn't catch so much as an old boot. The room is connected to Dan and Natalie's bedroom by a pair of new-looking sliding doors with electronic controls, now closed. When they arrived, James caught a glimpse of two beds — an adjustable hospital-style one with a hoist beside it, tubes, cables and whatnot, and a small, low single for Natalie. For Becks.

James is happy to be hauled up mountains by Brenda. But if something like this happened to him, and he could choose anyone in the world to look after him, it would be Becks.

The conger did not die in vain: even Natalie has to admit that Mike's slow-fried steaks with Spanish paprika are a triumph. The man can cook. When he produces two bottles of what he calls the queen of Riojas, James makes a poor quip about drinking red wine with fish.

'Whereof you know nothing —' begins Mike, a corkscrew materialising in his hand. 'Just trust me on this, if nothing else, okay?'

Dan is too tired to join the table for long, but he makes an appearance. He asks to taste the wine, which Natalie presents carefully to his lips, and then collects back into the glass: thin liquids make him choke. Everyone waits for his reaction.

'*I'm getting apricots,*' he says. '*Liquorice. Marmite. The faintest inkling of squid. Wait, that could be Nat's hands.*'

While the others laugh, Natalie reflects with private, loving irony that it has taken total paralysis and an electronic voice to make a comedian of her husband.

When the community nurse arrives to help settle Dan in for the night, the Mocks excuse themselves. Natalie gives the nurse her usual verbal report, playing down the boat trip as requested, then sees her out and gives Dan his goodnight kiss. Then she returns to the dinner.

'What about you, Bren?' Mike is asking as she opens the door. 'What is it you love so much about wandering off to the arse-end of nowhere?'

'I love being alone,' says Brenda, her back to the door. 'I love having no responsibilities except to myself. No obligations gnawing at me, no stupid misunderstandings, no boundaries.' Mike sees Natalie, and tries to cut his sister off. Both bottles are empty.

'I did warn you about Bren,' he says to James, with a laugh. 'Ah, Na —'

'James understands,' says Brenda, sharply. 'He feels the same way, which is why we get along. Right?' Natalie looks at James, who gives a noncommittal smile to them both. Right enough. 'I'll tell you one thing,' continues Brenda, oblivious, 'I'm *not* about to start squeezing out babies. Sometimes I feel I'd like to take everyone who has any kind of claim on me, shove them in a top hat, wave a wand and make them disappear in a —' she looks round, sees Natalie, and finishes her sentence in a softer, uncertain voice: '— puff of smoke.'

Disappear. Right. Natalie feels anger and sadness welling up copiously, without hope of containment. She turns, hurries out into the unlit kitchen, lets the sobs come.

'I'll go,' says Mike's voice, sharply, and then she hears chairs scraping and multiple footsteps. 'Brenda!' calls James' voice. Sound of the front door opening and slamming shut. Mike is beside her in the dark, arm around her shoulders.

'I'm sorry,' he says. 'She didn't know. She doesn't understand.' Natalie turns on him.

'And you do?'

Mike looks chastened. She's never seen that ginger crest of

his fallen like it is now. The look becomes him. 'Let's not argue,' he whispers. 'We're all making this up as we go along.'

James' face appears in the doorway, an apparition from the past, freezes and then retreats. His intimation, intended or not — that he was interrupting something untoward — is unworthy of a moment's thought, but it nevertheless tempts her involuntarily to compare James to Mike as she once compared him to Dan. Another stupid thought-crime — she commits too many, each adding its fresh cut to her bloodied self-respect (and people keep calling her a saint).

Mike is the shallower pool, of course: a picturesque but insubstantial lagoon of a man. Likeable, untrustworthy and emotionally retarded — or so she always thought. But after all he's done for them over the past eighteen months, for Dan but also for her — especially for her, perhaps — she might have to reconsider. This isn't the first time they've stood whispering in the kitchen with good intentions.

26. Circling scythe

'... on what small things depends our fortitude in dying ...'
Montaigne

Sometimes Dan and Natalie go for a walk around the block. This takes them past the canal, where Dan likes to stop and contemplate the scene. There are ducks, perhaps, a pair of swans, a cormorant even, but these days Dan isn't looking at the birdlife; he's looking at the water.

One day at a time, and he tries to make each of them worthwhile. When he's not being hoisted, shunted, medicated or otherwise feeling like a nuisance, he can read (but not for long); he can respond to his ex-colleagues' respectful requests for technical advice on the synchrotron apparatus he designed; he can write emails to Mike or James; he can classify a few more galaxies in the crowdsourced astronomy project to which he contributes; he can reminisce. His brain is kept supplied with glucose fuel by the liquid feeds, with oxygen by the assisted ventilation he's now hooked up to at night. As for his body, it's not entirely inert but visited by strange twitchings and shiverings, memories and imagined sensations of movement, itchings and achings. There is more discomfort and indignity than acute suffering. It's a life of sorts.

Natalie could understand him until the spring — several

months after anyone else — but then the last of his consonants escaped him and he had to resort to typing. For reading and browsing he uses an eye-operated computer, but for simple communication tasks his left thumb just keeps soldiering on, defying the doctors. Weakening of his swallowing muscles brought on the choking episodes which have been perhaps his darkest moments, but those are largely behind him now. This first available exit he passed by — chose life, and tube-feeding. He can still manage soups and smoothies by mouth: between them these cover an impressive array of taste sensations (not a rasher-of-bacon sensation, sadly, or that favourite warm-smacky glass of red). Saliva mostly exits via the corner of his mouth, but neatly now. Adapt, adapt, adapt.

The next exit opportunity seemed to be approaching fast when his breathing difficulties began, but these have now stabilised. He needs the machine they call the puffer — ingenious yet inescapably horrifying — only at night. The disease has a habit of galloping along with intent, then taking forty winks at the roadside. He might be in for the long haul. But what about Natalie? One day for him; one day for her. Her life, its possibilities — that he never did enough to encourage — all on hold. How much longer?

An aura of dread surrounds this place now, hangs over the glinting water. He could get here on his own, and there is no barrier. It would be a messy way to go, upsetting for Nat, but he's left it too late for the neater options: he can't take drugs by himself, nor can he ask Nat or Mike to administer them. (They see a lot of Mike, these days — he's always dropping by, always ready to help.) Dan thinks of those fish living their gloomy, secret lives at the bottom of the English Channel. Hauled up to their doom. Might he not reverse the process?

How much longer?

Meanwhile, James F. Saunders positions his new signboard prominently on the pavement. Chalked on one side: 'The human heart, O Chactas, is like those trees which do not yield their balm for the wounds of men until they themselves have been wounded by the axe. Chateaubriand.' On the other: 'Truth itself is always halved in utterance. Lawrence Durrell.' Plenty more where those came from.

The bell jangles as he shuts the door and turns the sign to OPEN. He inhales the cool, page-fragrant air. Upstart Books, of which he is now the manager and Brenda the proprietor following its fortuitous selling-up by his ailing employer — and a little help from Mike — occupies one of the prize spots on the main street in Wigtown on the Galloway coast. James is gradually honing the stock towards irresistibility (he is ruthless and well-practised when it comes to disposing of verbal trash). They have a permit to sell coffee and, after much trial and gull-fodder error, have learned to bake passable cakes. Simple website: up and running; Twitter followers: forty-six; upstairs flat: draughty but spacious.

His relationship with Brenda is an adventure in itself. During the summer, while paperwork was delaying the shop's reopening, they walked two hundred miles up the wild northwest coast of Scotland in nine days. He has never felt fitter or more exhausted. Brenda loves the shop. Her new boss on the Galloway estate has taken all his management courses and treats mental health issues sympathetically.

Last night, as James watched his old university magazine burn in the bedroom fireplace (while Brenda was showering off the residue of her own demolition work), he wondered whether any other copies survived, eleven years on, or if anyone would still remember his poem. *Every hour...* That clock still runs, perhaps. Meanwhile he and Brenda lean against each other like a couple of damaged spruces, in mutual gratitude and love.

Mike Vickers awaits the seven twenty-two, toes of his brogues on the yellow line, staring across the tracks at the near-deserted platform opposite. During his garden leave he rented a flat in Maidenhead, in between Reading and London. Dan and Natalie didn't ask why: they understand. He still uses the Paddington flat occasionally, as does his mother, when she's in town.

He persuaded Mij to follow him across to Crispin's new firm, and the soft-spoken, fridge-chested developer has become his boss in the small Soho office. He's learning a new programming language, building a sexy interface for the traders (Crispin's adjective) while Mij makes the thing actually work. The fund has only a handful of investors so far; there is no magic show — just Crispin and the other portfolio managers calmly presenting their evidence, explaining exactly what the various strategies do and what they don't do. Fees are low. The office mood is calm and focused. Pay cuts are the norm for new hires, and nobody, as far as Mike can tell, is rushing out to buy tapestries. He's an essential, competent cog, and it feels good.

In a few seconds, the fast train will hurtle through with a furious wallop of air and sound. Presumably death comes like that sometimes — the only warning an ominous humming of rails. Not always like the Grimpen Mire. Mike takes a deep breath.

Wham. In the blur of rushing train windows he sees his own crisp, sunlit reflection, not alone but standing in the midst of a multitudinous army of commuters. No superstar, high achiever or Rocket Jesus, not top of the class, but a minion, an underling, getting on with it. Some of these solemn-faced, drab-suited worker-bees may indeed be brain surgeons, or social workers, or brilliant, inspiring teachers. The admired. Others are facilitators like him: agents of this or that, telemarketers, baristas, project managers. If nobody facilitated, if nobody tinkered and sold things, the brain surgeons among us would have nothing to buy.

Onward, proud and peaceful commuter troops! Yours is a just and noble cause. Specialise, negotiate, delegate, innovate! Stand tall and facilitate! Help out here and there. Politely disregard the naysayers, the ideologues, the hypocrites. Keep the ball of prosperity rolling. Pay your taxes. Be a good friend.

Find a girl, settle down.

Mike Vickers, do your best! I promise to do my best.

As Brenda Vickers taps the trig, she notices that the stone balanced on top is weighing down a piece of paper — a photograph. She tugs it loose, glances — a grinning, grey-haired man with walking poles. A dead man. She thinks of her grandfather. Of Mrs McCready, too. Stuffs the photo in her pocket. Sorry, but not up here. Let the wind say his name instead.

A two-minute breather. She's learning to love this arse-end of Scotland. She was afraid she might feel hemmed in, with Glasgow sat sprawled between her and the Highlands like a vindictive troll, but these broad-shouldered, forest-skirted hills are a revelation: an unshowy, neglected, bleak Brenda-heaven. This fifteen-mile circuit is worth it just for the names: Murder Hole, Rig of the Jarkness, Loch of the Dungeon, Range of the Awful Hand. Sounds like a dinner party.

The Wigtown shop seemed to offer a new start — cold sweats and arcs of blood behind her. Last week's debacle with James' ex proved otherwise. Ah, well. James himself, at least, has come up trumps. He really was in love with her — Brenda — all along. The circumstances of their reconciliation — that letter sent by his little devotee, whom she later met over parkin and milkshakes — gives her a warm, cosy, sheltered-from-the-wind feeling. Maybe everything really does happen for a reason. She wouldn't suggest that to James, of course — they try to avoid both laughing at each other and giving cause. There are frequent lapses, but that's okay. They're on the same side.

Brenda has heard that from this highest hill in the range you can sometimes see Snowdon, a hundred and forty miles to the south — the country's longest direct sightline. The air is clear today, an ozone-tinted void, but not clear enough: she'll have to make do with the Isle of Man, the Irish mainland and the peaks of Arran, each fifty miles away or more, etched along the shining, circling scythe of the sea.

Natalie blends the soup in short, weary bursts, keeping one eye on the baby monitor that will flash if Dan coughs or presses his call button. Carrot and ginger — his favourite. Chilblains on her fingers, knuckles that bleed from the slightest knock, a split on the tip of her thumb. Marks of her trade. And yes — a baby monitor, recommended by the nurse.

She worked part time until Dan's first serious choking incident. When she explained her working hours to a supplier with whom she was arranging a meeting, the guy assumed she was 'another one of these super-mums.' It happened a few times, but she remembers that occasion because it was just about when their baby would have been born. Their one miraculous chance. She's never started the pill again, and nothing's happened. Teasing, irregular periods; half a dozen negative tests in the dustbin of her life. Dan says it's probably him — still likes to imagine her carting about some other guy's child after he's gone. But Natalie has always known she wasn't built for babies.

As she pours the last blenderful straight into a bowl for them to share, the monitor sings out, lights flashing. She picks up the bowl, spoon, napkin, and walks promptly but calmly down the hall to their room.

Dan's eyes are already fixed on the door as she enters. *Breathing*, he taps. She leans close, can hear and feel his shallow, laboured breaths.

'You need the puffer?' His thumb twitches assent. She switches on the machine, fiddles with the settings, untangles the tubes, carefully fits the bands over his head and adjusts the seal around his nose and mouth. It works by giving the air an extra push each time he breathes in. She holds his hand. After a minute or so, says, 'Better?'

The thumb twitches. It begins slowly picking out letters on his keypad.

Natalie — a pause, in which the puffer wheezes softly, then he adds, *my love* — another pause — *I think we are nearly there.*

27. Warm sea

'Neither men nor their lives are measured by the ell.'
Montaigne

Dan Mock savours the near-silence: Nat has turned off the puffer, just for a few minutes, because it keeps making him cough — or try to cough. His puckered lungs, full of bad stuff, twitch their feeble, rapid breaths. It has occurred to him that this is a sort of trial run.

He pushes his sluggish, reluctant mind along one corridor of thought after another, looking for the old luminous clarity that seems to have deserted him. Life hangover. He could listen to a piece of music. Something delicate that rejoices in a soundless room; something heartbreaking, while he still has a heart to break. He turns his eyes to the screen and scans his collection, but can't decide. Last chance for a last listen. No. It feels too late for that. Too late to worry about things he won't do, places he won't go, people he won't see. His eyes swivel up to his Hubble galaxies. Uncounted thousands of them in that postage stamp of sky. Teeming with life — maybe. But the meaning, the vision is slipping now.

His family were here today. His parents would be here every day, of course, but he and Nat talked months ago, agreed to set gentle boundaries. He guiltily prefers to depend on her than on them. They all understand now that the end is near; don't realise quite how near, perhaps, which is just as well. The atmosphere was serious but not grief-stricken. Nobody said much. Laura, his sister, surprised him by calmly recounting childhood memories. Little things: the time he ruined a birthday magic show; epic games of Monopoly and Scrabble; the prize stag beetle that escaped and found its way into her sock drawer. The past is a sock drawer. It was enough.

Two days later. Natalie Mock stands in the bathroom, but this time she's not looking in the mirror. So this is it. The doctor switched Dan's puffer to its more aggressive mode, not assisting but controlling. Said it had to stay like that now, said Dan would get used to it. He hates it. He can't communicate distress even with his eyes, but she could tell. And now he's drawn the line. Just like that. Refusal of treatment. She takes deep, slow breaths. If only she could breathe for him.

Mike, the GP and the nurse are in the kitchen, conferring in low voices. Dan asked them to wheel his bed into the front room, where his pictures are, and where slatted winter sunlight comes and goes.

Try not to fight me, he said last week, *when the time comes*.

Dan's consciousness flees before the oppressive discomfort, the tyrannical machine assaulting his lungs, and finds itself in a strange, whimsical corner of his mind. The gnawings and scrabblings of panic, of what he's leaving behind, of what he's forgotten, of what he never knew — these persist but are muted, blunted by a mantle of something like relief.

Perhaps, he muses, my legacy, my achievement is to anoint the lives of my friends with a mortal essence. To teach them that there is no masterpiece, no transaction by which you can cheat death; you cannot run to the hills, and you cannot look to your children. A child is a genetic extension, yes, but surely in every sense that matters to our humanity, a child is not a continuation but something entirely new. My love, you see that now. Death has to be absolute to make life thrilling.

This death is a gift, my friends. Use it wisely.

The doctor has said all the things she's obliged to say, and Natalie steps forward as the others respectfully make way and then melt out of the room. She looks into Dan's moist, blinking eyes. The old mood diagnostics — tone of voice, movement or the subliminal semaphore of the face — so painstakingly tuned over the years of their marriage, are useless now, when she needs them most. Disconnected. Dan's state of mind can be deduced only from the pauses before and between his answers. When the doctor asked him to confirm his decision, he didn't hesitate.

'Dan.'

Natalie. My love.

They sit for a while, his hand inert in hers except for a faint twitch of his thumb. His chest rises and falls at the puffer's command. The doctor has tried to set a natural rhythm, but how could it be natural? At last, Natalie manages to say it.

'Dan, do you remember Assisi?' Now he does hesitate.

Yes.

'Do you remember — the tiny little church where St. Francis died — with the vast Renaissance basilica built over it, like —' she falters. Dan is selecting words with his eyes.

Like an architect's delusion of grandeur.

She smiles.

'Yes, like that. Like a fantasy. I was thinking of that place.

That great, soaring palace of stone, built to honour one man who lived like a beggar, and died in a — a little shed, smaller than this room.'

Yes.

Natalie's sobs are coming like shivers, but she keeps going. 'Dan, I can't build a palace like that for you. Not out of stone. But I promise I will love and honour you just as much — as much as any of them. I'll build a palace for you, over you — inside — in my —'

In your thoughts. Yes. I know you will. A tear gathers in the outer corner of his eye, half-reclined as he is, then spills. Instinctively Natalie wipes it away.

'I'll build it, and I'll sit in it and think of you — and us, and all these years we had.'

Yes. But Nat. Build it over me. Not over you. Do you understand me. She nods; cries. *Build it with open doors. You'll want to hear* — he stops, looks at her, waits for a lull in the tears — *those turtle doves* — another long look.

She nods again, kisses his hand, his forehead, smells his hair. There is no need for a full stop.

Mike Vickers stands in a column of dread while the others make their arrangements. *If you feel you could do it,* Dan wrote last week, *it will be a great mercy to Nat. She doesn't really like the doctor, doesn't want her to be the one. And she herself — no.* The two friends discussed this once before, at the hospice. Conspirators.

'Afterwards,' wrote Mike, 'and in the years to come, I will make sure Nat is alright.'

I know. I'm counting on you.

The doctor nods and Mike steps forward, looking at Dan, not at Natalie. Never at Natalie. Dan's eyes follow him steadily, encouragingly. He reaches for the clips that secure the life-sustaining mask. Natalie sobs, but with restraint. As for Mike, he finds that he's not going to cry. He's going to do this — claim the last of his undeserved victories over his friend, the better man. He's going to do this and not cry.

The morphine is weaving its sleepy spell. Dan can hear the distant music of Natalie's voice, but not the words. He remembers — his body remembers — floating in a warm sea. Greece, perhaps. He was naked, the most naked he has ever felt, the sea a womb. Eyes closed, arms and legs gently paddling the void. And then, without warning: an eddy of cold water. A sharp, penetrating chill against which he had no defence. A moment only, before the uterine warmth flooded back.

That momentary chill was the chill of life. Up close, life is a magnum opus. But from a distance, it's just a cold eddy, fleeting and unheralded, in a warm sea of nothing.

His mind finds time for one last observation. There will be no fear, after all: no reverent hush, no chill, no halls of alabaster white. Just a warm sea; a drowsy, forgetful womb of peace.

Dyspnoea. Beautiful, hypnotic word. Sad peony. Pansy ode. Open days. Soapy den. Easy pond.

28. Yours absolutely

Natalie Mock drifts from one room to another. Dan is in all of them, and none of them. Oddly, stupidly, it's her birthday today. He's not here to. He's not here.

Mike is coming round in. To help. Now that the funeral is done and. Over. Mike said his few words very well. Couldn't have asked for. He said Dan was a cautious man. Planned everything, he said, except the best and worst things that ever happened to him. Dan did think that, yes. Their marriage a miraculous accident. Perhaps. Mike hardly mentioned the disease. Said Dan was everything he, Mike, ever wanted to be. His quiet genius an inspiration. No sense of humour, though. He said.

But now it's over. Maybe it's time to. Just a bit of tidying up. Sorting out. Putting away.

She perches on the edge of Dan's reclining chair — the chair in which he died. Died, yes: that's the word for what Dan did. She switches on his computer and types the password. There is the familiar background picture of a galaxy, but all the icons have disappeared. All except one — a document nestled in one of the galaxy's spiral arms. *For Natalie.* She clicks. A document.

Dear Natalie,

How do you say goodbye when it's forever? I give myself two
chances to get it right: in person and in this short letter.
If I get it wrong, I'm sorry — I know you will forgive me.

  You once suggested I publish a record of my illness, and
I refused, saying I would leave public introspection to the
artists. But I thought about what you said, and started keeping
a private diary. A place to say the things I couldn't say to you
in that stupid electronic voice, I thought. Something for you to
remember me by. I didn't write every day. I often felt better
after writing it, but as the months passed and the entries
multiplied, it occurred to me that the Dan presented in those
pages might not be the Dan I wanted you to remember. The
diary had become an outlet for all the self-pity and despair
that I was determined to conceal. It was a true likeness,
perhaps, but a partial one, and not my better side. I felt
I trusted your memories more.

  And you wanted us to have a baby. I said no: I gave you my
reasons. Then, for no reasons whatsoever, the universe said
no too. I thought about what you wanted, and about the
steadfast, generous love I couldn't understand and didn't
deserve, the love that wanted to open a path even beyond
my death. I contacted a fertility clinic and discussed the
possibility of leaving a sample in storage, a surprise gift for
you to use or not use after I was gone. But then I began to
change my mind. I sensed an alteration in you, perhaps. A
different cord of strength: a possibility that you would, after all,
build a future without me, as I've always hoped. My little
gesture might threaten that, I thought — might send you the
wrong message.

  These gifts, these parts of myself — the diary and the
DNA — I have decided not to give you (I deleted the diary

and dismissed the clinic). Why am I telling you this? Because I want you to understand that you already have the best of me, safe and sound. What you have truly lost could not be saved, and what you have saved will not be lost. The rest is nothing.

What can I say of us? I can only thank you for what we had: for our bodies soldered, glued together so snugly that rolling apart must surely tear the skin. For your limitless capacity to surprise me — seeming distracted, uninterested, unsympathetic for a moment, and then looking at me in that way you have, as though you saw right down to the bedrock. For the wise humanity that you placed alongside my pedantic reason. We were a good team. I'm sorry we were so skewed at the end, that you gave so much and I could only take.

Others have given you the support I could not. New bonds have been forged. You know how I feel about my friends: how long I've known them, how I rate their strengths and their considerable weaknesses. But what I think doesn't matter now. The world is yours, not mine. The world and the choice are yours absolutely.

I'm sorry we couldn't journey further together, grow old together. But I'm glad we did journey together, you and I. If true love could really perform miracles, as it does in the fairy tales — but it can't, of course. Or maybe it has.
Thank you.
With love,
Dan

Natalie stares at the letter through her tears. Reads it again from the top. Can't believe it. *Likeness. Clinic. Bedrock.* She doesn't want to close the file in case it's somehow lost; drags it to one side of the screen to see if there is anything else. But there is nothing else.

Nothing else. She looks up at the wall, where the portrait she didn't draw doesn't hang. *You have the best of me, safe and sound.* What did he mean? She gets slowly to her feet and drifts into the gloomy hall, where her eye is drawn to the small mirror hanging beside the coats.

It's just her puffy face, looking back. But when she sees her face, she can see his face too, as it used to be: magisterial, patient, brimming with nerdy exuberance.

'What *does* the F stand for, anyway?'

James F. Saunders peers out between the curtains across the broad, wet, lamp-lit street. Over the lowest of the shops opposite he can see faint headlights crawling along the coast road on the other side of the bay. He's learned that you can love two women, and be true to both of them. He quietly, copiously radiates gratitude for Brenda's change of heart — that she did not merely take him back, but sought him out freely, makes all the difference to them both — and wonder, too, at her strength and restless courage, and fierce solicitude for her vulnerability. Every night he lives out a parallel life with Becks in his dreams. Two emanations of the same self. The lost novel has risen again, inarticulate now, of no service to humanity, subsumed in the imperfect structure of his soul.

'James?'

As he turns from the window, James is aware of a slight sensation of pressure, a restrictive ache in his head or in his chest, or maybe both. He blinks and rolls his shoulders, and it goes away. The questioner is Mike, sat behind a sort of Giant's Causeway of tottering book piles. Economics, business and finance. Incomprehensible to James, and with offensive titles

— he was going to toss the lot, but since Mike's here he might as well check for any hidden gems.

'James? The F?'

James looks at Brenda, just in from her evening run, sitting on the floor with one lycra-clad leg outstretched, touching her toes; apple-cheeked, the sleet still melting in her hair. As she shifts from one stretch to another, her body leaves moist imprints on the floorboards. At the suggestion of her doctor, she has started a blog. *The Chainsaw Diaries*. The entries — a dozen so far — are a sort of piss-take, with careless snaps of the back of the van, muddy boots, bad weather, her packed lunch, surrounded by equally careless prose littered with typos, grocer's apostrophes and outdoorsy slang. After barely a month she has ten times as many followers as the pithy erudition tweeted by Upstart Books.

If he was dying, and he could choose anyone in the world to care for him, it would be Becks. Yes. But he's not dying.

'James?'

He turns to his friend — millionaire, player of the field, the one Becks loves — smiles broadly and replies with a Portuguese flourish.

'*Fortunato.*'

Natalie Mock waits while her mother fills the teapot, assembles the tray and carries it solemnly to the table. This potent, versatile ritual with its amulets, incense and porcelain song. When at last the two cups are filled and consecrated and stand between them, her mother heaves a slow, preparatory sigh.

'Well, my love. My poor love.'

'Well.'

'Here we are. You and me.'

Natalie nods slowly. But her gaze drifts from her mother's

broad, comforting face to the window behind her. A winged cloud has caught the setting sun. Without touching her tea, she pushes back her chair, walks round to the window and opens it. The burning angel is already fragmenting. Cold air has never felt so good.

The ancient sideboard clock drip, drip, drips, emptying one vessel, perhaps, but filling another.

Natalie's heart beats in time.